HEIDS UP

HEIDS UP

Neil Renton and Mark Fleming

Tartan Moon Publishing,
Edinburgh, Scotland

First edition published 2024 by Tartan Moon Publishing

ISBN 978-1-7396800-8-4

These short stories by Mark Fleming have been published before: 'The Nimble Men' in **404INK magazine, Issue 5: Space**. 'YCL!' in **Front and Centre**, a Canadian literary magazine, under the title, 'Kola.' 'Like Dolphins Can Swim' in the online literary magazine, **pulp.net**, under the title, 'Blue Lines.'

Cover portrait of Mark and Neil © Craig Steedman.

INTRODUCTION

Neil Renton and Mark Fleming met through The Changing Room, a 12-week support group designed by Scottish Action for Mental Health, 'aimed at increasing the social connectedness of men in their middle years and delivering a programme of activity that will reduce loneliness and ultimately improve their mental health and well-being.' The Changing Room was pioneered at Hibernian FC in Edinburgh before similar sessions were rolled out at over 20 other senior Scottish football clubs.

Attending these drop-ins, Neil and Mark discovered a shared interest in creative writing, both admitting they found this activity inspirational and therapeutic. This led to them bouncing ideas off each other, initiating short stories via prompts: they took turns texting song titles randomly selected from their phone playlists. Taking this a step further, they dug into their writing archives to revamp older work.

As well as stories, many containing semi-autobiographical elements, they wrote essays about how their musical tastes have benefited their well-being. Finally, they interviewed each other about their respective mental health journeys, transforming sometimes harrowing flashbacks into poignant memoirs. *Heids Up* is the result: a collection of flash fiction, longer short stories, essays, and descriptions of lived mental health experiences. This book will resonate with anyone who has faced issues of their own, directly or indirectly.

What makes this creative potpourri a further delight are

the authors' differing writing styles. Neil was born in 1976, and typically for a Gen Xer, has harnessed social media as a writing platform. Some of his pieces began as drafts composed on his phone, while observing people/situations during commutes. He cut his writing teeth as a journalist reporting on Scotland's Championship and League 1 and 2 matches. In a similar ballpark to Celtic-supporting Chris McQueer, Hibs fan Neil's Twitter-friendly flash fiction is bursting with dark humour and surreal observations. You can catch up with his Tweets @RentsFaeLeith. He is also passionate about his indie music, writing reviews of the gigs he regularly attends for Blinded by the Floodlights.

Born in 1962, Mark's creative writing journey began when he was a teenager immersed in the capital's late 70s post-punk scene, a fertile period spawning many local bands: Scars, The Fire Engines, Josef K, Visitors, The Freeze, and a host of others, all namechecked by Douglas MacIntyre and Grant McPhee in their book, *Hungry Beat: The Scottish Independent Pop Underground Movement (1977-1984)*. Mark composed lyrics for his band, 4 Minute Warning, as well as articles for fanzines, some of his prose ending up in an early edition of *iD*. (Post-punk was as much a catharsis for literary endeavours, not to mention fashion, as music!) There followed a side-step to poetry, then short stories.

The writer he cites as a particular inspiration is James Kelman. "A story of mine was included in the *Picador Book of Contemporary Scottish Fiction* in 1997, edited by Peter Kravitz, then head of Polygon. I not only met Jim at the launch party, he introduced me to some of Scotland's formidable literary talent, including Agnes Owens, William McIlvanney, Jeff Torrington, Alan Spence, and many others. I had to pinch myself!"

Mark also writes regularly about mental health for his blog, www.markjfleming.net, and has contributed to the Hibs Community Foundation website, *The Leither* magazine, and John Robb's music/culture website, Louder Than War.

Crucially, *Heids Up* does not represent the conclusion of Neil and Mark's collaboration. It is the start.

CONTENTS

THE STRAY
Neil Renton 15

SEAL'S BROKEN - BIRTH OF THE TWINS
Neil Renton 18

A NORTHERN SOULBOY
Mark Fleming 23

PANIC ATTACK ONE AND PANIC ATTACK TWO
Neil Renton 29

THE NIMBLE MEN
Mark Fleming 32

DUSTIN JOHNSON'S PERFECT SWING
Neil Renton 40

DOM'S DOSE
Mark Fleming 46

MANAGING THE BLUES BLUES
Neil Renton 51

KANYE WEST FAE LOCHEND
Neil Renton 54

MY YELLOW SUBMARINE
Mark Fleming 57

THE SCAB
Neil Renton 59

NO PURCHASE NECESSARY
Neil Renton 69

WONKY
Mark Fleming 75

LIMBS
Neil Renton 79

CHRISTMAS AT TIFFANY'S
Neil Renton 82

THE MAGICIAN
Mark Fleming 86

SONGS IN THE KEY OF STRIFE – NOEL GALLAGHER WRECKED MY MUM'S FUNERAL
Neil Renton 91

NEIL'S PERSEVERED 95

ROCK 'N' ROLL AS A LIFELINE
Mark Fleming 102

ALFIE AND THE MONSTER
Mark Fleming 106

SONGS IN THE KEY OF STRIFE – I'VE GOT 99 PROBLEMS AND BEING JAY Z IS ONE
Neil Renton 123

DOUGLAS ROSS COUNTY
Neil Renton 127

MARK'S ALL WRITE 130

KATA TON DAIMONA EAYTOY
Neil Renton 135

THE STRIKE
Neil Renton 139

YCL!
Mark Fleming 142

LIKE DOLPHINS CAN SWIM
Mark Fleming 154

COCK BLOCKED BY NICKY WIRE
Neil Renton 166

DEAD LAZY
Neil Renton 169

WE'RE THE FLOWERS IN THE DUSTBIN
Mark Fleming 172

MENTAL HIBEES – SICK OF HIBS
Neil Renton 176

TEN THOUSAND CROWNS
Mark Fleming 180

MENTAL HIBEES – IT WAS THE BEST OF TIMES
Neil Renton 190

SONGS IN THE KEY OF STRIFE – POUR SOME TUNES BY SUGAR ON ME
Neil Renton 193

EMPIRE BISCUIT STATE OF MIND
Neil Renton 197

THOUSANDS
Mark Fleming 202

THE WARS
Mark Fleming 207

SONGS IN THE KEY OF STRIFE – THERE'S NO BUSINESS LIKE AFTERSHOW BUSINESS
Neil Renton 215

I WALKED INTO THE DOOR AGAIN
Mark Fleming 218

CHORED
Neil Renton 221

SONGS IN THE KEY OF STRIFE – THIS MORNING A DJ SAVED MY LIFE
Neil Renton 224

RED HANDS AND STONE ROSES
Mark Fleming 229

WHAT'S THE EXCUSE THIS TIME?
Neil Renton 235

ELIXIR OF LIFE
Mark Fleming 238

THE MAESTRO, GEORGE
Neil Renton 246

PROTECT YA NECK
Neil Renton 249

GUERRILLAZ
Mark Fleming 252

BETTER LIVING THROUGH CHEMISTRY
Neil Renton 259

WORKING 9 TO MAMBO NO. 5
Neil Renton 263

DEAR TAN
Mark Fleming 267

BURNS NIGHT
Neil Renton 276

QUICKSAND AND CAFFEINE
Mark Fleming 280

SEAL'S BROKEN – DEATH OF THE TWINS
Neil Renton 285

THE STRAY

Neil Renton

When all else fails, there's always Sandy. Apart from when Sandy is sucking the face off a Welsh guy on a stag do, that is.

They're anchored at the bit where folk put their drinks before hitting the dancefloor. I'm not going to lie. I'm a bit jealous. That should have been me, if I hadn't spent all night looking for someone else. Now I've got no option but to trawl the dregs of Club Trop and see what's left with half an hour before the lights come on.

Me and Sandy have got history, almost an unwritten rule between us. If neither of us finds someone else, we'll get together. Teeth clashing, exchanging breath that smells of cheap lager and stained tongues brought to us by Blue WKD. We know nothing about each other. Jobs, ages, surnames. None of it matters. Only the agreement.

In fact, I'm not even sure if her name is Sandy. She doesn't look like a Sandy.

With her doing her bit for cross-country relations, I've got no other option but to go home empty-handed.

I put my empty bottle on the bar and say some random stuff to the barman. We were at the same school but in different years, so we know each other indirectly.

He replies, but I can't hear him so I'm just nodding and saying things like "No way", hoping it fits whatever he said.

I head to the toilet but change my mind. I'll have to make conversation with the attendant and listen to his promotional lines.

"No Armani, no punani." Dated lad culture stuff like that.

I'll hold it in until I get home. One last check.

I do a couple of laps of the club just to make sure there's no one else I'm remotely interested in. I've been running this race long enough to spot the signs and there's none.

Anyone female and still here is either already with someone, politely declining the advances of a desperate male or has their wingwoman doing the awkward work for them.

When I get to the top of the stairs, I nod to the bouncers. Inside, I'm hoping to never see them again. Outside, I'm saying "See you next week."

The taxi rank isn't too bad, and I cross Lothian Road to join it but stop. There's Sandy and the Welsh guy, hand in hand, already in the queue. They're either going back to her flat or to his Travelodge.

Fuck that.

I stoat down the road, two steps forward, one drunken shuffle to the side.

If truth be told, I don't mind my own company. I prefer it to being with others, to be fair. Just not all the time.

I pass a homeless guy who's in a sleeping bag that makes him look like a mermaid. He's got a bad business model for the modern cashless society, a paper cup expecting loose change. To his side is a dog.

He says something, but I ignore him as I've got my earphones in. There's nothing playing it helps in situations like this.

"Hey! What about yer dug?"

I stop and turn around.

There's Scamp, staring back at me, wondering where the fuck I'm off to.

"Aye, thanks for that, mate," I say, reaching down to pick up Scamp's lead. "You're a legend."

"Do Ah no get anything for dog-sitting him?" the homeless guy asks.

"Nah. In fact, I can see you've had a successful night. If it wasn't for Scamp, you wouldn't have made as much as you have."

I put a couple of fingers in his cup and gather a few coins that I pocket as Scamp reluctantly follows.

I've got a feeling he'd rather stay with his new best friend.

SEAL'S BROKEN - BIRTH OF THE TWINS

Neil Renton

"Seal's broken, lads."

"Fuck sake, Carpet," I snap. I'm no in the mood for him today, a stress-causing pest at the best o' times, never mind today. "You've got a bladder like a burst tea bag."

"Nah, I didn't mean that kind of seal. The singer Seal."

He does that thing where he looks away as he finishes his sentence, like it's a full stop. He's coming out of the pub bogs, drying his hands all over his jeans.

"What the fuck you on about?"

"Seal. Big guy. *Kiss from a Rose* and that. He was having a wee cry next to me at the urinal."

The train station pub is rammed with scarfers and others in green and white. I've got my new Gazelles on, and they're fucking hurting me. With Christine about to give birth to twins, this could be the last time I'm out for a while. I need to make the most o' wearing them, no matter the cost.

"You're fucking at it, Carpet."

"I'm fucking not. Turns out he's having some personal issues. Anyway, I told him he can join us for a pint."

"We're no starting the rounds again!" It's always a hassle keeping these tight cunts in check. Carpet's notorious, holds the door open when there's a group of us heading into the boozer so everyone else is at the bar before him. He's not polite; he's just tighter than a crab's erse and doesn't want to buy the pints before everyone else.

"We've got that spare ticket cause Kingy couldn't come."

"Wait! You've had a slash next to some crooner, and the next thing he's coming to the fucking Scottish Cup final with us!"

I'm no making any effort to talk to the boy. Nae offence, I don't care who he is or what he's done. He's probably a nice guy and that, but I've got enough to worry me without anyone else's problems.

Seal appears, and he's standing there, a big, tall cunt. He's casually dressed, got a mobile in his hand, and he looks upset, a tiny bit awkward.

He better buy a round. I've made sure Dempsey has, and this is sort of his leaving do since he's away to Oz next week.

Carpet introduces him to the lads; I'm last.

"Mr Seal, this is Keith."

"Pleased to meet you," he says and holds out his hand to shake. Not too firm; I hate insecure cunts who squeeze the life out o' you.

"You too, mate," I say.

"Can I sit there?"

"Yeah, sure." I adjust my seat at the high table, and something catches his eye.

"Whoa, nice Gazelles, mate. Really like them."

He's transfixed and can't stop staring at them. None o' the fake interest the rest have shown.

"Thanks, mate. Want a beer?"

We're crowded around two tables on the train. A few older Hibs boys ahead of us; I've nodded my head in their direction and asked if they're behaving themselves. They responded accordingly, not having a clue or caring who I actually fucking am.

I took the seat on the outside so I can stretch the feet and watch the Gazelles don't get crushed or marked. Carpet likes a random kick o' his careless feet under the table. Need to watch him.

"Thanks for the beer, mate," Seal says as he slurps the bubbles off the yellow tin.

"Ahh, don't mention it," I say. He's unaware I've taken it from Carpet's carry-out. As is Carpet.

"Thanks for making me feel so welcome. I was a bit down, but you guys have cheered me up."

"Listen, mate, it's cool. We're a bunch o' cunts, but good cunts. Much like you."

"Congratulations on becoming a dad."

"Cheers, mate. If I'm honest, I'm fucking shitting it. My arse is twitching like a nosey cunt's curtains. It's a big deal being a dad at the best o' times. But twins."

"You got any names?"

"Nah, not yet. Still working on it. One for a boy and one for a girl."

Seal sits up and plunges into a split-open bag of onion rings.

"I've always liked Ryan and Linsey. They're good names."

"Aye, they've got a ring, eh."

I make a dent on the can I'm cradling without realising the force I'm using. I know folk have got good intentions, but it feels that every time someone wishes me well, it gets me down.

"I've just met you, but I can tell you'll be fine."

"How's that?"

"If you love your kids as much as you love those trainers, they'll be the most cared for and looked after children in the world."

We clash the tops of our cans, and I think to myself, as fields fly past the window I'm looking through. That's a lot o' love.

*

"HIBEES HIBEES SING US A SONG! HIBEES! SING US A SONG!"

There's a divide in Dow's Bar. Celtic fans at one end, us Hibs fans at the entrance. There's nae bother; despite the tear gas incident a few years back, there never really is with us and them. Let's face it, everyone knows if it wasn't for Hibs, there wouldn't be a Celtic. They owe us everything.

Seal's loving it. He's got a massive grin on his face that's illuminating a typically unlit Glasgow boozer, and he's in the middle of us. He's getting loads of thumbs up from folk who get he doesn't understand Jakey Edinburgh.

"Mere," I say as I take his pint. "Go up and dae your thing."

He looks at me, then at the clearing ahead. He hands me his tumbler and whispers something to himself. Pep talk.

"Wait," I lean into him. "Give us something classic. Not any obscure B-side pish."

There's that smile again.

He goes to the front of the Hibs fans and holds his arms out.

"I DON'T WANNA DANCE!"

"DANCE WITH YOU BABY NO MORE!" Hibs fans join in with perfect timing, and once they've stopped laughing, our wee cousins from the west join in.

"What was that about?" I ask him.

"You've got to give the people what they want. And they wanted Eddy Grant."

*

The queue for the train is a lot less lively leaving Glasgow than it was getting there. I'm past the point o' a hangover, and I'm past the point o' caring about Hibs.

"Does that happen a lot?" Seal asks. He's munching on a haggis supper, and the poor cunt had to endure it without chippy sauce because of the cave people of Glasgow not having any.

"What? Hibs getting beat by Celtic? All the time. Not winning the Scottish Cup? A hundred years, mate. And it'll be a hundred more."

"Why do you put yourself through it?"

The queue shuffles up about half an Adidas, and I shrug.

"It's a good day oot at the football ruined by the football, eh?" Carpet shouts at me from behind the queue.

"Keith! I've got Maggie on the phone. Christine's gone into labour."

There's fuck all I can do about it standing in Queen Street. I look down, dejected, and clock my trainers. It's as if they're smiling back at me. Inspiring me. You've got this.

22

A NORTHERN SOULBOY

Mark Fleming

After pulling out the Sunday night 5-a-sides, Euan rubbed the ankle that was playing up again. A compound fracture in his teens had left him with post-traumatic arthritis which could flare up at any time. Twisting the screw-top from a Bulgarian red, he decanted what looked like blood into a half-pint tumbler, considered popping an ibuprofen to augment the 14.5% anaesthetic.

So began another alcohol-fuelled YouTube journey into his youth. Here in his lap was the parallel universe where he'd rewind his own highlights. 'Excerpt from a Teenage Opera,' by Keith West. More than a slice of psychedelic pop: like so many songs with the inexplicable power to resonate, a time machine for his spirit. He was five, besotted with the blond-pigtailed girl who'd moved in further up the street and who'd sing him the chorus: 'Grocer Jack, Grocer Jack, is it true what mummy says, you won't come back? Oh no no.' His last year at Craiglockhart primary. Mott the Hoople, Bowie, T-Rex, Middle of the Road on *TOTP2*. Glam rock and Sally Carr's hotpants hinting at the exciting world light years beyond homework and a demonic headmaster who moaned as he lashed his leather belt while surely shooting his load under the folds of his black cloak.

Fast-forward. The Pistols. Pretty Vacant. Johnny Rotten

perfecting a balancing act between not giving one solitary fuck about anything but somehow giving more of a fuck about everything than all the cheesy novelty acts and aspiring pop stars and pompous rock acts put together.

The term X factor had long entered the zeitgeist, but its true meaning was demeaned rather than underlined by panel shows granting a conveyor belt of desperate wannabes their craved 15 minutes in the limelight. Although pop music was inherently transient, the X factor seemed a valid definition for those performers who instantly stood out from the pack, their fame continuing to shine where peers merely flashed in the pan. Igniting fans' lives with excitement and making them obsess about owning their singles and albums. Inspiring gigs that would leave indelible impressions long after the tinnitus faded. The music that seized impressionable imaginations like a benevolent affliction, and especially where Euan's teens were concerned, dictating fashion sense.

So many apprentices at Telford had dressed according to whatever genre they were infatuated with. There was one lad Euan had chatted to in the canteen, Fraser Nelson, a former schoolmate, although both played down the enthusiasm of these reunions. Nellie, a painter and decorator, had been in Euan's registration class at Tynecastle High. Nellie was once a soulboy.

At the youth clubs, Euan's posse would glower from the sidelines, secretly envious of Nellie's captivating spins, twists, and backdrops, trying not to be seen tapping toes to the amazing Northern Soul anthems. 'Tainted Love.' 'Do I Love You.'

999's 'I'm Alive' would temporarily take the PA system hostage, prompting Euan and a handful of mates to leap into the spotlights like demented jesters. One time, an incensed Nellie led a mob chasing Euan and his pals up the road. They legged it to the Sighthill bus terminus where the driver refused to open the doors to four mad-looking kids with ripped jeans and egg whites through their spiked hair, gasping for breath, thumping on the doors. The poodle-permed driver gawked at the commotion, shaking his head, mouthing, *savages.*

Euan pictured Nellie commanding those floors. Spectators enthralled. The girls adored him. Euan could see why, going as far as to admit a man crush, although this observation was delivered with heavy-handed irony to pre-empt any homophobic jibes.

Back then, weekend youth clubs had been the centre of Euan and Nellie's universe. Sighthill. Carrick Knowe. The Chesser. St Martin's church at the foot of Ardmillan. The Merky at Fountainbridge.

At the core of the volatile tribalism, Euan and Nellie fostered a love/hate relationship which persisted for many months. The latter had been a given, an exaggerated public veneer presented to their respective mobs, punk rockers and soulboys, sub-cultures existing alongside each other at school, but like oil and water, never mixing in the playground or beyond. The former, driven by raging but confusing hormones, remained rigorously masked from the ingrained intolerance of their respective friendship groups – and families.

Nellie missed so many Monday registrations after weekend blowouts further afield. Often to be found holding court to the edgier fourth years smoking behind the sheds, he described coach trips to Wigan Casino where everyone would speed like jets at the all-nighters. Though warned not to wear his gear to school, he'd be standing there, arms folded, defiant as the black fists on the patches on his jersey. *Music for and from the soul*, he insisted.

Where Winford or McGrail, their history teachers, would drone on about Edinburgh's grandiose Georgian New Town, funded by plundered Jacobite estates, Nellie would deliver lectures about soul music. Still high as a kite, his chatter veering from enthusiasm into mania, chewing gum as if it was burning his tongue, he relished taking centre-stage. Slouched on the periphery, toying with the Chelsea and Buzzcocks badges pinned to his blazer, Euan would grudgingly listen in. He could still recall everything.

Nellie waxed lyrical about soul sounds spreading like wildfire through the US charts in the 1960s. During the mod scene, vinyl imports were brought into Liverpool docks by merchant seamen. Club DJs were soon lapping up this underground version of soul – *rare grooves* he called it. The scene took root in northern England where clubbers and record collectors were bypassing mainstream Motown. Lighting up clubs like Blackpool's Mecca. Manchester's Twisted Wheel. Dancers would drop blueys, then freak out to the tunes going beyond 100 bpm, hour after hour.

He went on to explain soul originated in the Afro-Caribbean communities; long before crossing the Atlantic eastwards, its roots were in the tribal rhythms, handclaps, dance shuffles, and call and response, retained as folk memories for the horrific journeys *westwards* across the ocean, Africa to the plantations; families crammed into the vessels sharks would trail.

Clandestine dances after sundown became a metaphor for breaking the chains.

The pair felt lingering hostilities wilting the more familiar Euan became with Nellie as a visitor when he dated Euan's wee sister, Carol. Over cans and furtive smokes, they also found themselves bonding over the musical tastes they shared, primarily Euan's older sister, Gillian's Bowie albums. Carol soon moved on, but the two remained friends.

Obstinately loyal to their rival gangs, behind closed doors, chemistry developed. This bubbled over one time Nellie's parents were holidaying in Ibiza. They spent a reckless weekend drinking, speeding, dancing, laughing deliriously. Soulboy baggies and punk drainpipes cast aside into a singular heap next to Nellie's bed, they also made love. Euan was adamant that was what they'd done, not simply shagged, as both did with girlfriends; to Nellie, Euan was just another of his fuck buddies, forgotten once his libido was satisfied. All these liaisons ceased when Nellie got a girl pregnant, becoming a devoted father to their wee lassie. Euan felt the meltdown of teenage heartbreak.

*

Well into his second red, Euan found, 'Do I Love You.' Heaving himself up, he stepped into the middle of the living room and began approximating the way Nellie once shuffled in and out of the flickering lights, knowing every eye was tracking him; Euan's most intently of all.

Nellie and his mates would dust the floor with talcum to prevent skidding. Euan's socks slithering along the floor tiles, he tumbled, his head smacking the skirting board, ringing like the time the Northern gang stuck the boot in next to the bus-stop.

It was Nellie himself who pirouetted into the drizzly night and jumped onto his leg splayed across the kerb. Even he cringed at the snapping noise. Euan could still see him standing over him, amazing eyelashes fluttering with his shocked look, telling him he was a punk wanker, but he'd never meant to take it that far. In a more hushed tone, he insisted he'd make it up to him.

Euan sat up groggily, rubbing his forehead while the music pounded. He joined in.

'Do I love you? Indeed, I do, hey. My darling, indeed, I do. Sweet, sweet darlin.'

He thought of Nellie. Not the way he fucked up his ankle. They were all teenaged and fired up with the same litre bottle of Smirnoff getting passed around behind the youth club at the start of the night, before the music separated them into their clans.

A few weeks ago, on Facebook, Euan had been looking up the schoolmates he remembered. Nellie got a mention. Seemed he'd been one of the painters on the Forth Bridge. Was struck by a train. The comments speculated about whether this was an accident or connected to what one friend referred to as 'dark thoughts' after his daughter died of an overdose.

Euan didn't have to pretend to hate this sweet, sweet, Northern Soul. In his mind, 15-year-old Nellie was spinning like a top, and when Euan screwed his eyes, he froze the image so Nellie's bellbottoms unfurled like flags, while the black fists on the badges sewn into his jumper clenched tight.

Music for and from the soul.

PANIC ATTACK ONE AND PANIC ATTACK TWO

Neil Renton

I'm probably not the only person who didn't realise they were having a panic attack the first time it happened.

I was in the basement of The Venue, a long-missed nightclub in Edinburgh. It was Disco Inferno, so there wasn't much to worry about other than figuring out who actually sang 'Play That Funky Music, White Boy.'

The week before, I'd been to see Oasis at Irvine Beach. My friends and I had been right at the front, as long as we could handle the squashing and lack of oxygen, before we eventually escaped. I'd hazard a guess that it was the only time I'd been claustrophobic, and it must have left a lasting impression on me.

There were a lot of similarities to the concert. It was dark, full of people crashing into me, and I wasn't sober.

My head spun around inside my skull and seemed to spin off my shoulders at the same time. I looked for a safe place to hide and catch my breath. It was horrible, but it passed, and my biggest fear was still not knowing who Wild Cherry were.

The second time I had a panic attack was much later in life, and it didn't take place in the lower level of a nightclub.

It was somewhere far more prestigious.

It was at Cliftonhill.

For those who don't know, it's where Albion Rovers play football. At this point, they were in the bottom Scottish league. I was sitting in the press box, which wasn't much of a box as such. It was a wooden bench covered in off-white and fluorescent green pigeon shit.

It wasn't the bird faeces that were causing me to panic. It wasn't the game I was about to cover for a national newspaper. It was the game the following weekend.

In her haste, the woman working on the sports desk had allocated all the writers two weeks of games. All going well, the following week I was about to cover a massive match.

You're probably thinking this doesn't mean much in the grand scheme of things, but it did for various reasons that I'll explain.

Alloa were two games away from winning the league. A victory in the game they were playing while I was at Albion Rovers would set them up perfectly for clinching the title at Berwick.

Reporting on a game where a team wins a trophy sounds top class. The problem was, my cushy twelve-paragraph copy suddenly became six hundred words, and I couldn't use swear words, so that's my vocabulary limited straight away.

My deadline wouldn't change; it'd still be half six. I'd never covered a big league-winning game before, and suddenly, I was back in the seventies and eighties where players were all in the same bath at full time. They'd be spraying cheap champagne or cheaper beer on each other, and I'd get soaked.

Then they'd throw me in the bath as a laugh, and my Dictaphone would get wet, and my writing pad would disintegrate. I'd end up naked, hoping someone had put the heating on because I'd need it. I'd end up walking back to Edinburgh all the way from Berwick, and I'd never do another football game again because I wouldn't be able to meet the deadline. I'd miss the only newsworthy story, which was a strange creature with moobs and a shy willy seen shuffling back up the motorway.

And as this hit me, I remember staring at the empty stand on the other side of the ground thinking, "You're not having a heart attack. You're not having a heart attack."

As I felt like I was having a heart attack.

It was a horrible feeling. With it being the home of Albion Rovers, there was hardly anyone there, which was just as well because I didn't want to draw attention to myself. So, I did that very Scottish male thing and pretended not to mind while I possibly died.

"Oh, it's nothing. Honest. I can't feel my right arm, but I'll learn to use my left…"

Anyway, things calmed down. I managed to talk myself down with an inner voice I wish had spoken up more often.

And what was even better was that Alloa didn't win their game, so they couldn't claim the league the following week.

Panic over.

THE NIMBLE MEN

Mark Fleming

'What have you been told about checking your phone in front of customers, Calum?'

I watch Kennedy's lips moving but hardly take it in. I've been staring at Emily's text for so long: *Cal. Was trying to explain b4 you rushed out. Still want 2 go on holiday but I'd rather go as friends. Would be best for both of us. We can chat later. Emily X.*

How incongruous is that kiss? Like an inmate being informed the date of his lethal injection, then receiving a menu to choose his favourite last meal. I shove the phone back inside the sporran, fingers wrapped around it. Squeezing until my palm aches. I try holding Kennedy in just as intense a glare. But my stare relinquishes, as it always does.

I mumble. 'It was important. But I've switched it off.'

'Good. Serving customers is what's important. Keep Scotland's history flowing, Calum.'

He strides towards the advance guard of the next geriatric coach party. I note the accents. New Zealanders. Several wearing All-Blacks rugby tops. Their haka would look more like the *Thriller* video.

This was supposed to be my last day manning this kiosk at the Culloden visitor centre. Due to start packing for Thailand tomorrow. Travel to Waverley on Saturday for the first leg of a year's backpacking. But Emily's bombshell has derailed everything. All the arrangements. New clothes. Travel pills. Vaccinations. Currency. Months of planning cancelled in a text.

Insisting we can still travel half-way across the world together because we'll remain friends? Travel companions? Maybe this is one of her episodes. It wouldn't be the first time there's been a wobble in our relationship. That time I went down on bended knee in a restaurant, and she simply guffawed with laughter. In time, she said. I think of sleeping in the same room and doing just that. How would a platonic thing survive each time we got melted?

My phone vibrates. Kennedy is elsewhere so I check it out. Another text: *Have to explain, Cal. There's a guy. Jack. From Melbourne. Games designer. We met online. He's coming to meet me in Bangkok. You'll like Jack. You'll get on just great. He's into history. I've told him all about your Highland battles. He can't wait to meet you, so he can get inspired! He designs war games. Imagine if he designed one based on Culloden, you could get royalties?!!!! LOL!! We can be mature about this, Cal. When Jack joins us, you can book your own accommodation. By then, you'll have met someone anyway. Defo. The beach parties are awesome over there, Cal. Lassies from every corner of the globe, in bikinis, eckied up. Your fucking guaranteed, mate!! We can go out on foursomes. Get chonged watching the sun setting over the Andaman Sea. X*

Foursomes?! My sincerest wish would be for Emily and her virtual lover to be arrested by customs after being forced to smuggle cocaine into Indonesia. Closing my eyes, I bunch my fists. Try breathing evenly, although I feel every muscle trembling. Opening again, I stare at the souvenir displays. Scotch terrier keyrings. Lion rampant mouse-mats. Loch Ness monster cuddly toys. Braveheart coasters. Scottish culture reduced to trinkets; the equivalent of Sitting Bull performing horse stunts with Buffalo Bill's travelling circus.

Two middle-aged men waddle from the cinema. Their accents remind me of *The Sopranos*. New Jersey. They hover, fingering postcards, then keyrings bearing Clan surnames. I clock regimental tattoos nestling amongst the wizened white hairs on one guy's tanned forearms. Not old enough to have survived Normandy or the Pacific but too young for Vietnam. Korea? They're joined by respective wives in leisure suits.

'Just think on it, Melv?' says one of the housewives of New Jersey. 'Two thousand men died out there, out in that field, just to decide who was the rightful English king.'

'Unbelievable, Jen. Bonnie Princes? Young Pretenders? What is this, Hans Christian Andersen?'

My mind flits back to Emily. How can you break up a real relationship based on a connection with someone you've never met? What if Jack is a catfish, a 60-year-old weirdo from Milton Keynes? Even so, when I think of the situation, he's real enough. Bet they've been Skyping when I've been out. You think you know somebody, but if you find out you actually don't fucking know them at all, you can imagine anything.

I gaze around. As a kid, my parents used to take me to the old visitor centre. The redcoat commander, the so-called 'Butcher Cumberland,' who ordered his men to slaughter the wounded on the battlefield, was portrayed as a rotund mannequin with rosy cheeks. There was also a dressing-up box with redcoats for his soldiers. Jimmy wigs for the Jacobites.

My phone judders. I snatch it. Her again. A call this time. 'What the fuck, Emily?'

The Americans watch me. Kennedy is hovering again, furious.

'Cal. Don't be so immature. We always agreed we could see other folk, didn't we? Christ, we're nineteen. We're far too young to get serious. There's a whole world out there. Anyway. You'll get on with Jack. I promise. Cal? Speak to me, Cal. I'm sure you'd rather I was honest? You're not gonna be a fucking baby about this, are you?'

I toss the mobile across the room. It cracks against a pre-1746 map of the Highlands. All the clan territories still there in a multi-coloured patchwork. I snarl at the nearest woman.

'That cartoon Nessie on your T-shirt? Tell me which is more farcical? That plesiosaurs could have survived the extinction of 99% of the dinosaurs 65 million years ago, continued to survive, right through the Ice Age that carved Loch Ness from the mountains, then live for another thirteen thousand years? Or the notion dinosaurs wore tartan fucking bunnets?'

'What did he say to you, honey?' her husband says. 'Sometimes I find the local accent is just goddamn impossible.'

'Search me,' she replies. 'Supposed to be English but it's anything but.'

Kennedy is rushing over, combover flapping, jowls wobbling. He sometimes reminds me of that Duke of Cumberland dummy; all that's missing is the white wig.

'What on earth has got into you, Calum?! You're not just demob crazy, you're crazy full stop!'

Said with a smirk. He's been gunning for reasons to get rid

of me before my last day and I've presented it, with loan shark interest.

'This boy's gone berserk,' pipes an American voice.

Kennedy stands between the tourists and me. Raising his hands in apology. I elbow my way past.

'Calum?'

I stumble against a display cabinet. A dragoon's pistol and a bayonet unearthed from the soil. I elbow a crack in the glass panel. A woman squeals.

'*Calum!*'

Next, I'm outside, stumbling across the moor. I can't think where I want to go, only what I need to leave behind. I run by the red flags indicating the government army's deployment on the morning of 16 April. Soon my legs are aching. Lungs struggling for air. But I keep on. Arriving at the blue flags, the Jacobite position, I halt.

A skylarks trills. Clouds are vast cobwebs smeared across powder blue. I gaze back at the red flags, imagine a young rebel, his terror-stricken vision darting from the cloud formations to the scarlet uniforms formed in disciplined ranks. His claymore gripped with white knuckles. Preparing for the order to rush towards those musketeers, and cannons primed with grapeshot. Offering his life for Prince Charles Edward Stuart; not through any deep-rooted political leanings, not necessarily through religion since the Jacobite army contained as many Protestants as Catholics, but simply because his Laird, his master, had aligned himself to this cause.

As for the government soldiers, swearing their oaths of allegiance to King George II and his German royal family, then putting their lives on the line for a government less than 3% of the population could vote for. They'd be watching the rebel army with trepidation, anticipating the feared Highland charge. But also aware of what volleys of lead balls travelling at 1,500 feet per second would do to human beings struggling over boggy ground.

Perhaps the rebel was praying for some horseman to canter through the dawn mists brandishing a white flag, bringing news the Houses of Stuart and Hanover were to be united by some marriage. That was how alliances were created back then. By weddings. Or killing.

Reaching into my uniform's plastic sporran, I snatch my lighter, spark the doob I'd prepared for my walk to the bus stop after my shift. I exhale towards the clouds. Now I delve into the pouch for the hip flask. Uncapping this, I drain the remainder in fiery mouthfuls. Leaning back in the undergrowth, I watch the clouds drifting in a fantastical procession. There's the white Ferrari I'll own one day. There are the Outer Hebrides, joined to a reversed Italy. I follow a jet trail, 12 kilometres high, until its white wake fades. The ground rocks gently. My eyelids transform to lead.

*

Twilight is enveloping the moor. Beyond the last clouds, the first glimpse of Venus and a dusting of stars. As the surrounding terrain dissolves into shadows, I switch my attention to the infinity of space beyond. Ten minutes later I can pick out The Plough, the Seven Sisters; brightest of all, the Dog Star. Lighting the joint again, I shift the red dot between the points of light, faster, creating dazzling patterns. With each passing minute, further reaches of the infinite majesty of space are being revealed. Hundreds of stars. Thousands.

Gradually, I notice curtains of green and blue light shimmering near the horizon. The Northern Lights. *Na Far Chlis*, as the Highlanders would've referred to them. The Nimble Men. I visualise the fighter again, the Friday night before the battle 300 years ago. Tartan shawl wrapped around his shivering frame, fingers hovering by a campfire, sucking on a clay pipe, gazing up at these stars. Inventing his own constellations; seeing bears, leaping salmon, pouncing kestrels. Creating his own mythology as soldiers on any battle's eve have done for millennia. Wondering if the Nimble Men might appear, gamboling across space. Placing everything in perspective, the majesty of the heavens versus the ridiculous sectarian squabbling of men on this tiny planet. Most of all, wondering if he'd be alive to lose himself in space the same time tomorrow, after it was all over, seeking the Nimble Men, leaping over these skies in their eternal dance.

Flashing lights by the centre. Above, an aeroplane blinks over the Moray Firth. Taking a final, lingering drag I notice torchlight by the red flags. The sound of barking dogs makes my hair bristle. I think of Emily snorkeling through the South China Seas, a tanned figure floating close by, ripped muscles dragging through the blue waters.

The wind stirs the blue flags above me. Black flags now. They flutter and snap. Torches carve swathes of heather from the gloom. One beam sweeps by. Catches me. Others home in. Flicking away the roach, I take a deep breath. Begin marching up the slope towards them. Quickening my pace from a stroll to a jog, my heart drums in my chest. Breaking into a sprint, I lift my face to the stars, shrieking like a proud Clansman.

A deep voice bellows. Torchlight envelops me, as if I'm being ambushed by paparazzi.

'Kennedy?! You called the fucking busies?!'

I don't even remember snatching the bayonet from the glass shards. As I brandish it in the night air, I feel the matted blood between my fingers and the hilt.

The crackle of a taser. 50,000 volts. I slump backwards, limbs jerking. Above the battlefield, space is a manic whirlwind, as if galaxies are being born. The Nimble Men won't stop.

DUSTIN JOHNSON'S PERFECT SWING

Neil Renton

Edinburgh loves a drama.

This morning, heavy rainfall has ground the city and the surrounding bypass to a halt. It's July. It's Scotland. We shouldn't be surprised. Instead, we need to acknowledge it's one of the many reasons why we're depressed.

Speaking of which, I eventually made it to the doctor's surgery for my regular check-up.

The weather threw me off track, and I ended up getting the wrong bus, jumping on a diverted 16 when I was aiming for a focused number 7. Then I was all out of sorts, standing at the entrance of Ocean Terminal, wondering how I was going to make it on time and realising that if I had stayed on the wrong bus, I would have been closer to where I needed to be than where I was.

I still made it on time, unlike one of the receptionists. There's an older one that I recognise; you need to get an apology in early for nothing in particular for her to show any empathy whatsoever. Theresa, according to her badge.

Standing meekly at the reception desk and at her mercy, I apologised for making it to the surgery on time and, in doing so, interrupted her from batting away flashing red lights like a dog's tail swatting away flies.

She looked up with her thin, over-made-up face long enough to tell me the doctor I was seeing was late. I apologised for this.

It's not as if I've got much planned. At some point, I'll be in tears. Probably sitting at home, staring into an abyss. In the shower I haven't switched on. In the bed I haven't made. In front of a blank television. Another Monday afternoon. Another Friday night. Another Sunday morning.

There's a series of issues I'm going to skim over in my ten-minute appointment. I'll plead to have the Edinburgh Leisure membership renewed that day, but free to help me out, which I never actually use.

What should I? The gym's full of beautiful people who don't break a sweat on the treadmill. I can't tie my laces without needing an inhaler.

My pass gives me access to council golf courses, and there are plenty of them in Edinburgh. I should really put the knowledge I've gained from all the articles I've read on the sport in the publications next to my usual seat.

Today I'm engrossed in Dustin Johnson's Perfect Swing. Last week I learned how to Putt Like Rory. It won't be long before they're sizing me up for one of those green jackets they get for winning stuff.

The other receptionist has turned up to bail her colleague out. She's younger and trying all she can to stop the aging process. She shakes her see-through umbrella and puts on the radio. There's a local station and the DJ is asking listeners to guess the year. Theresa greets Hannah.

"I think it's ninety-eight," Hannah says as she sits down, switching her work phone on and letting it ring.

"How come?" her work pal asks, oblivious to the fact someone is trying to make an appointment.

"Barry Banter gave a clue that it was the year Legally Blonde came out. I went to law school after seeing that."

"To be a lawyer?" Theresa asks, not hiding her shock.

"Yeah," comes the reply. "I saw it on tape and it changed my life."

It's just as well Blockbuster Video never had *Pretty Woman* that night, I think to myself as I devour John Ramm's Massive Drive.

"I'm sorry that the ingrowing toenail is still causing you pain, Mrs Hay, but there are no emergency appointments for today. If you can give us a call tomorrow at eight, we'll be able to see what we've got. I know, I appreciate you tried today at eight, but unfortunately, we're short-staffed due to the weather."

"Honestly," sighs Hannah. "That's all I get. Moaners."

"Eighteen in the queue. You're joking," Theresa tuts.

"Wait, changing my mind," Hannah springs to life. "Two thousand and three. Barry Banter mentioned it's the year the Xbox came out, and I got one for my wee brother on his birthday that year."

I flick my thumb up the spines of the magazines. I've devoured the golf ones so much that I'll have no other option than to start on the *People's Friend*. That's how often I've been here.

"Next up, it's a song from local band The Shan! Remember them? It's 'Lucky 15,'" shouts Barry Banter.

I'll never forget the first time I heard that song on the radio. Jo Whiley, Radio One. Robbie, The Raith Fury, was driving us up to Aberdeen for a gig, and he seemed intent to break either the land speed limit or our necks on the A90.

Next to Robbie was James, gloriously gorgeous. Cheekbones chiseled with the same tools that Michelangelo used to carve David. Model features that were too pretty to be hanging about with us under a mop of Mediterranean curls.

Eric sat behind James, eyes darting from side to side, not hiding the fact he didn't want to be in the beat-up Fiat.

And I was next to Eric, holding the seatbelt into a buckle that I couldn't clip, thinking that with any slightly wrong movement we were destined to die. And I hadn't felt happier before or since.

"Let me be your smile on a Monday morning/The glow that makes you feel good without any warning."

The unscheduled stop. Robbie searching under his seat for the Jelly Baby he'd dropped. James for a pee that was spraying onto the legs of a nauseous Eric. Me pinging the fence and working out album covers.

"What a blast from the past that was!" Barry barked. "I've not heard that song for YEARS! I tell you what, we could all do with a smile on this Monday morning, couldn't we?"

"Whatever happened to The Shan? They were a one-hit wonder!" Barry Banter's co-presenter Beth asks.

"Good question. I read an article in the *Evening News*, a 'Where Are They Now?' feature on forgotten local celebrities, and it said that lead singer Murray Doyle was last seen working in a call centre."

Everywhere falls silent for a bit. The radio station, the waiting area. Even the phones stop.

"Ah, that's a shame," sighs Beth as if working in a call centre was a worse fate than death itself.

"Two thousand! That was the year! I know for a fact because I hooked up with that Murray," blushes Hannah.

"No way! You could sell your story," her work pal says.

"Are you joking? No one remembers him. I'd get about fifty pence."

Both of them laugh and go back to the phones that have started ringing again. Hannah puts a patient on hold and turns to her colleague.

"I'm calling in the station and telling Barry. We'll get a mention."

She picks up her phone and taps the number with her acrylic nails, putting on loudspeaker so we all hear what she's doing.

"HELLO! You're live on EH Radio! What's the mystery year?"

"Barry! No way!" Hannah shrills.

"Way! Who's this?"

"It's Hannah! I know the year! It's two thousand!"

I don't realise I'm walking over to the reception desk in the middle of the surgery. I'm doing it with the purpose of Tiger Woods on his way to whatever titles he seemed to win on a regular basis. Big strides, arms like pendulums at my side.

I reach under the Perspex separator and grab the phone off Hannah. "Hi Barry, Hannah here is wrong. The year was two thousand and one. And to correct you, The Shan weren't a one-hit wonder. 'Lucky 15' got to number one in the national charts, back when it meant something. We had another two top ten songs and another one that made the top twenty. And this is the proper charts when people made an effort to actually go out and buy stuff. Queue up and everything."

"You're right. Murray Doyle is working in a call centre. He's currently signed off with depression as he battles suicidal thoughts on a regular basis. Like, every waking moment. He's currently in a doctor's surgery waiting to be seen by a GP who'll warmly shake his hand as he didn't expect him to still be alive.

"Oh, and Hannah, just to correct you. It wasn't Murray who you had a thing with one night. It was Robbie Hunter, the band's drummer. It happened down an alleyway off the Royal Mile, and he said you were so bad at blow jobs you scraped your teeth down his cock. The B-side he wrote, 'Queen of Nothing,' was about you, especially the lyrics 'She grates on me, she grates on me. She. Grates. On. Me.'"

The doctor has appeared and he's standing open-mouthed. I hand a shocked Hannah back her phone as Barry Banter spits out apologies.

At least one of us does.

DOM'S DOSE

Mark Fleming

In the lane outside the kitchen, I listened. Shrieks. Roars. Smash of glass. A bite-sized riot. I tugged my tab until its tip was a long glow. A stag *party*? Nah. Parties mean fun. We'd a party for my Nana's 65th last April. It came to me. A stag *dose*.

Sometimes they're sound. They lads from Dingwall last week were brilliant, celebrating Dougal and Chloe's nuptials. A hoot with Highland accents. They were a stag party. But tonight's table for 24 were up from Hertfordshire for Dominic and Arabella. Defo a dose. Poor Arabella's not on the radar. Would've been a healthy beep when Dom grabbed Karina's arse and made her drop plates.

Edinburgh's stag central. We put out the red carpet for final flings. Just before my fag break, that was literally, mind. The floor got splattered as a ching-fuelled argument led to punches then bearhugged apologies.

All night, their boorish attitudes and cut-glass accents have been putting me in mind of that photo from the papers: Cameron, Osborne, and Johnson, the architects of austerity, in their Bullingdon Club dinner jackets. Speculation about initiations. Abusing pigs' heads. Burning £50 notes in front of beggars. But that wasn't the worst of it.

Their voices getting louder, snarlier, swearier with each fresh bottle of fizz ordered with clicked fingers. That wasn't the worst. The actual words pouring from their mouths: strumpets, trollops, and some girl rattled so many times, 'It'd be like tossing a worm into the fucking Albert Hall.' That wasn't the worst. The best man offering me and Karina, 'Six month's wages in this roach-infested packie shithole' to come back to their hotel, a threesome so Dominic getting laid for the last ever time as a single would be something to remember, adding, 'What stays in fucking Edinburgh,' with a wink and a Jurassic Park belch. That wasn't the worst.

The best man hoisting the tablecloth. Above the crushed poppadoms and trodden salad, unzipping his flies, his cock like the alien poking out John Hurt's guts. That wasn't the worst. No matter how many times customers leered at my boobs, called Mo, 'Mahatma,' or Karina, 'the pokable Polack,' we just switched off. You have to. We've got used to long nights pandering to doses as well as parties. Even the doses tend to leave generous tips. The last shreds of a guilty conscience. The worst came later.

After their bill was settled, in cash, tonight's tip some kind of record for Mo's restaurant, Karina began clearing the plates from their chimp's tea party. I fetched the mop and pail. We heard Mo whistling Taylor Swift, popping into the gents. We heard Mo scream.

*

'The fucking smell, Amy. I'll need new air fresheners.'

'It'll be *so* worth it, doll.'

'Three Sisters?'

'Aye, doll. When the best man was organising taxis, he

said …' I mimicked his entitled accent. 'Three sisters for Dom the man! Even better than the Bengali Banquet's two spunk buckets.'

Karina grimaced. 'Still can't believe fucking tip they leave. I'm hitting the Fort on Sunday, Amy. Getting my new wardrobe from New Look.'

'As if that makes up for the rest of it, though, doll. All that cally bundled on the table.'

'Cally?'

'Money. Screwed into fistfuls. Like they were emptying litter out their pockets. That's what it's like for the likes of them. Something to just toss around.'

'I ken.'

I chuckled. Love her Polish Scottish. 'The best man even made a wee battle plan.'

'What you mean, Amy?'

'Using shot glasses.'

'What?'

'Like a general, organising his troops. He slams one glass down.' Posh voice. '*Maggie Dickson's.*' Back to Gracemount. 'Next glass.' Posh. '*Biddy Mulligans.*' Gracemount. 'Next glass.' Posh. '*Three Sisters.*'

I grinned at Karina, but my heart was pumping. As they'd been getting ready to shoot, I'd sneakily snapped them. Texted the photies to Daz, my big brother, head doorman at Biddies. Edinburgh can be a village. Their club rugby shirts were white, like the England strip with a different badge. Not a great choice for a pre-session curry then a binge but made them stick out like sore thumbs. Which was the point of stag uniforms. High-viz for misogynists.

Daz texted. *White boys just left, sis.* Sure enough, we could hear them long before we saw them, their drunken voices broadcasting their condition. Their status. Karina and I peered down. A reversal of the time the Old Town's classes lived in the same tenements but were separated by distance from the open sewers: them in the Heavens; us, their wage slaves, cleaners, butchers, miners, cooks, bakers, soldiers, chambermaids, and waitresses, nearer Hell.

I hollered. 'Show us your pricks, you pricks!'

'Where'd that come from? Up there! Some Jock slapper! Up on that bridge. You fucking dirty cow. Time for another show, boys.'

I thought of Mo, holding the toilet door open for us to see, hand trembling so much the door was squeaking on its hinges, the funny noise reminding me of a midgie or something. Except tears were streaming down his face.

'Bloody bastards, they are. No different from their ancestors, feasting at grand tables while their punkah wallahs wafted away the stench from Purba Bardhaman, my father's home, the millions starving during the famines.'

Moments ago, after receiving Daz's text, I'd sketched around. Oblivious revelers. Nobody would've noticed Billy Batts in Karina's boot, let alone a bread crate filled with weird balloons.

They'd wrecked the condom machine, a few strewn over the floor. The mirror was smashed into shards. The blocked toilet was overflowing with shite and puke. When Mo had stumbled away to phone an emergency plumber, I'd pulled on kitchen gloves. Started filling condoms.

There, his voice echoing under George IV Bridge, the best man was flashing again. My third missile caught him across the side of his head, coated his white shirt.

'Welcome to Edinburgh, motherfuckers,' shouted Karina.

A guy next to her grinned, delving into the balloons. 'Gardy fucking loo!' His mate grabbed one. Other passers-by were clocking us. Filming the carnage. Starring Dominic's dose. We were all chucking the missiles. Chorusing, 'Gardy fucking loo!'

MANAGING THE BLUES BLUES

Neil Renton

If Walter knew how much of a hassle it was managing Chelsea, he'd have told them to bucking ram the job. He wasn't even officially in charge until Monday and it was already a pain in his arse, having interrupted his Sunday routine of a pint with his pals in the Dockers.

It seemed like the whole of the world's media had decided onto Academy Street and the surrounding area. Vans with giant satellites were stationed all the way up to the Tesco car park as journalists phoned in copies on one mobile while typing furiously on another.

Everyone was desperate to catch up with the seventy-eight-year-old pensioner who had just been appointed as boss of one of the most prestigious teams in football. And as with many things in life it was his grandson's fault.

Ryan had recorded clips of his grandad's reaction to watching The Blues and thanks to social media the videos went all over the world. Walter's rants at the inability of a bunch of highly paid professionals went viral.

"If he didn't spend so long in the tattoo shop, he could spend some time training!"

"Bucking HELL! He didn't even move for that penalty!"

"Did you see that? Well, he never! Useless!"

There was such a public support for Walter and his opinions that when the Chelsea board made the decision to get rid of their third boss in a month, the unanimous decision was to bring him in.

Walter sat in a corner of the Dockers opposite his usual seat which pissed him off even more. That Roy Keane fucker was in it with the Scouse and the Manchester ones. All crew neck sweaters and black trainers with big white soles. Show offs. Walter didn't like Keane, he wasn't a fan of grumpy cunts. Anyway, he was willing to bite his tongue and put his preconceptions to one side long enough to be interviewed by the three of them.

He also wasn't happy about having to drink Belhaven Best from an illuminations green water bottle but he had to appease the sponsors who didn't like him consuming alcohol in front of the cameras.

To his left was Wullie, Walter's long-time pal now employed as a translator. Many people, even those whose first language was English, had a problem understanding what Walter was saying most of the time.

"XG3?" Walter screwed up his face. "The only goals I'm worried about are the two on the bucking pitch."

"You get that, boys?" Wullie asked. The room nodded cautiously.

"How will you handle a dressing room full of egos?" asked a smarmy reporter Walter had taken an instant dislike to after the journalist had coined the headline 'Chelsea Pensioners Appoint OAP.'

"Av've manned the door o' The Dockers oan a Saturday night. When yea' had tae split up Agnes and Lorraine fightin' o'er the bingo then nothin' fazes yea."

"What do you say to those who are questioning your £32 million a year salary as being too much?"

"Too much?!" Walter replied. "Have you seen the price o' drinks in London? Ah'm paying three pound sixty for a pint o' Best. £32 million widnae even get me a fifty pence mixture doon there."

"Excuse me! Walter!" Bonnie Scotland, Only Fans! Would you like to collaborate with me? I was thinking of filming a special called Tossing the Caber."

Walter looked at her confused. She had the appearance of having showered with creosote. He leaned into Wullie who got his phone out and showed him images.

"Porn star?" Walter spluttered. "What happened to the glamour girls from years ago? The Sam Foxes, The Maria Whittakers. Ah've got bigger tits than you."

"You get that, lads?" Wullie asked.

The silence from everyone in attendance said it all.

KANYE WEST FAE LOCHEND

Neil Renton

Walter smiled to himself as he sauntered towards the fantastic pish he was about to have.

To be honest, he was a little disappointed after getting sacked from the Chelsea job, but the £12 million payoff cushioned the blow.

His buddies had decided to take him to The Dockers on a Friday afternoon to cheer him up. The company was brilliant, with everyone in top form. He'd had a good kick of the ball, and now the ball was kicking him back full force, square in the bladder.

There were two guys standing at opposite ends of the urinals. Walter could have slunk away to the cubicle to have a pee, but despite his small stature, he was more than capable of holding his own. And with two hands at that.

To his left stood Colin, a big brute of a man with a hooped earring and arms covered in Celtic tattoos. To his right was Donald. Not as tall as Colin, he stood swaying on his feet as the steam from his pish clouded up his glasses.

Walter broke the silence with a rasper of a fart and a question.

"Here, any o' you cunts heard o' some cunt called Kanye West?"

Colin and Donald pondered this as the pair of them pissed as if they were running a bath.

"Nah, why?" Donald asked.

"Ma grandson Ryan is away tae buy a pair o' the boy's trainers. Three hundred quid!" Walter spluttered.

"Three hundred quid! Fir trainers! Ma last car cost less than that!" choked Colin, both on the vitriol of his own words and the odour of Walter's stench that was currently turning his nostril hair to ash.

"Exactly. Ah know Ah got ma payout fae Chelsea and Ah could give him the money, but it's no the point," said Walter.

"It's the principle, eh," Donald said.

"Wha's wrong wi' Skechers? Ah got these in the half-price sale," said Walter, showing off his footwear with pride.

"Wait. Kanye West? I know the name. Big ginger streak o' pish fae Lochend. Works on the bins," growled Colin. "Dae ye want me tae put the feelers oot on him?"

"Ah just want tae know wha' he's playing at, selling his trainers tae kids for three hundred quid," Walter shouted above the drone of the hand dryer. "And I also want tae find out, when he sells ma grandson his trainers, how is he gonnie get hame in his bare feet?"

*

Walter was in his fucking element. The Belhaven Best was flowing like a tsunami of turgid-tasting barley. He'd picked a winner in the syndicate bet, and he was holding court at the back of The Dockers with his account of what he'd actually done with the polo shirts Chelsea had provided him with.

He stopped laughing and unfolded his arms when he noticed Colin ambling towards the table with a Tesco carrier bag.

Colin nervously asked Walter for a word, and the pair of them retreated to the empty function suite at the back.

"Walter, Ah dunno what came o'er me. Ah hink it might've been cause I never had anything tae eat before Ah started drinkin.'"

"Aye, that'll be it," mused Walter as he noticed Colin's gut struggle to be contained by his forty-four-inch waist jeans.

"Anyway, Ah was ragin' aboot yer helpless grandson,"

"He's twenty-two," interrupted Walter.

"So Ah went lookin' fir Kanye West. Y'know, tae speak tae him."

Walter felt a wee bit ill as he glanced down at the bag Colin was holding. Was that a red haired-sized head inside it?

"An.'.?"

"Well, obviously he denied that it was him ripping off folk with his expensive trainers an' said Ah had the wrong man. That's when Ah flipped an.'... Ah'm sorry, Walter, Ah really am!"

Walter did his best to console the Big Unfriendly Giant, but it was like trying tae cuddle a pylon.

"Ah went a bit tonto an' Ah gave him a shoo-in. Then Ah took his trainers aff him and gave him a shoo-in with them."

Colin meekly reached into the bag and pulled out a tatty grey trainer with a hole blossoming through the big toe. Walter couldn't believe Ryan was willing to pay a three-figure sum for them.

"The cunt is a proper rip-off merchant," said Colin. "His trainers have the same 'S' on them as yours."

MY YELLOW SUBMARINE

Mark Fleming

Revolver, The Beatles (1966)

Dad was born in 1921 in Monaghan and brought up in what was then called the Irish Free State. Mum was born in Craigentinny, east Edinburgh, in 1932. I came along just as Britain was entering the Swinging Sixties.

This era of heady youth culture typified by screaming Beatlemania, the mods and rockers, and Twiggy in Mary Quant mini-skirts, passed my already middle-aged folks by. I do remember there were always records playing at home; not The Beatles or The Kinks, film soundtracks such as *Calamity Jane*, *South Pacific*, *The Sound of Music*. And Dad's comedy albums, Bob Newhart, Shelley Berman, Tom Lehrer, or The Goons on the radio. But one slice of 60s pop that did lodge in my fertile childhood mind was The Beatles, 'Yellow Submarine,' the double A-side with 'Eleanor Rigby,' released the same day in August 1966 as their 7th studio album, *Revolver*.

Chronologically sitting between their rock singles, 'Paperback Writer' with its upbeat, chiming guitars, and the psychedelic anthem, 'Strawberry Fields Forever,' 'Yellow Submarine' was a novelty song. Ringo Starr took the lead vocal, while producer George Martin, who'd previously worked with The Goons, added comical nautical sound effects.

At the time, John Lennon's remarks about The Beatles being

more popular than Jesus, together with the band's public stance opposing the Vietnam War (not to mention allusions to barbiturates sold in yellow capsules) led to 'Yellow Submarine' being banned by some US radio stations. But as it was released two weeks after I turned four, the only soldiers on my radar were Captain Snort and Sergeant Major Grout in *Camberwick Green*.

The song inspired me to produce my version of its subject, a lurid collision of yellow felt pen which did look as if it could've been produced by someone zoning out on sedative-hypnotic drugs. I should say, *does* look, because my dad framed it, and it took pride of place on the wall at home for many years. It's still in a drawer, somewhere.

THE SCAB

Neil Renton

Sophie stood at the kitchen worktop as the world around her exploded into chaos.

"There should be a channel on the radio where they don't read the news. Just music. Nice and happy songs," she said.

"You could put on a playlist," her husband Dougie noted while he shuffled packets of cartoon figures around.

"Just an option. Do you want to be depressed for the rest of the day? Question why you've decided to raise a child when the planet seems intent on killing itself? Or do you want the latest songs from Taylor Swift and Ed Sheeran?"

"What sort of playlist do you want? I'll put it on for you." Dougie knew when to quit while he was ahead with his wife, and even when to cash out when he was nowhere near the top.

"That's the thing. There's too much choice on the likes of Spotify. Genres I've never heard of that creep into my Wrapped at the end of the year."

"Where do the Mars Bars go?" Dougie asked.

"Blue bags. Put two in the pink ones over there." Sophie raised her eyebrows in mock disgust. "You know whose parents that is."

"Too much choice," Dougie smiled.

"Like this thing they've been going on about. Some disease that's killing people in about five days by covering their bodies in a scab. Do we really need to know about this? Surely they'll find a cure by the end of today and we'll all be fine."

"Mummy," Molly came into the kitchen, with the family dog Simba trying to keep up.

"It's a big deal, Sophie," Dougie said. A rogue mini tube of Smarties had accidentally opened and he had no option other than to clear up the mess.

"You know what's a big deal? You've put the lollipops in the wrong bags. Sugar-coated bitter ones should go there. You'll need to do them again."

Sophie's parents didn't have much, which meant Sophie didn't have a birthday party until she was 18. Even then, it was a low-key barbecue with a carefully selected small group of friends and her boyfriend at the time. A crate of Becks between them all, when everyone was too polite to admit they hated the taste.

She'd watch with envy from every Little Marcos to the Trampoline Centre to Shandon and Hibs Club celebrations. She didn't want Molly to be that child. Always invited, never the invitee.

"Mummy."

"It's just a birthday party."

"It's not just a birthday party. You don't get it, Douglas."

"Mummy. Look. I've got something to show you.

*

Sophie cradled an ailing Molly in the Royal. Her daughter's limp head rested on her chest, while her legs dangled lifelessly over the side.

Molly lay still. There was a faded tattoo transfer that had become engulfed by the scab. When Molly first showed Sophie, it was like a candle wax seal you'd get on an envelope centuries ago. Now it was as though the youngster had coloured her own arm with black tar. Every time Sophie had the stomach to glance quickly at the incrustation, it grew. It was more alive than Molly.

"We need to do something. My daughter is dying."

"I'm really sorry, but there's nothing else that can be done," said a consultant with a jittery twitch in his eyelid. Since they'd been at the hospital, they'd been seen by everyone from students right up to the heads of departments. Now it was the turn of this guy to talk a lot but say nothing.

"There must be something."

"As we've already gone over, we'll keep her in the high-dependency unit, monitor her progress and continue to seek advice and guidance from the finest medical experts already working on this outbreak."

"Five days they say you have when you get it. There's four left."

"We'll do all we can. We'll get her a bed in a moment."

"It's her birthday next week. She won't live to see the age of six, will she?"

Blink blink BLINK.

"Believe me, she's in the best place."

*

It can't be that difficult to drive.

Sophie had started to learn in a manual car. Her parents were going to give her their old Jazz when she passed her test, but she had no other option than to give up when the world went into Covid lockdown.

Dougie's automatic should be easy to get the hang of. It was early, birdsong being the only noise. No nosey neighbours judging her manoeuvres.

Molly was buckled into the back, wrapped in her comfort blanket to keep her shivering body warm.

On the passenger seat, she dumped the supplies: cans of cheap, shop-brand energy drinks, birthday gift bags, and a helium balloon. Lastly, Sophie placed a cake—Molly's favourite, lemon drizzle.

Simba peered out of the window, tongue hanging out of his panting mouth. Please don't bark. Dougie was fast asleep, Sophie made sure of that. She didn't want any risks to be taken.

*

She'd switched off her phone, then driven over it, then stamped on it, then buried it in a wooded area when they stopped for a comfort break.

You couldn't be too sure.

All she had were the directions she'd written on the back of a receipt.

This was definitely the place.

She took a right and guided the car along a man-made clearing. If the car breaks down, if it gets stuck, they're fucked.

As she looked back to check on Molly, pale and sweating. The Scab glared back.

They're already fucked.

You'd expect there to be ambulances, signs, even if they're temporary: 'Hospital this way.' Nothing.

There was a grand-looking house just over there with a farmyard next to it. She'd ask them where it is. They must be close.

Sophie climbed back and kissed Molly's clammy head. Every time she looked at her daughter, Molly appeared to be closer to death.

She was too exhausted to cry.

Sophie rang the doorbell and knocked on the door. Then she did it again, more rapidly and forcefully.

There was a sound behind the imposing green door. Words were spoken before the door opened.

Initially, there was a bit of confusion. A young guy, glasses, short-sleeved business shirt, chinos. He stood for a bit, then it clicked for both of them at the exact same time.

"You must be Sophie," he said.

Sophie covered her mouth. She wasn't sure what was going to come out.

"Doctor Kennedy?" Sophie offered her trembling hand for him to shake.

"Please don't be offended if I don't return the gesture," the doctor said.

Sophie looked down and noticed why.

*

"I got the disease just over two months ago," Doctor Kennedy said. "South America."

"And you took matters into your own hands?"

The doctor grimaced. Sophie immediately realised her mistake.

"Sorry," she said, trying not to look at his right arm, shortened at the elbow.

"It's okay. I'm used to it. But yeah, you're right, I decided to amputate the limb."

"And that was two months ago?"

The doctor smiled and nodded.

"And you're still alive?"

He nodded.

She hugged him, covering his shoulder in all kinds of fluid that had been living on her face. His left hand patted her back.

"Come on, I'll show you round."

The doctor pushed Molly in the rickety wheelchair. Like a lot of the equipment at the makeshift hospital, it was basic.

The ward was housed in an old stable to the back of the farm. Seven beds were occupied while loved ones sat around them speaking words of comfort. Medical staff roamed about, checking levels and giving thumbs up to the patients.

"Here's Molly's bed," the doctor pointed. A couple of porters helped her onto it.

"I can't begin to thank you," Sophie said.

"Please. There's no need."

"I don't have my phone to get onto my banking app and get the money." Sophie wondered if Dougie had blocked it. Were the police aware at this point? She didn't have any concept of awareness.

"It's cool. We've got computers here. Let's not worry about that just yet. What's going to happen is my staff will get Molly examined and settled and we'll sort something for you," the doctor winked and grinned. "It's been some experience for you."

*

"Mrs York, you'll need to come with us. There's been a complication."

"What is it, Doctor? I thought the operation went well? You said it was a success."

"Come with me," Doctor Kennedy instructed.

Sophie unwillingly left Molly lying in the makeshift bed attached to a drip. The bandage on the stub of her arm had absorbed a bit of blood, but apart from that, she looked fine. A peaceful sleep for the first time in days.

The doctor hurried ahead as they left the temporary ward and headed to the house. The cold night air cut through them. Sophie called out for answers, but he didn't reply.

Sophie grabbed him as they got to the entrance with a force she didn't think she had in her.

"Tell me what's wrong."

"There's a drinks reception and you're not there."

The doctor led Sophie into the main house. Inside, everyone was smiling and laughing. There was a mobile phone playing Ed Sheeran songs. Family members of patients danced with staff members and drank alcohol from paper cups.

"What about—"

"Molly? She'll be fine. The operation was a success. She'll be tired and need plenty of rest, but we did it. We got rid of it."

"Fuck! You're a fucker!" Sophie cackled hysterically. "For a moment I thought something had gone wrong."

"No. The only thing that's wrong is you haven't told me if you're red or white."

The first cup didn't even touch the sides. A decent white too. Next was a warm lager, then a straight vodka. She couldn't remember if she had any of that energy drink left in her car. Wherever that was.

"I needed this, Doctor," Sophie said.

"And what Molly will need is a strong mum. You can't be there all the time for her. You need to look after yourself and care for yourself as much as you do for her."

Sophie nodded. She wiped her cracked lips with the sleeve of her hoodie and caught her reflection in the mirror of the hall they were chatting in. Instantly, she felt aware of her neglected appearance.

"Oh, don't call me Doctor Kennedy. Call me Luke. I'm off duty."

*

The doctor was told his presence was required in the living room where coffee table dance music played. Sophie followed like a lovesick puppy, moving with no rhythm. She couldn't get the beat, too knackered, too early days drunk.

He was younger. She exchanged idle chit-chat as one of the nurses poured her a large one. No idea what it was; it didn't matter.

They kept bumping into each other with glances. They'd look away, then back at each other, giggling like kids.

Sophie left the throng and stood in the doorway. Luke was in the middle of an adoring pack hanging on his every word. He motioned towards his stub and started a Mexican wave of belly laughs.

He saw her. Neither of them looked away this time. He excused himself and followed her out the door up the stairs covered in darkness.

She let him into the first bedroom she could find. She didn't know who it belonged to. She didn't care.

*

Sophie woke with a woman screaming.

It took her a bit to get her bearings. She was on the right-hand side of a bed, which was strange in itself. All she had on was her bra. She jumped up on unsteady legs and put on her clothes that she could find.

Then more screams started. Sophie flew down the carpeted stairs three at a time with her stomach churning with guilt. Dougie and Molly.

She hurried as fast as she could along the wet gravel with one bare foot and made it to the entrance of the stable. She wished she hadn't.

Lying on a bed was the corpse of a man, once aged with Sophie. His partner stood next to the body, missing a leg but covered entirely in a black scab.

Two beds up, the charred and blackened remains of a pensioner. Everywhere covered in a scab, including her wide-open eyes.

Molly.

"Molly! Molly!" Sophie shook her daughter. The parasite was slowly crusting over her body, edging its way to her neck.

"Mummy, I don't feel well," Molly coughed.

Where was the doctor? Where was the kind nurse who told Molly stories about unicorns and fairies?

Sophie went outside, where others stood confused. All family members and loved ones. None of the medical team was to be seen.

Back into the farm. People were either dead or dying. Shrieking or silent.

Out to the car, keys in her hoodie. Opened it and took all she could out of the back seat and back in.

"Molly," Sophie said as she placed gifts on her daughter's bed. "I know this isn't what we planned.

NO PURCHASE NECESSARY

Neil Renton

I fucking knew there would be a tour. It's all about paying attention. It was there for everyone to see if they read the email promoting the last album. It's no point panicking now. We all had a chance to get an early ticket. Sign up for pre-sale access. I scroll to the bottom because I'm tight and I know my way around stuff like this. I didn't need to pay for a CD when I'll stream it for free.

It'll be a proper military operation. Work laptop, mobile phone, multiple browsers. I'll book a half day for getting them and then a full day for the actual gig.

I check my Ticketmaster account to make sure I haven't forgotten my password. Bank card details are up to date. Log out, close the internet, and back up and check again. This time, shut down the computer, full restart, then power on. All good.

I've got time to get a new mouse. It's a tiny bit sticky; clicks don't respond as fast as I need.

*

Initially, the pinch is through my jeans, but just to make sure, it's on the bare skin of my arm.

It's real. The discomfort proves it. Still feels dreamlike, but it happened.

That wasn't as hard as I thought it would be. Relatively simple. Almost an anti-climax. I like building fear and drama, and there wasn't any. Not today, anyway.

There was that moment where you get in, and it thinks a bit about it, and you select how many you're after, and it's contemplating it again, and you're praying to the Lords of WiFi with your toes folded as you choose the amount. There's no bargaining or negotiating; instead, I'm in the Gods, Live From Heaven, bleacher nosebleeds.

Instantly, there's an alert that comes through confirming it. Screenshot it. All feels authentic.

It's ages away, and anything can happen between now and then. But when it comes, it'll be worth it.

*

I've let myself down. Again.

I had one too many. I knew I was at that stage, but I still had that drink. Last night, I ignored the warnings of the bus tracker. Today, I've wasted the morning and didn't go to the gym.

I'll need to arrange other things so I can go tomorrow.

I only have myself to blame. No matter who else was involved.

Now I have a dilemma. Do I order myself a takeaway, knowing that it'll be missing items that I really want, as they always seem to get it wrong? Realising that after the first initial bites, it doesn't taste as good as I fantasised? Or do I make myself one of my world-famous toasties?

Technically speaking, it's not a toastie machine; it's a panini maker. I don't have a panini, maybe used it once for that when I got it, and there was a novelty factor. Ever since then, it's been bread.

It still lives in its original box. I take it out and catch the wriggling cable. I pretend it's a plug-headed snake.

The bread is in date but it's starting to go hard. I really can't be arsed going over to the shop and having a conversation against my wishes with whoever is working.

Orange cheese. Proper fatty stuff. That'll do. I can see it now, oozing over the side, then it'll go hard, and I'll get to it when it cools down as if it's some sort of pudding.

I get the butter to add to the army I've assembled.

Then it hits me again.

The butter is in a different formation. Swept from the side in a gentle, flowing manner. Even, like a well-mowed lawn.

It used to be butchered to fuck. Chopped and chiseled. The middle would be gutted, scooped as if it's a beast that needs to be put out of its misery before it does the same to you. Completely covered in the memories of burnt toast.

I've lost my appetite.

*

An issue doesn't exist until you admit there's a problem. Then, when it's out in the open, it can take shape.

The question is: at what point does it get too big and cumbersome?

You can get help if you choose. Help yourself if you can; that's even better.

Everything is temporary. Even if you've lost your way.

*

You can't start again on a Tuesday. Fuck that.

Has to be on a Monday. That's the way things go. It's probably an ancient proverb. Found inside a smashed fortune cookie.

I can wait until next Monday and do what I like until then. And the thing is, it won't be as bad as what it should be because I know it's bad and I'm doing something about it.

Next Monday.

*

I could do with getting out, seeing people. I could do with keeping the plans I make and not canceling them in my head as soon as I do, then right at the very last moment revealing my intention of not actually fulfilling them.

I've been going through all superhero films. The good Marvel ones, obviously. Even the misfiring DCs for a sense of balance, admiring their effort if not the finished article. Nice grey palettes.

If I had a superpower, it would be the ability to see if things were actually going to be fine. Those many, many things I worry about.

What though if it wasn't going to be good? Then what? What would I do?

Or worse still, if I surveyed all that was before me and acknowledged there was nothing left to cause me to be stressed, what would I do?

I'd worry more.

*

There was no motive. None. Just an idle check. Maybe it was realising how many junk emails were actually in my normal inbox, while a few worthwhile gems had been filtered away. Needed something to do that felt like I had a purpose.

Manoeuvre the new me through the apocalyptic landscape left by the old me.

And it was right at the top.

A reminder.

We know you've not heard from us, they said. We've got it all in hand and we'll be in touch in due course. Gene holding email.

We've not forgotten about you.

*

What's the worst that can happen?

No one will get hurt. No one will die.

I unmute the chats. Gentle 'Hi' before I hide them again.

I bet they'll talk about me behind my back or in the other groups they're in.

The thing is, who's to say they haven't been talking about me when I was quiet?

My trembling fingers type, then change their mind.

No one gets hurt. No one dies.

What if no one responds? I'm just ignored? They've maybe not spotted my silence. How would I feel?

I can't win. It's not about winning, though, is it? It's about making the most of what you've got, especially when it's pretty much fuck all.

Alright. How is everyone?

There's a bit of an out-of-body experience which observes me hit send. I push down on the app until it shakes with a cross in the corner.

Before I get a chance to delete it, a reply comes in. Then another. Then an emoji in my original message.

Calf's so tense I need to shake them to stop the cramp.

Onto the next chat.

*

I've accidentally broken the bracelet.

It's snapped, and the beads are trying to get away. Escape to freedom or to someone else who'd look after them better.

I've got my hand covering the scene of the crime. I'm rolling down my sleeve to hide the debris. It's getting a bit cooler now. I'm not the only one struggling with the summer temperature. I'm going to try and gather all the letters and symbols before they're seen by the stranger who kindly gave them to me.

I'll take a moment tomorrow, clear a bit of time. There'll be videos and stuff to help me there.

*

Usually, fireworks make me jump. Not tonight. They're afraid of me. I capture them just before they disappear.

I can't remember when I fell out with fireworks. Seven, eight at a push. Big kids throwing them into the bonfire at the top of Thorntree Street to scare us younger boys and girls. One flew inches past my face and exploded just behind me. By the time I was at lunch the following day, I had to put out the flames it had left in my hair with my bare hands.

The crowd are up and moving towards the exits. I follow them and try not to look at that one seat that's been empty to my right for the whole thing.

74

WONKY

Mark Fleming

'*Unbelievable.*' The three of us keep parroting.

I add, 'What are the chances?' Although the chances of mates from donks ago passing our old local and bumping into me are odds-on. I'm ayeways here. In this seat. Grandstand view of SkySports above the corner where we used to play arrows. Hilary stacking my Grolsch's before the previous yin's finished. Like the old days, I'm first pished — well, topping-up from yesterday pished, so sluggish more than laser-staring allcomers — but fired up enough to keep throwing my arms around this pair of beautiful bams.

Dan. Only back in Leith clearing stuff out his Ma's after she got moved into a care home. But still the joker. He says, 'Mind you. I ayeways think, for a city of half a million punters, it's fucking *amazing* how often your paths cross with cunts. You should ken, Kev?'

'Eh?' I squint to focus on his unfamiliar bald pus.

'Any cunt wanting to shag away from home's better waiting for the Cabbage in Europe, eh. When you can fucking pay for it. Hide your tracks.'

Draining my bottle, I shrug. You don't see folk for years, but they still pick up the edited highlights through the Grapevine. Anyone other than Dan would've got a sore lip for making light of it.

Kirsty found out about Jax and me after her cousin, Chantel, getting driving lessons in Joppa, spied us exiting a B and B, all over each other. Wrong place, wrong time. Later, I turned into my street to find my carefully rehearsed alibi about the management training course obliterated by Kirsty's smoke signals: the pyre in our front garden telling me to *fuck right off*. The flames would've looked the same if my wardrobe was from Primark, but the smell of my smouldering £739.99 CP Company windcheater is something I'll never forget.

Fitz can still bore for Scotland. After the long-lost backslapping, he spent the first two Mick Jaggers banging on about his BMW X3 going in for a service, which is the only reason he popped in. Now he'll need to collect it the morn. He can name every car he's ever had, right down to the engine spec, but gets his ex-wives mixed up.

Now we're onto serious reminiscing about our youth, the stories this bar could tell, and other bars, shopping precincts, train and tube stations, Cessnock to Millwall. The time the Prestonpans lads joined us for the semi against Aberdeen, drinking with us the whole day, only to turn on us in the Terrace Inn and fucking wreck the joint. Dan the Man spiked one of their drinks with microdots, mind. Some boy he said kept noising him up. Like most stuff he did in his 20s, on the spur of the moment, now sounds well sketchy.

The tales flowing like a ruptured dam, we chat about all the radges we knew, the decades making exploits legendary. Mostly living in four-beds in Gilberstoun, a couple of years away from becoming full-time golfers, their 2.4 kids now with 2.4 kids.

Moments of silent introspection when we drop the names who never got beyond needle-sharing.

When it's my next round, in the mirror above the gantry I spy an older gadge coming out the bogs. Despite the white locks, I recognise him. Saft Si. I track him skulking behind a table of tourists. New York City. I can still clock different accents a mile away. Before this pub got gentrified, used to be second nature when you were sussing out weegies or teuchters on match days. The Sherman Tanks are poring over Fringe flyers. Saft Simon pauses, points at their brochure, his filterless voice shouting how shan the Festival is for locals. As they ask the slow cunt to speak slower, he's already dipped a handbag. While they chuckle at his accent and try introducing *shan* into their conversation, the sleekit thief has slipped a fat wallet into his back pocket.

'Mind Saft Si?' I ask, setting up the shots.

'Seen him earlier,' says Fitz. 'Part of the fixtures and fittings. Still collecting the glasses in here for beer tokens?'

'Lonely boy,' adds Dan. 'Sad as. We've got a past, but we've grown up, eh. That's what life's about. That sad cunt's forever stuck in the Eighties.'

'Forever stuck at his mental age when he was in the remedials,' says Fitz, twisting his limbs in grotesque shapes the way Donald Trump does when mentioning mental health issues.

Clinking glasses, we sink the shorts. When the whole bar lurches like a waltzer, I slap my hand on the table.

'Awright, shagger?' says Dan.

'Ayeways,' I reply, winking. 'Your shout, Fitzpatrick.'

Fitz heads to the bar, stopping to spraff with regulars. Giving those and such as those, the few ex-lads, more aggressive handshakes. Dan is repeating a Kevin Bridges routine. Doing the weegie accent. Cracking himself up. Making it harder to follow. 'Pity he's a fucking Septic fan,' he concludes.

I stare into the galaxy of empties sparkling against the lights. In a city of half a million, it might well be another 10 years before our planets align like this again. If ever. I fire a glance at Fitz. Only just got served. Trying it on with the manageress, Hilary. Another constant.

She's lost a lot of weight over the years, but as kids we called her Hilary Artillery. She'd been a few years above us at Leith Academy. When she first started here as a young barmaid, she gave us all a go at the end of the night, across the pool table. We'd joke we were like flies on a hippo's back. A rite of passage, like getting a kicking off the ASC sheepshaggers. I notice Saft Si nodding at her, thumbs up. When he passes the wallet, she strokes the back of his hand, whispers into his ear. After last orders they'll be last to leave.

I never thought I'd be so jealous of the people who never moved on. When my head's spinning on my empty bed, Saft Si and Hilary Artillery will be on the pool table. No wonder it's ayeways had wonky legs.

LIMBS

Neil Renton

Let me tell you just how bad a footballer I am.

I'm shocking. Brutal. My first touch is so bad that my second is an apologetic raised hand.

Here's an exchange that took place with my primary school football coach as I trundled off the pitch at half-time:

"Neil, I'm taking you off."

"But coach, we don't have another sub to replace me."

"Neil, I'm taking you off."

Let's not blame me entirely. Let's blame gravity for bringing down my dear old mum.

She tripped over a portable fire that was inexplicably in the middle of a living room (don't ask) while holding baby me. Maybe she fell on me like a wrestler in tight pants, or perhaps I landed badly on the floor, but somehow, I ended up with a broken right leg. I can't quite recall the details as I was only a few months old and more concerned about the suffering I was going through. Completely not my mum's fault. It was the seventies. These things happened.

Anyway, despite physio sessions where I played basketball with kids in wheelchairs, my right leg never fully recovered. As a result, I can't really kick with that foot; I have to turn my whole body to angle a pass. If watching me kick a ball is painful, try being the person kicking the bloody thing.

It hasn't stopped me from playing football, though. If nothing else, I'm enthusiastic, but that's not going to get me very far—or further up the pecking order when it comes to being picked.

From a young age, I cursed myself by giving up on getting better. I could have improved, practiced, worked on my weaker foot. Instead, I just gave in.

But my defeatist attitude didn't stop me from earning a runner-up medal. Which is impressive but wait until you hear how I earned it.

If my selective memory serves me right, I was about five. It was at Butlins in Ayr (don't ask, it was the eighties), and we were there from Monday to Friday because it was cheaper than going over the weekend. It wasn't Disney World, but a holiday was a holiday.

Anyway, there was a wee football camp, and I loved it. I'd go along daily, play a game with teammates who were thankfully far better than me, and they carried me all the way to a cup final.

But there was a problem.

The final was scheduled for our last day there, and there weren't enough pitches because the older kids were playing. So, someone came up with a plan.

We'd play the cup final on an ice rink.

And we wouldn't have any appropriate footwear. There were no skates—maybe in case they burst the ball. We'd just wear those cute black rubber plimsolls that you got back then (don't ask, it was a generation before fashion).

So off I went, to the biggest game of my life. I had it all to play for.

And I hated it.

Due to the incident when I was a baby, not only was I robbed of all footballing skill, but it had also stolen my balance. I was quite literally like Bambi on ice.

I couldn't run, and I didn't like sliding in case I fell, which I did a lot.

Instead, I spent most of the game clinging to the wall as the whole spectacle whizzed past me like Tom Cruise hanging by his bright white fingertips to the side of a plane as it takes off in one of those Mission Impossible films.

The match itself was like another movie. With discarded limbs and pools of blood, it resembled the opening of *Saving Private Ryan*. Carnage everywhere.

Weirdly enough, the opponents must have been used to it, as they managed to beat us 5-1.

I've still got the runner-up medal. It's the only one I've got for playing. I keep it tucked away in a box in a cupboard that I fondly look at and caress when I'm searching for something else.

And I've still got the scars—both physical and mental.

CHRISTMAS AT TIFFANY'S

Neil Renton

She didn't look like a twenty-year-old Tiffany.

More like a thirty-two-year-old Jenny to her live-wire pals. Jen to her dejected ex. Jennifer to her posh and unsuspecting parents.

"Come in," she greets me at the door like I'm an old-time friend and not a first-time client. Cotton trackie bottoms and a hoodie. There's a stirring caused by this, but it isn't what we agreed.

Magnolia walls. All the doors are closed. There are a couple of framed generic pictures in the long hall. All is still.

I shouldn't be doing this on Christmas Day. I shouldn't be doing it on any day. I'll tell Michelle that during the present drop-off I had to have a word with my brother about his behaviour, and she'll roll her eyes. I'll say not to tell him that I told her about the chat I had with him, and that will be the end of the conversation about a lecture that didn't actually happen.

It's a short life. And one that today has brought me a Lynx deodorant gift set, some novelty socks, and a couple of box sets that I've already given away to charity shops. A short, sometimes unrewarding life.

I follow her straight ahead into the bedroom. Inside, the blinds have been lowered to let in a crack of light and nothing else.

She wakes the sleeping telly from its slumber as the DVD logo ricochets around the screen. Tiffany presses play, and a big black taxi driver gets in the back of his cab to the excitement of an over-made-up, under-dressed passenger.

"Get comfortable," she commands. "I'll be back in a minute."

Everything is calm. Neutral-coloured sheets and pumped-up pillows. I get down to my underwear as quickly as I can, making a careful pile of my belongings so as not to lose anything. Imagine explaining that to Michelle.

I lie back in the middle of the bed. I want this to last as long as possible, but at the same time, I also want it to end as quickly as possible.

The bedroom door opens and Tiffany enters. Right on it. She's squeezed into a white shirt, wee black skirt, and heels.

And a problem. Stockings.

"What happened to the tights?" I ask. "We had an agreement."

"I couldn't find any clean ones," she whispers seductively.

"Put on dirty ones," I say.

"I'm not that clarty."

"We had an agreement though. That's what I paid extra for."

It's a Mexican stand-off. Me on the bed, wrist placed near my stiffy. Tiffany, shoulders shrugged, tugging at her skirt.

"I don't have any tights I can wear."

"Well, I'm not paying for this."

"I could go out and pull these up really high and come back in?"

No.

"Okay," she grudgingly exhales. "There's a corner shop open. I'll pop over and see what they've got."

My heart beats faster, pumping blood all over my body.

"Thanks."

"The thing is, I can't just leave you unattended. And you can't come with me. That's a bit weird."

"Clearly."

"So, I'm going to handcuff you to the bed."

"Fair enough," I say.

She goes into the bottom drawer of her bedside cabinet. Through a pile of dildos and lube, she brings out a pair of serious-looking handcuffs. No fluffy bits on these ones. No mercy.

I'm fastened to the bed, and she goes out again and comes back as her previous incarnation of a mum doing the school run.

"Are you hungry?" Fake Tiffany asks. She can get me a snack when she's out. I wonder what her going rate for a Mars Bar is?

I'm fine, I say. I've got a pair of George from Asda pants on, a gift last year from one of the kids, although Michelle would have given them the actual cash. Imagine spending your hard-earned pocket money on a set of novelty briefs?

Trying to burst through the material is a pre-cum erupting Viagra volcano of a dick. Hardly the eighth wonder of the world, but a marvel in its own right.

"Right. Back soon. I've told Chuckles I'm away out and to behave."

She leaves, then there's the click of the front door, and it's just me.

And Chuckles.

Tiffany's pimp.

What is he doing? Sitting in the spare room, edge of the bed? Maybe in the living room, muted telly. Reading the subtitles in between playing solitaire. Seven foot fourteen inches tall. The type of build that makes American footballers wish they'd taken up soccer instead.

She won't be long. Which is usually what I'd say about my dick. I can almost see the veins.

The bedroom door opens. Chuckles. It must be.

Silence is broken by a gentle pressing of the carpet, but the pimp is nowhere to be seen.

Then he springs onto the bed, and I shit myself.

Chuckles isn't a bloodthirsty gangster. Secured to a bed with an allergy to cats as one ventures slowly towards me, I wish he was.

THE MAGICIAN

Mark Fleming

Frank was marching as to war. A band piping the boys off to the frontlines. Fluttering banners cracking in the wind. The boots segued into different drums, then Steve Jones' power chords introing his all-time favourite album with 'Holidays in the Sun.'

A sideways glance. Moira was snoring. Probably what had woken him. Accustoming to the full moon filtering through the Venetian blinds, he noticed her curled lips. As if her expression had frozen just before her novel slithered from her fingertips. Her nightly ritual. Historic romance. Her other one. Pointing out his failings. The gardening he loved but what else was he going to do now the jobs were dwindling with the shortening days? The same every year. Arguments about money. The same every day. Making sure the bills were paid wasn't nearly enough to fund spa breaks with her friends, the monthly manicures for those talons clutching the covers. Worse still, the defeats he failed to admit to with Moira's 22-year-old daughter, Chrystal.

Why couldn't he be more like Greig next door? Not a fiftysomething digging out weeds until sundown; a normal Joppa citizen who went to an office in a smart suit or hot-desked from his conservatory, juggling figures on spreadsheets. Last holiday in Kuala Lumpur. Wherever the fuck Kuala Lumpur was. Greig whose appearance always melted Moira's stony features.

And brought a coquettish smile from Chrystal that curdled his guts. Moira only ever sneered or smirked at Frank. When her imagination sought affairs with 19th-century landowners, he knew Greig's would be the face she conjured beneath manes of hair.

These thoughts whirling through his mind, Frank recalled his vivid dream. Then realised he could still hear footfall. Primeval fear lanced through him. There it was again. Boots crunching. Gruff voices. Swear words. Torchlight. Slithering from the duvet, his fingers were shaking so much he had to take deep breaths before poking the slats apart. At least two men outside. Not even attempting stealth, brazenly trudging through the pansies he and their youngest, Emma, planted the previous weekend to complement the crimson dahlias and Governor anemones, all shades of crimson, her favourite colour. That was what instilled a sudden resolve.

Moira always parroted how much she wished he'd change. Grow a pair. Although she clearly preferred him the way he was. So easy to manipulate. Dominate. Much shorter than him, she still managed to look down her nose. Especially that time she'd informed him she'd sold his punk vinyl to some Gumtree collector to go towards her gastric band op. The thought of Emma's careful work crushed into the dirt crushed Frank. Now was the time. Here was the opportunity for Frank Dunbar to be the changingman he was forever promising himself and that beautiful 10-year-old.

He sped downstairs, into the kitchen. Through the window, torches flashed like a duel in the *Star Wars* films Emma loved watching with him. Further inspiration. Easing open a drawer, he groped in the darkness, fingers curling around a steak knife's handle. Approaching the back door, he savoured the way the flickering beams winked against its blade. Igniting his inner Jedi. Creep up on them or a sudden charge? Against the evil Empire, they had to make those bold decisions all the time. He pictured Emma's wee grin, poking into Maltesers, their furtive secret. Moira hated sci-fi and forbade giving Emma the sweet treats her self-inflicted diabetes denied herself. Emma would expect him to charge. Bracing himself, he shoved the door aside, leapt down the steps. Clumsily. Hitting the patio, he sprawled, the knife clattering into the gloom. Torchlight bathed him and he stifled the humiliating shriek that would wake everyone.

Mysterious crackling voices accompanied their approaching steps. Summoning the final vestige of his evaporated courage, he peered up at the men who were surely about to put him in intensive care. Hi-Viz vests. Two burly policemen ages with Crystal.

'You alright there, sir?' An inked arm reached out, tugged him to his feet.

'Eh, aye. Scraped my knees.' Blood spattering the paving, he realised he was naked, their torches creating an even more grotesque shadow.

'We've had reports of a housebreaker,' said the thinner one, matter-of-factly. Almost bored.

'Confused reports,' said his partner, the Robocop of the two, thickset, tribal artwork flourishing over his forearms. 'Someone at the station was monitoring Porty People on Facebook, rumours firing around of a hoodie lurking around here. These corner houses are the only yins in the cul-de-sac with a lane leading out the back. My colleague thought he saw someone skulking down here. You seen anything?'

Frank flinched; the question sounded like an accusation. 'No, officer. Only came out to investigate when I heard something.'

'Is that right? In future, don't come out to investigate when you hear something. Phone emergency services. Pensioner got whacked across the back of his head with a hoe in Dalkeith last week.'

'Oh.'

The other one yawned. 'He might've run over your garden, climbed up and over your shed. Is it the Harry Lauder Road on the other side?'

'Aye, that's the Harry Lauder over there, other side of that massive beech.'

'We're nowhere near the fucking beach,' snapped Robocop, flashing his torch at Frank's bits. 'Anyway. We've radioed back-up. With dogs. Just in case. You can go back to bed, sir. Sorry to have startled you.'

With that, they barged back towards the blue lights pulsating against the opposite houses, the disjointed walkie-talk fading. Shivering, Frank waited while his pulse diminished. Just as his heartbeat was levelling, he was aware of another figure watching him, and the rhythm began drumming all over again. From behind his neighbour's rhododendron, a wiry man emerged, balaclava exaggerating his white-eyes. They both listened to the cop car squealing off, then the lad snatched up the knife. Frank instinctively drew his quaking hands over his balls.

'I've not seen you,' said Frank, fighting to control his quavering voice.

'What?'

'Listen. My stepdaughter used to babysit next door.'

'*What?!*'

'So, I know they keep a spare key under that pot of petunias behind you. And he keeps the fob to his car in a glass ashtray in the hallway.'

'Why you tell me this?'

Frank couldn't place the accent, wondered if it was his real one. 'Why? He's so entitled. And I fucking *detest* him for the way he looks at my stepdaughter.'

'I get picture. Is dog in house?'

'No. You could grab the fob, head past those clowns poking around the bushes on the Harry Lauder, be on the A1 in five. I'm just going to check on the flowers those polis destroyed. They're my wee lassie's.'

He strolled towards the flowerbeds. Against the moonlight, he smiled: the confusion of boot prints had avoided the pansies so lovingly poked into the soil by Emma's little fingers. Surely by chance rather than design. He crouched to them, inhaling their gorgeous dusky fragrance. Greig's Tesla didn't make a sound. Frank had made it vanish.

SONGS IN THE KEY OF STRIFE – NOEL GALLAGHER WRECKED MY MUM'S FUNERAL

Neil Renton

I'll never forgive Noel Gallagher for spoiling my mum's funeral.

He didn't turn up with the Primrose Posses and start a drug-filled fight with brother Liam, rolling about in the cemetery and crushing carnations left by well-wishers. He didn't piss Jack Daniels over the cucumber sandwiches at the wake. The ones without crusts but that curl up because no one wants them. He didn't wear Adidas trainers and an olive parka when the dress code was black suit and tie. He didn't even turn up changing the lyrics to (What's The Story) Morning Glory?

In fact, he didn't ruin my mum's funeral. I did. But as always, I like to blame others for my mistakes and the inevitable demise they cause.

You should try it one time. Just don't blame me because I'll pass that buck to someone like a multi-millionaire Mancunian singer-songwriter I've never met before.

I don't think a son ever recovers from his mum dying. They spend nine months carrying us around in their bellies and the rest of their lives carrying us about in any other way they can. They're pillars of support, always in your corner even if you've backed yourself into it without any space for another.

They'll always find a way.

My mum was there for me when I needed her. Even if I didn't deserve her. So, given the chance, I wanted to repay her in a small, tiny amount. I wanted to make her proud and to make her remembered.

And, in an office above a Masonic Hall in Leith, my chance to shine broke through the dust-covered windows.

We were arranging the order of service, and we needed music. That's when it hit me. As I loved music, I was going to honour my mum in the most spectacular fashion by making sure there was a song that was suitable for her.

My mum (my dear old mum whose face I can see as I type this and I want to see her face in real life) loved the Bee Gees. To be honest, anyone with half a clue about life would feel the same.

Noel Gallagher, one of my musical heroes, did an interview in Melody Maker. It was just when Oasis were breaking through. He had to pick ten songs for an imaginary jukebox and one of his choices was a Bee Gees song.

I'll pick that, I thought. I put forward the title and the guy helping us sort stuff out took a note of it, and we continued organising the service.

What could go wrong?

The funeral was a funeral. Everybody whispering in that tone they usually keep for phoning in sick from their darkened bedroom. People sorry for our loss. Some words spoken as a tribute. A loving and fulfilling life condensed into a few minutes.

Then came my moment. The song played that was special to my mum so we could close our eyes, bow our heads and think of her.

Which we did.

I won't keep you in suspense any longer. The Bee Gees song I picked on the ancient advice of Noel Gallagher was 'You Don't Know What It's Like.' It's a beautiful song. If you don't believe me, go on. Give it a listen.

It's a song that has a time and a place. And as it started, it hit me why Noel recommended it. The time and the place was on a Friday night, over a bottle of wine with that person you love and you're about to love all night long.

The time and the place wasn't on a Tuesday morning at your mum's funeral.

It's a love song. A different kind of love song.

A fact I soon realised.

The tune gets off to a fitting start. "There's a light. A special kind of light. That's never shone on me." That was appropriate as my mum was about to be cremated.

It went from bad to worse. "I'm a man!" Barry Gibb screams. "Can't you see who I am?"

"I can't see," I can imagine my dear old mum saying. "I'm dead."

Then there's more taunting from the falsetto legend. "You don't know what it's like to love somebody, the way I love you."

Again, my mum was probably saying from the discomfort of her coffin she was spinning in, big problem with the emotion being returned right now.

When songs get played at funerals, there's never usually a reaction other than sobs and eyes dabbed with hankies. This response was even more subdued.

Deep down inside, I think my mum would have approved of the selection. Maybe had a laugh from the unforgiving corner I'd managed to back myself into.

I hadn't intended to fuck things up, but I did. To the point that the only way I could have made an even bigger mess was if Noel Gallagher had said his favourite Bee Gees song was "Stayin' Alive."

NEIL'S PERSEVERED

We've all got mental health, but the first time I was aware of my own being an issue would be back in 2012. Initially, I wasn't aware mine was deteriorating. But physically, I felt done in.

There was so much going on in my life. I was in a job I was struggling with. My mum was diagnosed with cancer. There were also all the responsibilities that come with being a dad, which I sometimes struggled with. I began feeling dizzy all the time. I had pounding headaches. One side of my face felt numb. I remember almost fainting at work, asking if I could go home. To my mind, the thought of a man fainting carried a stigma, so I didn't want anyone to see me fainting at work! I made a doctor's appointment, and they did tests which didn't reveal anything. I was told I didn't have to worry.

I'd always been a bit of a joker, the guy who'd try to get punchlines in. First in the pub, last to leave, all that. But, at my work at the time, my team had moved. I'd been in a much nicer office environment; now I was staring at a wall and sitting close to the toilet, watching people going for a piss every few minutes. Things came to a head one weekend. I can date this: Saturday 17 March 2012, because Spurs had played Bolton in the FA Cup quarterfinals. The match made headlines because Bolton midfielder, Fabrice Muamba had a cardiac arrest on the pitch. His heart stopped and he was effectively dead for 78 minutes. At work, I was reading all these papers about Muamba collapsing, like Johnny 5 from *Short Circuit*, consuming everything I could about this boy collapsing and dying and then surviving. The tears were rolling down my face.

So, I had another checkup at the doctors. I explained I was still getting headaches, and my face felt partially numb. I felt like I was going to pass out all the time; it felt like I was drunk without having had anything to drink! I told her how any time I was getting out my seat, I had to plan journeys so I wouldn't bump into anything. When I mentioned the Fabrice Muamba situation, this prompted her to ask if I'd ever felt depressed. I was like, 'Depressed? Me? No way. I'm the life and soul of the party!' But at that point, I burst into tears.

That was the first indication I needed to do something about my mental health. It still felt alien, opening up to talk about it, compared to what it's like now. So, I'm thinking, I've been diagnosed, I'm struggling, help me. Where's the instant fix? It had taken ages to get to this realisation, which was great, but why had my journey to this point taken so long? There was no one thing that had triggered me. I had a brilliant upbringing. A loving family. I was well supported by great people around me. Family and friends.

In the past, I'd tried stress control groups, going along to a six-week course to listen to people discussing mental health. I just sat in the furthest away corner, arms folded, thinking, 'Why would I want to make pals with depressed folk?!' Then I heard about the Changing Room.

This SAMH-run programme was launched in 2018 at Easter Road, when Neil Lennon was the Hibs manager. Pardon the pun, but it's mad to think that even as recently as five years ago you'd never really get men talking about mental health. Neil was a pioneer for that. I thought I'd go to see what this Changing Room was all about. It was a big intake, so I missed the first course, but went on the second one. It really changed my opinion about mental health. I could see people I recognised who went to Hibs games. For want of a better term, it 'normalised' mental health struggles. Recognising someone I could be pals with can have issues really brought it all home.

Just being there was a massive empowering and enlightening experience. It was also so important that it was held at Easter Road, a place where I had so many memories, good and sad. I suppose a football stadium can be a bit like a surrogate church or cathedral, a place where people can go to feel part of a community. And they can worship! In these familiar surroundings, we all felt encouraged to open up. You just feel safe straight away. And that was the reason I got involved in it. When SAMH's Pher Nicholson and Robert Nesbitt were trying to work out what to do for the 12th week, after the 11 weeks of guest speakers and quizzes and so on, they had this lightbulb moment of inviting us to head around the pitch in pairs for a chat, on what has become a staple of the Changing Room experience, the 'walk and talk.' Because it's a side-to-side thing, as opposed to people looking at you, you feel far more relaxed about being open about what you're feeling.

Joining the Changing Room made me appreciate stuff more and gave me the inspiration to want to help others. So, I decided to become a volunteer. But. The irony was, at that point my mental health was massively sliding, getting to the stage I was suicidal. I was helping out. Going along to sessions. Listening to people describing their issues. Discussing speaking to professionals. I wasn't doing any of that. I just thought I'd fight my own battle. And day after day, I ended up losing that battle.

So, I'd started as a participant, then became a volunteer, and then I was struggling, the worst I'd ever been. I knew how to deflect these feelings. People would ask how I was, and straight away I'd answer, 'I'm alright, how are you?' Anything to take the focus off me. I'd been to the doctor about my physical symptoms and was tested for multiple sclerosis. When I heard that was a possible diagnosis, I remember leaving the doctors and thinking, 'My life's over!'

I underwent further tests, and at that point, I also hated my job. My mental well-being was like a roller coaster. My depression had dipped in 2012. Came back up again. I joined the Changing Room in 2018. Then it dipped again. By 2019 I was at my lowest point. As a volunteer, I was giving out advice, trying to be a role model for people with their own mental health challenges. I was struggling, and this was made so much worse because I was now convinced I was dying anyway.

I remember leaving the hospital in January 2019. January's always a horrible, bleak month, anyway. Metaphorically, I'd been running towards the edge of a cliff for a while. Things that would stop me would be my wife and kids. They were like a barrier, but then I'd think, 'I can just jump over that.' I was getting closer and closer to that edge. When I took my youngest daughter to school, we never chatted as we normally did. I was also in tears because I'd decided the only way out of this was to take my life. I said goodbye, hugged her tightly in the playground. I thought, 'Right. This is it. I'm going to do what I need to do.'

I was at the bus stop, knowing that one bus would come to take me to the hospital to get the results of my latest brain test. The other bus would take me to the place where I'd convinced myself I was going to finish things. I'd timed the buses, so I knew the hospital bus was due, while the other bus was still seven minutes away. The bus for the hospital was stuck at the lights. The bus to take me elsewhere was now five minutes away, getting closer all the time. I was thinking, 'Am I actually going to end up doing this? The first bus better hurry up. My life is hanging by a thread and it's all down to the LRT bus timetable!'

The hospital bus arrived, and I went on to see the consultant who told me I did have a brain condition, but not multiple sclerosis. It was depression, which could be treated. The doctor was really concerned about me. I sat outside the Western in tears. I was signed off work for three months, absolutely wiped out. One Thursday, as I was taking the bin out, I was thinking, now I need to be honest. Taking the rubbish out was like a metaphor. So, I sat down with my wife and said two words. 'I'm struggling.'

I just spoke to her – at her – for about an hour and a half. She knew I'd been going through something and was a big support, but she'd no idea my mental health had got as bad as it had. I went to the doctor and was given a safety guide of who to contact when you're having suicidal thoughts: GP surgery. NHS24. The Samaritans. The Royal Ed. I was invited to add names and numbers of other people I could count on for help. So, I put my wife's name and number. I also wrote down The Changing Room. Even although I hadn't known the guys there as long as my family and friends – and no disrespect to any of them – but everyone at The Changing Room knew what I was going through better than anyone else, and I knew I could reach out to any of them. Likewise, I'd expect the same from them.

That support from The Changing Room was a massive help. If it wasn't for them, I'd be wondering how to get rid of that stigma. So, I was really starting to feel better and decided I wanted to do more. I volunteered as much as I could to help out. I got together with Dave Thomson, and we talked about what we could do to help guys over and above the 12-week Changing Room programmes. We came up with the idea of monthly drop-ins under the banner, 'Supporting our Supporters.' Just to be there for any guys needing help. To let them know there's always hope, and that suicide can never be an answer, no matter how bad things get. There are solutions that we can work towards. I've been through a challenging time, personally, but as one of my mates said, 'Always remember, everything is temporary.' Whatever stressful situation you're facing, keep it in perspective. It's only temporary. Our mental health is something we need to be united to face. Although the stigma's getting better, it's still there, especially with young men. There's so much pressure on them compared to when we were younger. We never had social media and the desire to need to look better, to have more money.

The main thing with The Changing Room is just to give people the support they need, especially in the current climate, after COVID, and with things like independence, Brexit, the cost-of-living crisis; all these external factors that can impact your stress levels, your anxieties or concerns, your mental well-being. We've all got mental health, but sometimes it can seem as if the struggles we face as middle-aged men are harder than anything we've faced before.

Family and friends. The Changing Room. Stuff I've been doing with SAMH. These have all massively helped me. Hibs are part of the reason I'm still here, and my kids have still got their dad. You go to The Changing Room at Easter Road and there are people you see who you've known throughout The Changing Room sessions. So many good people, with shared experiences, with a common bond. And it's not just about Hibs. I've got pals involved with Big Hearts, which is brilliant as well. It goes way beyond football rivalry. As I said at the outset, we've all got mental health.

ROCK 'N' ROLL AS A LIFELINE

Mark Fleming

Queen II, Queen (1974)

My early 70s adolescence coincided with a golden period for pop. *Top of the Pops* beamed a succession of ever-gaudier musicians into living rooms every Thursday, clumping around in stack heels, sashaying in sequins and eyeliner. David Bowie. Alvin Stardust. Mott the Hoople. Roxy Music. Marc Bolan and T-Rex. The Sweet. Suzi Quatro. Wizzard. Slade. And decades before the truth came out, Gary Glitter. Back to my childhood drawing board again, when Wizzard's 'See My Baby Jive' spent four weeks at number one in the summer of 1973, I was inspired to draw a portrait of their singer, Roy Wood, using every crayon colour in the pack for his facepaint.

On Sunday afternoons, I listened to the Radio 1 chart rundown presented by Tom Browne, consigning all these glam hits to cassette. Included amongst my compilations was 'Killer Queen' from Queen's third album, *Sheer Heart Attack*. The lead single from their next album, *A Night at the Opera*, was a game changer for my burgeoning musical tastes. Described by Freddie Mercury as a fusion of three separate songs, 'Bohemian Rhapsody' was like nothing else in the charts, a six-minute epic teetering between theatrical pomp and hard rock.

On Christmas Eve 1975, the BBC broadcast Queen's appearance at London's Hammersmith Palais. I watched, captivated, as this triumphant gig bridged the gap between my tastes, from an adolescent into pop to a teenager into rock. Around the same time, I borrowed *Queen II* and *Sheer Heart Attack* from an older lad who lived opposite, along with his Status Quo albums, *Piledriver*, *On the Level*, and *Blue for You*; and then Queen's *A Night at the Opera*, *A Day at the Races*, and Black Sabbath, Deep Purple and Led Zeppelin albums from an older cousin, David, during visits to Helensburgh.

Newington Library had opened that March. As well as books, this offered upwards of 7,000 albums and cassettes: soundtracks, classical, folk, jazz. And rock. Previously, buying albums on pocket money was a luxury. Now I had access to a universe of headbanging delights and could freely borrow and tape as many titles as I wanted.

So, my 14-year-old musical tastes intensified, cassette recordings of twee chart music - everything from Slade to Lieutenant Pigeon to Chicory Tip to David Essex - being feverishly taped over with eardrum-perforating rock 'n' roll like AC/DC or Motörhead. Inversely, my passion for my football team, Hibs, waned, from molten to lukewarm. Why? Because, at that age, something happened. I got seriously fucked up.

The British Isles summer heatwave of 1976 is often cast up as the hottest of the 20th century. Reservoirs dried up. You could fry eggs on the tarmac. But it seared into my adolescent consciousness for an altogether more nightmarish reason. Attending a Sunday School picnic organised by Cairns Memorial Church in Gorgie, at Carberry Tower in Musselburgh, I was dragged into an outhouse by one of the church staff and sexually assaulted. So disgusted by this ordeal, I never told a soul about what this nonce cunt had done to me; not the friend who'd invited me, nor any of the responsible adults present that day, nor any of my family. Internalising the horror, attempting to deny it had even happened, seemed the best way of coping. The only way. But I believe that fucked me up far worse in the longer term. It might even have done something to my brain chemistry, the butterfly effect eventually leading to the violent bipolar swings which came along in my 20s. Sliding doors moments, eh? If only I'd thought of an excuse not to go to the picnic I didn't even want to go to when my pal phoned to ask me if I wanted to go.

A major aspect of the seachange in my musical tastes was surely down to escapism. And of all the bootleg recordings I created, *Queen II* was a fabulous escape; one album I continually went back to. A couple of years later, the band went on to be denigrated by the punk generation as symbolic of the banal, empty bluster of much of early 70s rock, revolving around whimsical lyrical imagery and overblown musicianship. But at its core, this album was multi-layered hard rock, fully deserving its masterpiece credentials.

'March of the Black Queen,' consisting of various segueing sections, was a precursor to 'Bohemian Rhapsody.' 'Ogre Battle' was an up-tempo rock song resonating with one of my other mid-teen obsessions, speculative fiction (I was devouring novels by Isaac Asimov, J. R. R. Tolkien, and John Norman). Elsewhere, there was 'The Fairy Feller's Master-Stroke,' inspired by the pre-Raphaelite painting of the same name Mercury admired in the Tate Gallery, Mercury dazzling with harpsichord flourishes and, like so many Queen songs, demonstrating his incredible, effortless vocal range. *Queen II* climaxed with 'Seven Seas of Rhye,' a sweeping, hook-laden song, their first single to make the charts. And the first record I ever bought.

ALFIE AND THE MONSTER

Mark Fleming

As Donnie fixed masking tape to the poster, those glinting eyes seemed to be watching him. Once the sheet was secured to the lamppost, he stepped back, wondering what Alfie was seeing right now. If anything.

Brad had tried everything else. Left Alfie's favourite toys in the garden, alongside a bowl of water, and treats. For foxes or gulls to pillage. Because cats were more active after sunset, the pair of them had paraded through the neighbourhood, calling his name. Both Donnie and his son were diffident, found that onerous. You often saw these posters around Portobello. There was one outside the Turkish baths, sun-bleached, the name almost erased. Lucky. Irony, more like.

Even if a reward was being offered, how many were ever retrieved? He'd read the chances of unchipped cats ever being found were less than 5%. Alfie was a rescue cat, had endured abuse, been fished from the Water of Leith. He was nervous, never strayed too far. All it would take to entice any cat into a new home would be some old biddie putting out tastier treats. New home, new name. Equally likely, Alfie had been pulverised by a speeding car, dumped in the nearest wheelie bin. Then he thought of hawks. He thought of chicks tearing into the regurgitated meat.

A gaggle of lads, Brad's age, scuffed by. Rooted to their phones, none gave the poster a second glance.

*

Donnie was roused by gunfire. He aimed a fist at the wall. The salvo continued. His fingers tightened. Released. Reaching under his pillow, he fumbled for the half-bottle. Swirled the whisky around. He slugged, then heaved himself up. Tempering his unsteady footfall, he cursed as a framed photograph of his wife, Jenny, toppled. Glass splintered. Another machine gun burst. A muted explosion.

He hauled Brad's bedroom door open. Lounging on his bed, the boy was jamming his thumbs into his console, pulping zombies. 'Hey, Dad.' Focused on his bloodbath.

'Just cool the beans, son. It's nearly eleven.'

In a mocking tone. 'Siri. Middle-aged translation. *Cool the beans?*'

'D'you finish your assignment?'

'The morn.'

'Thought you said it was *due* the morn?'

'Morn's afternoon, Dad. Plenty time.'

'Morn's afternoon?'

Brad answered with emphatic finger taps. Donnie watched a grenade pitching towards a crowd of shambling characters, their dumb expressions tracking this missile. Like so many conscripts lumbering over some desolate Ukrainian plain. Thousands of fresh graves above the bones from Operation Barbarossa; above the bones from Konotop, 1659, when Ukrainian Cossacks fought for Russia against Crimean Tatars. Donnie had read all that in a previous essay. Brad got an A. Was smashing his Sixth

Year modules. Donnie always tried playing down his praise, knew the lad got so easily embarrassed.

A livid yellow flash. Viscera coated the screen, slithering down. Donnie noticed bruising around Brad's cheekbone.

'You been in the wars yourself, lad? Looks like you've got a keeker coming on?'

Self-consciously, he touched his skin. 'It's nothing, Dad. Collided with a goalpost at training.'

Donnie sighed. 'About the assignment?'

'Aye, aye. Nearly finished it. Anyway, Dad. Supposed to be a scout coming to my game the morn's night, mind? Might not have to be worrying about assignments. Know what I read in your paper? Top Rangers players can make 1.5 mill a year.'

'I seen that. At Parkhead they're on 1.9. Imagine a Celtic scout coming to watch you one day.'

'As if you'd want me playing for *them*.'

'Money talks, lad. Doesn't sing party songs. But whoever the scout's reporting to, all you can do is give it your best shot. And avoid jumping into the posts, mind.' He observed his son's pursed lips. 'I know the football's important. But how many promising kids actually make it?'

'I can juggle, Dad. That Liverpool player you were telling me about.'

'Eh?'

'From the 70s? A winger?'

'Oh, aye. A Dubliner. Steve Heighway. Signed by Shanks. Before that, he got a 2:1 in politics. His teammates cried him Big Bamber. After Bamber Gascoigne.'

'Eh?!'

'Used to present University Challenge.'

'That's the point, Dad. I'm not going to sack my studies if I get offered a contract. Got to have a Plan B, as you keep banging on.'

'Just make sure you get your Plan As and Bs in the right order.' Donnie scowled at a demonic figure his son's crosshairs were seeking. 'Reminds me of my boss, that one. Tony McClay. Go on, son. Blow his fuckin' napper off.'

*

Turning into this street, mansions loomed, the ornate balustrades, finials, and cornices constructed during the Empire nestling beyond gleaming cars. Wiping his palm across the windscreen, he murmured. 'The state of this. Never mind the rats scurrying off the railway. This avenue's plagued by status-symbol vehicles.'

A woman steered a buggy to the kerb, chatting on her phone but glaring. Self-conscious about talking to himself, he shut up. Braking, he gestured for her to cross. While she pushed by, he studied all the chunky tyres straddling pavements. When the pedestrians were safely on the other side, he let out a sigh. 'If you could see this lot, Jenny. Some just double-parked. Like they're taunting wardens to fix tickets. Which they'll pay online without a second thought.'

Halting in the road, he hit the blinkers, glancing at the dash clock. Hurried around to the rear doors. After too many corners taken too quickly, parcels were strewn. Rummaging, he sought the package addressed to 25A, a PS5, one of several in his Aladdin's Cave. This property had been subdivided; the flat was down a path. No security light, so he tugged out his phone.

Fumbling to activate the torch, he blundered into a flowerpot. Cursing, he grasped at the plants, doing his best to force them back into their container. 'Don't need customer complaints on top of McClay fuckin' whinging about delivery times.'

He stabbed the buzzer. Felt his heart beating. Pressed again, longer. AC/DC blared. 'Riff Raff.' Vigorous thumping was no match for Angus Young. He poked a note through the letterbox saying he'd return in the morning, yet another added to tomorrow's schedule. Returning to the street, he noticed someone testing his van's rear door.

'Away from there, ya thieving fucker!'

Fury exaggerated his Irish accent. A wiry youth leapt into a car which sped off. Donnie didn't catch the plate. McClay would have held him responsible for not securing his vehicle. Locked inside his cab, his shaking hands delved into the glove compartment, feeling for the hip flask.

*

'Just wanted to put a washing on, Brad. Your blazer. I noticed it was manky. Someone been chucking eggs?'

His son jolted, tugging earplugs. Harsh techno. 'Alfie?'

'No, lad. All quiet on the feline front. But speaking of quiet, you'll only keep yourself awake listening to that ... Racket. Sounds like white noise with a beat.'

'Dad.'

'Try Brian Eno.'

'Who?'

'Used to be in Roxy Music.'

'*Who?*'

'*Brian Eno.* Electronic stuff. First introduced to him when I was a bit older than you, by my mate, Sandy Reilly. One of kind, he was. Crazy. But crazies need their quiet moments.'

'Brian Emo?'

'*Eno*. Ambient. Dead relaxing. When I had time to kill, made the long hours go by, so it did. You could just listen, drift to other places in your head. For hours. You needed that, or you would go crazy!'

'Sounds *awfy*, Dad. Hippy music.'

'No way, son. Anyway, was someone chucking eggs at you?'

Silence for a moment. 'No. A few of the S6s were mucking around. Got caught in the crossfire.'

'You'll need to be quicker than that taking the ball to the by-line for a cross to the far post, lad.'

'*Obvs*.'

'Also. You'll want to look your best for this scout, you know, when the time comes to sign along any dotted line.'

'Probably not come to *that*, Dad.'

'Listen. Say this gadge's done his five levels. Say he's top of his game. Imagine you did get signed up to play for the mighty Glasgow Rangers? They're sticklers for tradition. Have you noticed our managers never wear trackies on the touchline? Always tin flutes. Goes *way* back. Way back to Bill Struth, manager from the 1920s to 1950s. Even before *him*. Can you imagine? A manager for 34 years? Lucky if they last that many *days* these days. And Struth was old school. Like Jock Wallace. We never signed Italians or Colombians in them days. Clowns crossing theirselves before running onto the hallowed turf.'

Aware the drained flask was running his mouth, he clammed.

'*Tin flutes*, Dad? Appropriate.'

'Suits, I'm talking about.'

'Was gonna rinse my blazer.'

'I'm putting a wash on before my next shift. I'll check the instructions. Should probably take it to a launderette.'

'Uh huh.'

'Listen, son. If things don't go so well.'

'*Don't* say that. Told you, Dad. You'll jinx it.'

'*Listen*, son. Don't really care if the scout's impressed or not. Well, I *do*, obviously. But it won't be the end of the world.'

'Dad.'

'I know, I know. There's always Plan B.'

'Aye, aye.'

'What I *was* building up to say is … Your Ma would've been fair proud.'

But the monotonous beat was activated, plugs back in, the world shut away.

*

The essay title was 'Video Games and Violence in Contemporary American Society.' Donnie skimmed through the pages.

"There is an average of 1.19 mass shootings every day in the USA, but conservative commentators will use every possible excuse, from mental illness to video game addiction, rather than confront the real issue, the fact their country's Second Amendment legislates for gun ownership as a basic right of its citizens …

He flipped pages.

… psychopaths fail to draw a distinct line between reality and fantasy. Far more people spend their leisure time enjoying computer

games than watching movies or listening to music; the gaming industry is set to turnover $257 billion by 2025, with first-person shooter games accounting for 20.9% of the total. Players can become immersed in simulated warfare where they are encouraged to use a variety of lethal weapons. Contrast this with war in the real world, with social media providing 24/7 access to genuine military horror …"

The alcoholic haze elevating his pride, tears came. When he heard the boy on the phone to mates, he'd listen to the Edinburgh accent but smile at the syllables reflecting his County Antrim roots. *You can take the boy out of Belfast.* He'd heard that repeated so many times. Compared to the eloquence of his schoolwork, the lad's conversational voice was so different. Wasn't that always the way? Depending on who you were talking to, if you were working class you'd switch, informal to formal. Toffs only spoke one way since they didn't believe in impressing anyone. When Donnie had brought playground slang home, his father cuffed him around the ear. Especially if a swearword slipped out. Then he'd overhear his dad in the pub when he was waiting outside. Every fourth word worth one of his skelps.

Picturing his old man, a memory surfaced. His dad in the suit he rarely wore, orange sash around the folds of his neck. Perched on his knee, Donnie was mimicking the way his dad was whistling along to the band tuning up at the end of the street. Winking at him, his dad touched a finger to his lips, yellowish brown from his cigarettes. Lifted the glass from the table. Allowed him a sip. It was like swallowing fire.

*

Her dyed crimson hair cut into an angled bob, the headteacher looked so young. He would've put a week's wages on tattoos nestling. Snaking around her arms? Below the nape of her neck, like Jenny's? The notion tickled his dick. Forced him to sit up in his chair, cross his legs.

'Brad's normally such a quiet boy,' she said. 'Not forthcoming when teachers ask questions. But polite when asked directly. Which is why this was so out of character. Again.'

'Again?'

'Yes.'

'When I got the phone call, the school office said there'd been a fight? I appreciate you have to take these things seriously, but I had to get away from my work. I'll need to make up the time.'

'Mister Cameron.'

'Donnie.'

'It had broken up by the time staff intervened. He won't even say who else was involved. But. The reason I asked you to come over. It's not the first time Brad has been involved in something like this. And his attendance has slumped, just this past term. I just wanted to find out. Is there anything you could shed light on?"

'I'm … I'm taken aback, Miss Sanderson.'

'Kerry.'

'I'm taken aback, Brad's quiet, as you said. Shy. Loves his football. I'm gobsmacked.'

'Quite so, Donnie. Our pupils are maybe not quite so prone to antisocial behavior when they progress to S6s. But no one is immune. It follows so many of them throughout their lives. We have high hopes for Brad as a history student.'

'Aye. He's that academic. Far, far more than I *ever* was, Christ's sake.'

Her mobile phone buzzed. Glancing at the caller ID, she stabbed a button. 'I can tell by your accent school wasn't around these parts, Donnie?'

'South Belfast. But I've lived in Scotland for years.'

She nodded. 'I believe Brad lost his mum at an early age?'

'Aye. Jenny died when he was just at nursery. We were married in Northern Ireland. Decided to start a new life here. But. Jenny was hit by a car mounting the pavement. The driver was on drugs. Cocaine. He got three years.'

'That's tragic, Donnie. I'm so sorry. It must've been hard.'

'We managed. But … I just don't get it. He hasn't said anything to me. Not a word. I certainly had no idea about him bunking off.'

'This is a problem, Donnie. We're only party to rumours. There's been friction with another lad. There's a girl involved. A girl who was …' Her gaze shifted a fraction, now focusing on a calendar behind him. 'Pregnant. *Was* pregnant. But, as I say, we're pretty much in the dark about that side of things. Her family are religious. Just wanted everything swept under the carpet. If there is trouble and Brad is involved, nobody, not Brad or anyone else, is willing to broach the topic. There's a ridiculous code of silence.'

Donnie felt he was sinking into a well of confusion. He'd no idea what to say to any of this. All he could focus on was the hip flask he needed to tug from. His glove compartment. His safe place. 'He's been really upset about losing his cat,' he finally murmured. 'He was really attached to it. Alfie.'

'Alfie?'

'I chose the name. After somebody I knew back home who died suddenly.'

*

He gulped the whisky. Years before, he'd watched a film starring Elizabeth Taylor and Paul Newman. *Cat on a Hot Tin Roof*. Not his usual choice, but Donnie always liked Newman because his father enthused about being taken to see *Butch Cassidy and the Sundance Kid* at the Strand by *his* father, Brad's great grandad. The ornate picture house had portholes in the foyer, its architect influenced by the Harland and Wolff shipyards where only Protestants would get the jobs.

Donnie had watched the Western himself several times, had the DVD. He was always struck by the ending. Butch and Sundance bursting from their hideout to be felled by scores of Bolivian soldiers. The director freeze-framed their defiant last stand. You didn't see the aftermath of the maelstrom of bullets. In a modern re-telling, Redford and Newman's characters would be drenched in blood, like red snow angels, their iconic Hollywood faces shredded beyond recognition. In *Cat on a Hot Tin Roof* Newman was Brick, a former star athlete who turned to alcohol after a spinal injury finished his career. Brick described drinking until he felt a click: that moment the darkness would dissolve.

Donnie grinned. He'd clicked again. Now he tapped into Facebook, navigating to Kyle Matthews' page. In some photos you could glimpse the reckless teenager Matthews had once been. Hamming it up for mates. Brandishing bottles like firearms. Dancing on a table in some beer garden, the

Mediterranean a glistening blue in the background.

There was a time these images had incensed Donnie to the point of tossing the laptop across the room. There was still a web-like fissure across the screen's top corner. Why should Matthews have the right to act so cavalier after what he'd done? Donnie would also focus on the more recent galleries. Kyle and his attractive fiancée, Heather. In their wedding photographs, Kyle resplendent in Highland regalia. Shots of their kids. Robyn. Then Cassie.

Stalking this man on Facebook, he realised the answer to his question lay in Kyle's children's infectious smiles. Nobody should have their whole life defined by one moment of madness, in Kyle's case when he'd opted to twist the ignition key into a car while high on Class As. The possibility of redemption was a cornerstone of the justice system and the lad had served his time.

*

Scuffing along the gravel path, he skimmed inscriptions on the tombstones. Ian Tainsh, Royal Scots, died 1919. To have survived the horrors of the trenches, only to last another year. At least he'd have had a proper funeral, not just stacked in French pits. Elizabeth Fraser, 1862-1962. Had she been proud or indifferent at receiving Her Majesty's personal greeting card? Passing Elizabeth's resting place so regularly, he'd made up her life story. Her father had been a redcoat fighting Russians in Crimea, her son, Boers. She would've seen juddery cinema newsreels of early flying contraptions seldom lifting off the ground. Watched footage of Yuri Gagarin. Gained the right to vote. Outlived millions dying in global warfare.

Now Donnie could smell garden refuge burning in allotments on the opposite side of the graveyard wall. He felt the ground shifting, had to thrust out a hand to a stone cross to steady himself. His eyes smarted and the stench hauled him back to Scout camp, lighting fires with green branches that produced meagre flames but plumes of cloying smoke. He recalled hoisting the Union flag. "I promise that I will do my best, to do my duty to God and to The Queen, to help other people and to keep the Scout Law." Some altered the words, promising to *fuck* the Queen. But the boys were united in avoiding the predatory stare of their Scoutmaster, Fingers McCann. *For God and The Queen*. The legend emblazoned across the mural of balaclava'd gunmen on the gable-end of Jenny's street.

Tears coursing down his face, he blundered on until he reached the row. In the encroaching gloom, he counted the headstones. Crouching to grasp the wizened blooms from the vase by Jenny's plaque, he peered towards her inscription. Her name, the dates, the words he could remember choosing from the funeral director's catalogue as if it was yesterday, UNTIL WE MEET AGAIN. He reached out to touch this and felt as if he'd been cattle prodded. A single word had been spraypainted in lurid crimson, oozing down the flecked granite like blood.

He read it aloud. '*Slag*.'

*

Donnie was riveted to his son's actions, tracking his runs off the ball, glee coursing through him whenever he won a tackle or threaded through an inch-perfect pass. Minutes before half-time, a defender needlessly handled. Stepping up, Brad placed the ball on the spot.

Donnie noted the scout, level with the box. Lanky, cropped hair, pointing an iPad to record the moment. If tonight's spectacle was merely the first rung up a tortuous ladder, Brad was smashing it. The boy was a natural attacking midfielder, his fluid motion and confidence both on and off the ball a delight to watch. He consistently prompted applause. Donnie was also pleased to observe a posse of females shouting encouragement from the sidelines; one of them, a redhead, always loudest.

This must be the girl. Olivia. His son rarely discussed her, his only revelation being she'd recently gone out with someone else in the team who hadn't handled the split well. Brad's headteacher had alluded to that backstory but when Donnie tried broaching it, the boy had clammed. Pregnancy? He'd heard something. Ancient history, but.

'Bury this, son,' Donnie shouted.

The defender murmured to Brad. He reacted, gazing beyond the goalposts. The referee's whistle piped. Brad's foot made contact, but his attempt was half-hearted, the ball striking the post, trundling back towards him. Trapping the ball, he composed himself, ready to slot it past the flailing keeper, only for the other lad's studs to go through him like a bull crashing into a cape. Even from 30 yards, Donnie heard the splintering of his fibula and could see the shattered bone piercing the skin. Brad squealed.

Donnie rushed towards his son. In the erupting melee, the referee's whistle was pitifully inadequate for restoring order. The red-haired girl was hysterical. 'Fifty fifty ball.' The other player laughed, like a hyena hunched over a carcass.

Brad's eyelids fluttered. 'In one of the trees … Dad.'

'Don't talk, son.'

'No, Dad. I've just noticed.'

Frowning, Donnie gazed into the branches. He could make out crow nests among the stark tendrils. One looked different. Resembling rags. He knew it was a black and white cat. A cord had been wrapped around its neck and tossed over the bough it was now hanging from.

Looking to the tree, the boy grinned. About turning, resigned to marching from the pitch, he flicked his middle finger. Donnie noticed the crimson stain. In that horrible moment, he visualised him at the back gate, offering a scrap of chicken or tuna. A flash of black and white fur, collar tingling. Scooped into a bag.

He got to his feet. A red mist familiar to his own younger self igniting, he stalked after the boy. Quickening. He would pounce on this bully, punch him into next week. He would target the bull's eye, his Adam's Apple, punch him into his next life. He could already see him writhing in the mud, gasping like a landed fish, the fatally swollen trachea turning his mouth blue. He could. He would. He fucking *would*. He screamed his rage. Screwed his eyes shut. The world, which had spiraled around him so often, out of his control, needed to stop.

Deep breathing, he sought his headspace. Brian Eno's 'An Ascending.' Playing in his mind, the YouTube video he would watch glassy-eyed while thinking of Jenny: Earth from space, Scotland appearing through clouds to the right of the Irish Sea; his new home, the old one far behind. But he couldn't stop the nightmare flooding back. Pictured the moment he emerged into sunlight for the first time in so long. Spotting Jenny and his parents through the unruly knot of photographers waiting for them all to ease through the turnstile after the Good Friday Agreement had emptied the Maze. His side furtive in baseball caps, hoodies, shades. The other side had all left earlier. They'd heard them being greeted by party poppers and champagne corks.

And the instant he once tried and tried his hardest to justify but always knew that because he never could, his every sinew had to be devoted to suppressing it, to denying it, to lying about it, to running away from it. Now, for the first time in an age, he'd raced right into it again. Could see, hear, feel everything. Cloying fag smoke. A car alarm a block away, its beeping synchronising with his racing heart. His neck itchy from loose strands after that morning's trim at Uncle Davie's barber shop; tugging on the balaclava made him recall childhood nits. Gripping the door handle so tight to mask the shaking, his knuckles were white. His sinister reflection. His Royal Stewart tartan shirt. Sandy snapping, '*Get it fuckin' done.*' The carjacked taxi's diesel engine idling. Rattling. His crazed pulse as he skulked through the allotments. The tantalizing aromas. Basil. Mint. Chives. Tomatoes. The stout figure emerging from a glasshouse, intent on a seedling. The photos he'd studied confirmed. Alfred Docherty. No connection to any group. Just someone from the area as a reprisal for one of theirs the week before. He squeezed the 9mm pistol's trigger. And again. And again. And again. The panes shattering. Holes drilling in the structure's rickety frame. In meat. Then, as the man tumbled, standing behind, a wee lass, five or six, maybe. '*Grandpa!*'

Before he fled, he registered her clutching her own seedling in its pot, a tiny orange flower shaking in her terrified grip, like a candle. Gaping at him. This monster who'd haunt her for the rest of her pure, innocent life.

SONGS IN THE KEY OF STRIFE – I'VE GOT 99 PROBLEMS AND BEING JAY Z IS ONE

Neil Renton

At the age of forty-two, I decided what I wanted to be when I grew up.

I wanted to be Jay Z.

What comes to mind when you think of him?

Rapper. Businessman. Inventor of his own colour. Owner of a basketball team. Married to Beyoncé. Once played a gig in the Southside Library.

The last fact might have caught you by surprise, but it's true. Or it was in my head anyway.

At the height of my lows, I was signed off work, but I was too embarrassed to say anything. I was going to the cinema, but it was costing me money. Not only was there the ticket price, but throw in the Poundland run for snacks and mini bottles of Irn Bru, and it was all adding up. A nightmare for someone like me who doesn't like spending his own cash.

I was randomly bumping into people I knew, which made me think they were suspicious of what I was up to. If I stopped for a moment to prevent myself from overthinking, I would have realised they'd be too busy living their lives to worry about Mine. The library seemed like a good idea. Who goes to one nowadays, I reasoned. Sad but true. I'd go, get some peace from my thoughts, and rock up the road, imagining I had been at the job I was signed off from as if nothing was wrong.

I based myself at a wee round table, surrounded by books on music, films, and other arts, as opposed to boring stuff like history or geography. I had a To-Do List, which was a joke. There were sandwiches that I'd prepared as if I was going to the office. I'd sit on the bench outside and throw them to the ants, making various medical appointments that I couldn't decide whether I was going to attend.

Leaving for a spot of fresh air was something I enjoyed doing. For one, there seemed to be fewer wasps than there were indoors. It was also quieter, so I liked to escape the absolute shrill of the place. When I was a kid, a library was a place of solace and tranquillity. Not anymore.

They're full of parent-and-toddler groups singing nursery rhymes and banging granite tambourines on the concrete floor. There's folk clattering the lids of a broken printer in the vain hope that it'll work. And no one seems to be able to talk in tones less than people discussing their mundane working days through the adverts at the cinema. That loud.

To be fair, I could have been Jay Z in the Southside Library. Complete with a full backing band consisting of DJs, hyenas on backing vocals, and the London Philharmonic Orchestra, and we'd be struggling to be heard above the elderly guy who was having problems plugging in his laptop charger.

When I wasn't in the great outdoors being chased by giant, buzzing terrors that had escaped the confines of the library, I was at the table. My table. And for some reason, I wasn't Neil Renton from Leith.

I was Jay Z from Brooklyn.

How did this happen? It's not as if I was possessed by the spirit of the big man as he was very much still alive. For some reason, I assumed I was him.

Remember his Glastonbury performance? He was trolled by Noel Gallagher beforehand, who questioned why a rapper should be headlining such a prestigious music festival and British institution. Jay Z didn't give a toss and instead came in to a sample of one of Gallagher's best-known tracks, the Oasis song 'Wonderwall,' pretending to play guitar. Outstanding.

His stage presence mesmerised me. I have none. If you don't believe me, ask the good people at The Stand Comedy Club in Edinburgh, who provided such feedback during a stint I had on their Red Raw Open Mic Night.

I could have learned a lot from Shawn Carter, and I was transfixed by the recall. If my memory serves me right, he did a lot of walking that Saturday night, and some of it was backwards.

It's a difficult thing, walking backwards. Try it when you get a minute. Preferably not while reading this. And not at the top of stairs—nine out of ten people who fall backwards down stairs die.

But give it a go when you're in a safe space. Walking backwards, not falling down the stairs. It requires confidence, self-awareness, and balance. You need to know where you're going when you can't see where you're going.

So there I was, convinced I was Jay Z. I'd initially pace the area, picking up a decent speed. Then I'd stop, play to the audience of a barely used pad and nervously chewed pen. And I'd walk backwards around the table.

At this point, my mind was massively out of control. I didn't know what I was doing. I didn't care. I didn't breathe; I just panicked. In. Out. In. And I think Out.

If I read, I'd regain some sort of moral compass. Off I went to the fiction section. How hard could it be to pick a book with so many of them? Maybe 99 at least. I went forward, took some side steps, then a wee bit backwards.

Really fucking hard is how hard it was to pick a book at that point. Where do you start? What category gets your interest? It's a commitment, reading. You're giving up your time to be entertained or educated. Or both.

Irvine Welsh. He'll do. You know where you are with the big man. But there weren't any of his books. Back to the drawing board. Back to the table I was circling. Back to walking backwards.

Thankfully, me thinking I was Jay Z was a minor blip. And it's probably for the best I'm not really him, as everyone will tell you.

Especially Beyoncé.

DOUGLAS ROSS COUNTY

Neil Renton

Nothing ever happened in the thirty-third minute of a football game.

That's why Ryan always chose to go get his steak pie from the food kiosk. The stalls at Easter Road were quieter at that point, with maybe a stray pensioner confusing a foreign student by asking for a Bovril, or an overweight kid fleecing his dad's bank card for a packet of Haribo and a Mars Bar chaser.

It was part of his routine. Check the scores from the other games, moan to strangers about how bad Hibs are, and no doubt pick the wrong queue to stand in.

Ryan cradled a pie as he headed back up towards his seat in the West for the remainder of the Hibs and Ross County first half when disaster struck.

He had lifted the tin foil container up for a closer study of the strange pastry worm that had broken through the shell when he dropped it. Maybe it was the heat of the pie, about two and a half degrees cooler than the surface of the sun. Maybe it was the fact he was worried about what he was about to put in his mouth. Whatever it was, it spilled from his grasp with the clumsy grace of vintage Ma-Kalamby and landed with typical Hibs luck face down on the ground.

Ryan couldn't just ignore it; Leave No Man Behind was his motto when it came to food. So he swooped down and picked it back up. No one will have noticed, he thought to himself, standing in front of a thousand eyes transfixed on the pitch behind him as he blew on it then bit it.

One person did notice. And that person was Douglas Ross, the part-time lineman and part-time Conservative MP, running the line that afternoon right next to where it happened.

"Oi! You, you manky cunt! Did you just pick that up from the ground and eat it?" Ross gasped.

"Eh, nah," Ryan mumbled through a mouthful of roasting pie.

"You fucking did!" Ross barked in a tone that made the fans in close proximity take notice.

"Aye, but it's alright, it's my pie," said Ryan.

"Doesn't matter, you're a clarty wee bastard," Ross said.

"Nah," pleaded Ryan. "Five-second rule."

"That was on the ground for about a minute, fucking disgusting."

"It wasn't."

"It was. And I know how we'll check. REF! REF! VAR! FUCKING VAR!"

Referee John Beaton sprinted over with a look of concern on his face. He listened intently as his assistant briefed him on the fallen pie escapade.

Beaton then fingered his own ear so he could hear the viewing team over in Glasgow give their verdict. Ryan delicately picked at the crust as the game was halted for the checks to be done.

Then the ref drew an imaginary box in the air and jogged to the television at the side of the pitch for a closer inspection. Meanwhile, the giant screens at Easter Road flashed up VAR: POSSIBLE FOOD EATEN AFTER BEING ON THE FLOOR FOR LONGER THAN FIVE SECONDS.

The obligatory full house waited in silence as the decision was made. Beaton studied his watch and the footage at the exact moment to time how long it had been on the ground.

Eventually, he blew his whistle and headed back to the pair.

"The pie was on the ground for four point three seconds. No offence committed."

Cheered on by the eruption from the fans, Ryan punched the air in delight and almost dropped the pie again, which would have been both funny and tragic. Meanwhile, Ross threw his lineman's flag down on the touchline in a petulant huff.

No one seemed to notice or care that Hibs went on to lose the game. Ryan's result was the only one that mattered.

MARK'S ALL WRITE

Mark Fleming knew something wasn't wrote when he lost the urge to write. At the age of 25, it wasn't just his creativity that was affected by his mental health slump. His love of music also faltered as he became disoriented from reality.

"I've always been into writing," Fleming says. "Back in the punk scene, I was writing lyrics. I was writing a lot and even got a couple of things published.

"But then I started to lose interest in creativity, writing, and music. All the records I used to play religiously just gathered dust. My health got worse and worse, and I ended up on the bipolar scale."

We're sitting in a quiet pub on the west side of Edinburgh. It's not too busy, but the waitress keeps checking if we need anything, making sure our nachos are to our liking.

Despite the sensitivity of the conversation, Mark doesn't hold back, even when she's within earshot. He's hidden his emotions for long enough.

"I was doing far too much overtime but partying like I was still a student," Mark continues. "I was still living at home then. My mum would say I was burning the candle at both ends, but I thought, 'Fuck it, I'm enjoying myself. This is life.'

"Everything crept up on me, though, and I got agoraphobic. I couldn't go out. I was signed off with stress."

Even while managing multiple tasks—like the pressure of moving house and getting the perfect angle of the chicken bun he's ordered—Mark seems unfazed. But it wasn't always like this, especially when he couldn't explain what was wrong.

"At the time, my parents didn't know anything about bipolar disorder. No one had heard much about it. They came with me to the GP because I couldn't articulate how I was feeling.

"The doctors said it was a depressive episode and gave me some pills. I became disillusioned. There was a light in the garden going on and off, and I thought it was a searchlight. I thought a gang was after me. I just hid away in my room."

Things quite literally came to a head when Mark decided to take drastic action. After metaphorically banging his head against a brick wall, he physically threw himself against his bedroom wall in an attempt to reset his mind.

"One night, I thought the only way to get through it was to reboot," Fleming says. "I thought if I knocked myself out, everything would go back to normal.

"I launched myself at the wall, thinking, 'This'll sort me out.' I ended up bruised. My dad heard the commotion, and while my mum called an ambulance, he sat on me. I woke up the next day in a locked ward at the Royal Edinburgh Hospital. I thought I was in prison."

The Royal Ed has a reputation as a grim asylum—a place where Batman's Joker might rub shoulders with Randle McMurphy. But that couldn't be further from the truth. It was here that Mark began to rediscover his love for life—and for writing.

"I remember having a pad," Mark recalls, "and my sister brought me a pen. I started writing again. She took the pages to work and typed them out for me.

"A psychiatrist saw the stories and found them interesting. I told him I'd had stuff published before, and he encouraged me to stick at it. It took time, but it helped get me back on an even keel."

Mark and I met through The Changing Room—a programme that helps men tackle their mental health through football. It's not just supporting a terrible football team that we have in common. Music, writing, and wearing tracksuit tops when we're arguably too old to do so are other traits we share.

"When I came off medication, I wanted to fill my life with positive things as a safety net," he says. "That's when I found out about The Changing Room, and I knew it was what I wanted to join.

"We've all got empathy for each other because we've all been through something similar. That's been a huge help."

I can relate to another factor that's helped Mark through dark times: his tunes.

"One of the best coping mechanisms is music," he points out. "I get my headphones on and chill out to anything.

"It was a eureka moment when I was in hospital. The guy in the next bed had a Walkman, and I called my mum and told her to bring mine in. It was the first time I'd phoned home in weeks—I'd been too zoned out on medication.

"When the Walkman arrived, I started listening to all my old cassette tapes. I used to tape John Peel's shows off the radio—a real mix of stuff."

We might be sitting in a place surrounded by alcohol, but neither of us needs it to keep our spirits up anymore.

"I don't drink as much as I used to," Mark says. "There was a time when I was still binge-drinking. But now I'm no spring chicken, and I've decided to take better care of my health."

For the first time since I've known him, I can see his eyes start to well up—when he talks about the support his family has given him.

"The fact I've been open with my wife, Karen, and my daughter is positive. I try to put things into perspective, and my wife is great at that. She can tell when something's up. She'll ask if I'm okay when I'm looking a bit down, and I do the same for her.

"We recognise when we're not as buoyant as we usually are."

Writing has helped Mark turn a corner in his life, and now he's using his talent to help others.

"A lot of folk my age are thinking of retiring, maybe taking up golf. But I quit my job in the civil service to become a freelance writer. Then, in the last year, I became a life celebrant.

"I want funerals to be a celebration of someone's life. Bereavement and grief are brutal stresses to go through, but if you can give a fitting tribute to the person they've lost, you feel like you've given something back."

What would Mark say to his younger self—the moment before he hurled himself at his bedroom wall?

"Don't!" he laughs at the obviousness. Then, taking a moment to chew over the question while biting into a chip, he adds, "I think I'd do what my dad did—grapple me to the ground."

"The worst thing about mental health is keeping it bottled up. Opening up is the answer.

"All those poisonous thoughts in your head aren't real. You've got your whole world in front of you."

KATA TON DAIMONA EAYTOY

Neil Renton

I was five when Mitch came swaggering into my life.

It turned out he was two months younger, but he came with the confidence of an adult decades older. I was in my street, kicking a half-burst leather ball against a factory shutter when he approached me. He sniffed a giant marker in his tiny hand before scrawling his name in capital letters on the wall. "Who are all the pies? Who ate all the pies? You fat bastard, you fat bastard, you ate all the pies," he shouted at me.

"Pass me the ball. I play for Hibs," he demanded. I did what I was told. I was too scared and intrigued not to. He picked it up, tossed it in the air, and blootered it high into the grey sky. Eventually, it landed on the other side of a barbed-wire fence across the street.

"That wasn't smart," he said, as if trusting him was my fault. And it was. We spent the next forty minutes trying to clamber in without being sliced to death or getting covered in vandal paint. We never did get the ball back.

At that moment, I decided I should try and stay as far away from him as I possibly could. We were inseparable until his death.

There was an attraction to Mitch. He was a liability, capable of starting a fire in an empty, rain-soaked matchbox. But he was enduring with it. You couldn't be too unhappy with him for too long. His dimpled cheek, with more personality than most could muster in their entire bodies, made sure of that.

*

It's raining, but Paris still looks fantastic. It's just noise and kinetic energy everywhere you go. They don't suffer fools or tourists gladly. I've no idea how Mitch coped.

I'll find out, though. Through socials, I've tracked down a singer called Manon who was the last person I've managed to find who'd been with Mitch before he died. She's agreed to meet me in a Scottish pub, the same one where Mitch took her. You can take the boy out of Leith, but you can't take the Leith out of the boy. Twitter refreshes. Hibs holding Celtic to a goalless draw. Gutted to be missing it. It's not the game I'm longing for.

When you book a one-way plane ticket, why does no one question it? "Why aren't you planning on returning?" There should be a pop-up that asks that question. "Are you okay?" "Do you need help?" "Can we contact someone on your behalf?"

Of course, people do intend to come back. There's a perfectly good reason as to why they've not planned that return journey. 99%, I'd say.

Still, there's the 1%.

He wasn't a classic beauty, but that didn't stop him from being the centre of attention. Especially with women. Big Dick Energy they call it nowadays. If he could bottle it in an aftershave, it would be the most popular spray on the fragrance counter, and he'd have shagged all the girls selling it.

Manon is very much a typical Mitch type. Gorgeous. Stunning. The best-looking person you've seen since the last Mitch conquest. Jessica Rabbit lips. Bambi eyes.

She speaks fondly about Mitch. Didn't know him for too long, but he clearly left an impression on her. She's upset. Her eyes start to glisten when I ask about his last hours.

"You know when they say they died peacefully in their sleep? That was not Mitch. He did not go quietly."

I'm proud as fuck.

*

His funeral was a proper send-off. His dear old mum and dad, people watching. Standing Room Only, they kept saying, as if the number of people who attended to see you off defined the life that came before it.

All the boys back together. Even Shanks, who I hadn't seen in ages. Shona seemed to take Mitch's passing hard, harder than most. Shanks did that uneasy comfort thing that Scottish husbands do so well. Rubs and pats.

That's when I decided to go to Paris. Tennents in one hand, phone in the other, trying to get flights. Return flights. Not one-way ones. C'mon, I asked. Who wants to look for the answers to what happened?

No one replied.

*

It's been good. Closure of sorts. Therapeutic. I managed to interview a couple of folk for the podcast, so I can write it off through company expenses. But in general, I'm glad I came. And it wasn't just the bit where I stared at Manon, although that helped.

137

There's more questions that will never be answered. Never mind. Bottom lip disappears as I sadly file away a fleeting memory of Mitch.

I've got a day before I leave. Doing all the wanky tourist shite.

Jim Morrison's grave. Me and Mitch in The Citrus Club, dancing to 'Peace Frog' and screaming at the top of our voices "BLOOD IN THE STREETS IN THE TOWN OF NEWHAVEN" as if it was the one with an EH postcode instead of an American zip. Debating if putting on weight made rock stars better. Morrison. Elvis. That's two.

Then I see it on the tombstone. Green ink. The handwriting. Bold capital letters for everyone to see. Leaving a mark. Leaving a legacy.

YOU FAT BASTARD.

Fuck it. I'm not going back tomorrow.

THE STRIKE

Neil Renton

"Shabana, will you join us in going on strike?"

"I was thinking more along the lines of getting a cappuccino."

Shabana stood at the vending machine as the precious minutes of her morning break slipped away. Blocking her path to a refreshment were an angry-looking Declan, an oblivious Charlie, and a worried Ryan.

"You can't drink from here. These machines are inhumane and perfectly exemplify how this company is treating us badly," Declan said, his arms folded tightly.

"Do you think this industrial action will take long? I want to get back to my desk before a manager sees us," Charlie asked.

"It'll take as long as it takes for the executive board to notice that enough is enough. We're not putting up with these horrible conditions any longer."

"Why are you striking?" Shabana asked.

"They recycle the cups," Ryan said, raising an eyebrow.

"What's wrong with saving the planet?"

"You don't get it. They're taking the cups out of the actual bins and putting them back in the machine without cleaning them," Declan replied.

"They can't do that."

"Well, how else do you explain me getting a hot chocolate, and this came out?"

Declan lifted the cup from the machine's tray for Shabana to examine.

"Hot chocolate?"

"No, look at the rim."

"At the purple stuff?"

"Exactly. And what colour lipstick does Frances wear?"

"Rouge?"

"Purple. So Frances has a coffee this morning, number twelve from the right-hand machine because that's her favourite. Then, when she tosses the cup in the bin, it ends up back in the machine. So when I get my hot chocolate, I get the cup she's lipped to death."

"And what's this got to do with Charlie and Ryan?"

"I really don't want to be part of this," Charlie said, turning to look at a blank wall.

"Yeah, I'm not sure why I'm here," Ryan added. "Initially, it seemed fun handing out leaflets and organising marches. Now, I'm not so sure."

"Wait. I've got an idea."

Shabana punched '40' onto the number pad of the vending machine and ordered herself a cappuccino.

"There you go, there's your lipstick."

Declan, Charlie, and Ryan stared at the second cup Shabana was holding and the purple dusting on its edge.

"So, no one here had a cup, smeared it with lipstick, and put it back in the machine, did they?"

No one answered.

"Yet my cup has this mysterious lipstick. Although it's not really lipstick, is it? It's the colour from the Vimto I ordered before. A little bit of its powder got onto the next cup."

The three of them stood with mouths as wide as a paper cup as Shabana took a sip of her coffee, smacked her lips, and headed back to her desk.

"Oi, where are you going?" Declan called out as the others followed her. "Vimto? Fucking Vimto? This is Scotland. It should be Irn Bru. I'm off to HR to report this racist bile."

YCL!

Mark Fleming

When the alarm bleats, Dimitri just heaves the duvet tighter. Sophie scratches the ink band around his arm until he groans. 'Proud of your tat, eh, Dimbo? *All about my individuality, Soph. Aye, right, mate. Page after page of they Celtic knots in the Tribe catalogue. With your spindly arms. Reminds me of school sports day, eh. When we had to chuck quoits over a stick.'

'Mmmh?'

'Get my breakfast while I shower, Dim.'

When she persists digging at his skin, he lets out a longer moan, burying himself under the covers.

'Boys with more get up and go in the Walking Dead last night, eh.' About to tug his tumbleweed hair, her phone beeps. 'Danni girl?' Stares at the text.

*

Typically, the 24 was late, so she speedwalks up to the care home from the stop, then swipes herself in. Creeps past the manager, Mags Laidlaw's door. But it's open.

'Eh. Morning …'

'Sophie. About time. Straight to Betty Stevenson, now.'

Her order's cut short by her phone. Cradling it, Laidlaw pokes around in a plastic box crammed with odds and ends. Snapping at whoever's at the other end, she wafts her hands at

Sophie, making her feel like a bad smell.

'Old boot,' she murmurs, heading to the lift, jabbing the third floor. Along the corridor, snores. Coughs. 'Fraser Mallan, your lungs are pure hacking, mate,' she calls as she passes his door. 'You sound like the crows that fixed me with their beady eyes when I passed the main gates.'

Sophie enters Betty's bedroom. 'Danni.'

Danni's at the window, watching the sunrise. 'Blackford Hill's on fire this morning, Soph. Beautiful.' About turning, she marches over to Sophie and they hug.

'Your yacks are red raw, Danni girl. You look ripped, though I ken your only vice is WKD Blues.'

'Her bed alarm went off, around twenty to six, Soph. I've come in to check. Soon as I clocked her, I just knew. Dr Inglis suggested she might've had a spasm, enough to trigger her alarm, eh. He says cause it was sudden, it'll be reported to the Procurator Fiscal.'

'This is *so* shan, eh?'

'Look at her, Soph.'

'Trying not to, Danni girl.'

'No, *look* at her, Soph. Her face. It's *changed*. Even in just a couple of hours. It's no Betty anymore.'

'Ayeways wanted to go in her sleep, eh?'

Danni nods, reaches out, brushes her cheek. 'So cold.'

'Poor Betty.'

'Listen, Soph. Liam'll be waiting for me. Needing my kip. Need a fucking drink, more to the point. I started giving her a bed bath. You can finish.' She steps over and they embrace again. 'Catch you, Sophie.'

'Aye. Same time the morn, Danniella, pal.'

As Danni's footsteps recede, Sophie turns to the bed. Betty looks asleep. But her eyes are a wee bit open, as if trying to focus on her. From countless bed baths, Sophie can recognise her body like reading a map. Below her wrinkles, the veins are its road network, still gorged with blood. Red cells trapped inside the gridlock of their pointless journeys.

Steam curls and weaves from the plastic bowl on the chest of drawers. 'Imagine that was a witch's potion, Betty. Maybe toss in an eye of a bat, see if it'd bring you back, eh. That witch in her office down the stairs could probably cast a spell or two, mind. Nah. Fuck that. Seen enough zombies on the box last night.'

Poking inside disposable gloves, she plucks the sponge. Wrings it.

'I hate it when a patient goes, Dimitri,' Sophie says aloud, rehearsing how she'll tell him later. 'While you were sparking up your first doobie-do, I was washing a cadaver on twelve fifty an hour.' She leans in closer. 'I'll have you looking your best for the undertakers, Betty.'

Sophie catches herself in the bedside mirror, tears trickling down her freckly cheeks. She clocks the purple and green streaks she was in too much of a rush to notice earlier. 'Dim helped me tint my jet-black locks last night, Betty. Cool as, Dimbo. Dye proper worked this time.'

The detergent catches the back of her throat. Reminds her of the smell in the bogs in Opium after somebody's hurled and they swamp the tiles with bleach. When she gave Betty her previous bed bath, Sophie's hair was peroxide. Almost white.

After that, she wheeled the elderly woman down to the TV lounge. They watched *This Morning*.

Sophie smoothes the sponge up and down her legs. 'Bones with a shiny layer of skin, Betty. Like this is a waxwork of you, mate. But I can imagine you dancing. I really can, Betty. Dancing in the Kings Theatre. You telt me how you were a dancer, there, a chorus girl you said, when the war was on. I can see you on that stage, mate. *Everyone* smoking, as they did in they days. You and all, soon as you came off stage, in the dressing room. With your cigarette holder. And when you were up on that stage, mate, I can imagine most of the lads in uniforms, trying not to get caught drooling over youse. I could see it all. Easily. When you telt your stories about the old days, I could see it all so clearly, Betty. It was like … like you were painting pictures with your words. You've some photie collection, eh. Flicked through your albums over many a cuppa, eh, mate? You giggling at some of the memories, eh. The stories beyond the freeze-frames. Me picking up on your excitement, eh. You explaining who's who. All they names, eh. All they people long gone. They'll be waiting for you, mate. Loved the way you could mind the names. Couldn't have told me who Dermot and Alison were interviewing yesterday morning, but you could travel back in time. Decades. Seen all your photies in Darth Laidlaw's office. You've hardly had any visitors since I started here, eh. If no next of kin shows out the woodwork, sniffing around for your Will, they'll wind up in landfill.'

Sophie rubs into the bloated stomach. 'Stretchmarks like Cramond beach when the tide's out, eh. Here, Betty. Might as well tell you. Dimitri's turning into a right wankstain. I know you'd laugh if you heard me say that. You liked telling Darth Laidlaw where to go, eh, mate? But Dim just *uses*. In the old-fashioned sense of the word, I mean. Give him a roof over his head and all I ask in return is he visits the jobcentre once in a blue moon.'

She dunks the sponge into the basin.

'Know what's even worse, Betty? He's not even a great shag. I might very well sack him soon. The night, why not? Seeing you this morning, like this, Betty, that's the icing on the cake. Put me on a right downer, eh. That's *it*, by the way. I'll tell him straight. After Emmerdale, mind. Not provoking any nasty drawn-out scenes before my programme, eh.'

Sprinkles trickle towards her crack. Sophie pokes into her belly button. 'How tickly is this? You'd usually be creasing yourself, eh. Giggling like fuck. If anything could bring you back, mate, it'd be this, not CPR. If you were still a teenager, bet you'd have your belly button pierced, eh, Betty? D'you like mine? Never did show you, ayeways meant to.'

Prising open the buttons of her blue tunic, Sophie tugs the material aside. Flashes her navel-ring. 'Dim's treat, Betty. He eBayed a dose of his old boy's records to cover it. Happy Mondays. 808 State. The Roses. Thank you, Madchester! My Ma'll kill me! So what, Betty, eh?!'

Working into the tiny white weeds between her legs, Sophie chews from a Juicy Fruit discovered in her tunic, then spits out foil. Hums a snippet of Bring Me The Horizon. 'Dim plays them to death. I know he's been playing them cause when I get back the Bluetooth speaker's cranked the fuck up. Their singer Ollie's a ride, but.'

Sophie delves the sponge between the body's legs. Noticing the brown smear, she paces back to the bowl. Rinses it a good few times, squeezing until her fingers hurt.

'I can mind everything you were telling me on your birthday, Betty. After you'd taken your meds. Sounded a wee bit of a ramble but I could tell by the tone of your voice it wasn't. It was heartfelt, eh?'

Sophie dumps the sponge in the bowl. Stares out the window where the sunrise has gone from red to gold. 'Wow, Betty. Pity you missed this yin. Your last yin, yesterday, was so dull in comparison. Grey and drizzly.'

Plucking out her moby, she captures a few snapshots. Turns to Betty. 'You shared so much with me. Highs and lows. Well. You're going for your final flit, mate. And what'd your last word of advice have been? I mind one of your sayings. I'm going to borrow it. Tell Dim we were just a hiccup in the drink of life. Except. Well. It's not always that easy, eh? I'm in love with him, Betty. What d'you say to that?'

Betty farts. Jump-scared, heart pattering, Sophie chuckles. 'Christ, Betty. Laidlaw would've had to scrape me off the ceiling, there! My pulse is doing a BPM Danni could dance to, mate.'

She imagines Betty's eyes flickering open; hears her infectious laughter, mischievous as a schoolkid at the back. But she also recalls Laidlaw lecturing with her mouthful of Morningside marbles and impersonates her. '*Even after the heart stops, Sophie, other functions continue. Hair still grows. Fingernails. Acid persists at the bowel contents, creates gas pockets.* Still the most comical thing I've heard for yonks, mate. Like you were summing up my immature dickhead of a BF. Not just that. It's like your message from beyond, eh. What you think of the way Darth Laidlaw talks to you lot. The way Dim put it when I mentioned it to him. Like a Nazi officer at the station platform outside one of they camps. You, *that* queue. You, *that* queue. But tell you what, Betty. From this bed, you've shared your life with me. First stage performance. First crush. Through to your grand finale, the sun on fire outside your window. Hope you seen some of it. The last thing you ever seen, eh.'

Footsteps approach. Unfamiliar voices. Sophie bends down to Betty. 'Aw. Your wee face.' Kisses her cold lips. 'Bye, Betty. You were a mate. Ayeways.'

Tugging the sheet over her wizened tits, she notices a solitary white hair jutting out. 'One of the undertakers might be a horny old cunt, Betty. Giving you the glad eye and that, eh. Might even be kinky. Into that necrophilia. You might get another ride yet, Betty, eh?'

Sophie tweaks the hair. When Laidlaw's right at the door, she shoves it into her tunic. Laidlaw and two guys in black suits enter, the men wheeling a trolley, wheels squeaking. Sophie can't watch them lifting Betty off the bed. Up till now, she's coped with her lying still; imagining she's like a coma patient where you can still talk to them. She knows it's nothing like that but also wonders if maybe Betty's spirit's still close by, if that's what happens. But when these strangers position themselves to haul her off the bed, she's not the person anymore. She's just another of today's bodies to get loaded into the back of their van, stacked into some container in a mortuary within the hour.

Sophie struggles to hold it together. Her insides are

churning. Whether she's on the verge of greeting or giggling, she has no idea. So, she stares at her husband, Kenneth's handsome face in the bedside wedding portrait, recalls something Betty once told her. The Arctic Ocean contains so much salt, it doesn't freeze but still gets way below freezing point. Hypothermia only takes minutes.

'Thanks, Sophie. You can head to the kitchen now. Start serving breakfasts.'

*

At the bus stop, Sophie sketches left and right, unfolds the Rizla paper. Breaking open a snout, enough for a one skinner, she empties the baccy shards, then delves into her pockets for the last crumbs of the 16th. She notices the white hair stuck to the clingfilm. A sob rushes up out of nowhere and tears are streaming.

'All I've got left of you, Betty. Know what? I'm popping it into the spliff. Dim would *love* that. When he's stoned, he stares right through me, like he can see me, but *can't* see me. Then he'll mumble: Soph. I can see. Clear as a bell, babes. I can see how *everything's* connected. We're *all* the Cosmos, Soph.'

Sophie sparks up. As she sucks the first drag deep into her lungs, she hears the hair crackling. She believes it adds an acrider scent to the smoke. She inhales even more, holding it in, holding onto this piece of Betty's DNA long as she can.

'Fuck me, mate … I feel the soles of my trainers leaving the deck … feel like I'm levitating, Betty.'

A hearse halts at the junction ahead. Sophie recognises the two undertakers, the one driving now wearing a top hat. A bouquet is propped by the coffin in the back. 'MUM.' As she watches the black car driving off, heading for Mortonhall, she's picturing Betty's wedding photo. Betty radiant in white, hair long, auburn. Kenneth in his navy-blue uniform. Buttons polished. The biggest smiles of their lives.

When the hearse is gone, she flashes back to Betty's birthday in May. She blew out the candle on the cupcake Sophie presented while a few of the residents who were awake in the lounge sang 'Happy Birthday.' As Sophie was tucking her in later, the excitement of the day and the solitary glass of sherry she was allowed prompted the centenarian to be entertainingly talkative. Sophie inadvertently pocket dialed, recorded minutes of chat on a voice memo. Today's events have now imbued this accidental mp3 with poignancy. Sophie feels as if she is now holding treasure in the palm of her hand. Hitting 'Play,' she closes her eyes, imagines Betty is seated beside her in this bus shelter.

When I was dead young, Sophie, I mean, so young I didn't really understand what I was getting into, I only did it cause my big sister, Blanche, did it. We joined the Young Communist League. The YCL.

Check you out, mate! Raising your fist like that. YCL … sounds like a gang!

Well. When I was a lot younger than you are now, hen, we were a bit like a gang. Rioting on the streets.

You? Rioting, Betty?!

Aye, hen. Rioting. Outside the Usher Hall when Mosley the blackshirt arrived in Edinburgh to give a speech. Some of the older men in the YCL went all the way to Barcelona to join the Brigades. Women, too.

Brigades?

Aye, hen. The International Brigades. Fighting Franco. A lot of them died fighting Franco. Fighting the Nazis.

Christ, Betty. Dim and his mates spend hours killing Nazis on Call of Duty. Spain? You'd struggle to get them out their fucking bedrooms.

Youngsters these days. I was married at your age, Sophie. Nineteen, I was, when me and Kenneth got wed. Got married in St Ninians in Corstorphine.

Kenneth? Not Ken or Kenny?

Never Ken or Kenny. Kenneth. See him in that wedding photie? He was so smart in his naval uniform. I was pregnant at the time, but too early to show.

Twins, eh?

David and Alexander. But. Me and Kenneth didn't even get a wee honeymoon. One night in a hotel. The following day, he sailed out from Leith. He was shipped out on the convoys.

What's that?

On the convoys. Merchant ships. They took supplies to Russia. Weapons. They were on our side, see.

The Russians?

Aye, hen.

Did he bring you souvenirs from Russia?

No, hen. Kenneth's ship was torpedoed. Lost by the Kola Peninsula.

That sounded weird, mate. Lost.

Lost at sea.

Lost. Like a bus-pass. Or that pack of seventeen Regal dropped out my pockets in a cab after our Christmas night out. Ha ha. Sorry, though, mate. I shouldn't be making light of it. Poor Kenneth.

Tell you something else about the war. Well, before the war. Blanche telt me. Telt me about Winston Churchill. The great British war hero. There was a General Strike. Nearly a revolution up here. Churchill wanted to send English soldiers into Glasgow to machine-gun the strikers. Keep our lads confined to barracks in case they sided with their people before their crown. See in Italy. Their blackshirt leader. Il Duce?

Doochee?

Il Duce! Mussolini. Churchill cried him a genius for the way his soldiers ended strikes. With machine guns.

Nearly a revolution, eh? Revolution reminds me of Rezerection, Betty. That was a mega rave held at Ingliston, according to Danni. Her Ma and aunties went to that. Bet your Ma was never off her face, Betty.

Off her face?

With drugs, mate. Pills. They'd take them to stay up all night. Dancing.

I could dance all night in my day. At the Palais. No pills needed, hen.

Was that ballroom dancing. Like on Strictly?

That's right.

Ingliston was all about raving. Not my scene, Betty. Hate that hardcore shite. I met Dimitri at Opium. The first time we did it we were listening to Nirvana. Lithium. While I jumped my first bones. What was yours? Some scratchy 78? Vera Lynn? More to the point, Betty, was it a sample or an extended dance mix, eh? With Dimbo, I blinked and missed it.

My Ma and Da liked dancing. Ma said she stopped dancing when she met my stepdad. Clive hated dancing. Clive said men who danced were fairies. Can you imagine, Sophie? That waste of space sent me out to work when I was only thirteen. Da died in an accident at work. No welfare in they days. It was tough for women back then, Sophie. I doubt Ma ever had strong feelings for Clive. She had to marry him for her family. Later, after I was married. Well. Sophie, I've never told anyone *this. You just didn't in they days.*

You can trust me, mate. My lips are sealed. Here. We'll need to get these curtains sorted. They hooks are broken. I have reported it, Betty.

I was found wandering the streets, one time. Greeting my eyes out. My bairns were getting too much. I was cracking up. The social nearly took the boys off me. Not only was I a widow at nineteen, there was no such thing as post-natal depression, either. Only madness. Specially when it was women cracking up.

Happened to my sister, Kathryn.

Sophie presses 'Stop.' Tears are trickling down her cheeks.

'It's too much to hear your voice, mate. You'll break my heart every time I hear you.'

Suddenly, she visualizes Kenneth, but right at *his* end. Lifejacket keeping him afloat. A tiny dot in a periscope, one of many, their ship sinking behind. Kenneth bobbing in the waves, focused on a vision of his love, her swanlike legs kicking into the spotlights.

Sophie's head whirling, she senses how Kenneth would have felt during these final minutes. Seconds. She feels each wave raising her. Lowering her. Lifting her. Lowering her.

Her finger on 'Delete.' Pressing slightly. Releasing the pressure. Pressing slightly. Releasing.

'We're all the Cosmos, Betty.'

LIKE DOLPHINS CAN SWIM

Mark Fleming

Liz doodled a square on the napkin. Inside this, a rectangle. A bed. Not for comfort, just somewhere to lie. Lifting her coffee, she blew into the froth, took a sip. She added an oval to the rectangle. A pillow. After another slurp, she placed a stickman on the bed. Higher up, she drew a small square. Into this square, a tiny circle. A window into the world outside, the sun shining. This room would be depressing otherwise. She gave her stickman a smiley face. Inside claustrophobic cells, you needed happy thoughts. Otherwise, you'd go mad.

'Still no sign of your friend, Mum?'

Liz shook her head, scrunching the napkin. Watching the crowds outside The Cameo, she studied the titles on the illuminated sign. Which one was Victor planning to take her to? He'd announced it'd be a pleasant surprise. From the timings, she'd narrowed it down to two. She hoped it wouldn't be the one she'd already seen.

Nikki stacked white cups until they curved upwards from her grasp like vertebrae. Clutching them to her apron, she rose, exaggerating the danger.

'Careful with that lot, sweetpea,' Liz said, lifting the magazine, thumbing through. Prada jacket. Costing more than she'd spent on clothes this year. Pandas. Just under two thousand left in the wild. She'd seen more people strolling past the café this afternoon. She dug into her jacket. The letter she'd written still needed a stamp. She read it again.

Dearest John, I was looking forward to your letter so much I read it then wrote this reply before my coffee got cold! I've always believed in fate. You know, before we hooked up, I did dabble in dating apps. Once upon a time. But that was so impersonal. I've had a few close encounters of the absurd kind! My daughter laughs at me writing longhand. You crack me up, mum. Who writes letters apart from someone in a Jane Austen movie? You text me often enough, she says! I much prefer this way, John. More personal.

Guilty about using the past tense about the apps, she folded the letter away. A balding man was lingering by the foyer, wearing what could be the grey bomber jacket he'd described. She felt her butterflies landing, folding their wings. Her gaze was drawn to his paunch and sagging chin. He'd lied about his age. Par for the course. She still yearned for new adventures, not settling for things.

Victor described himself as an IT professional. This meant another office drone who stared into a screen. If he spent 40 hours a week being dull, perhaps the wife he'd claimed had died of cancer might in fact have absconded with a neighbour due to his uninspired lovemaking. When teenage girls flitted past, he made no attempt to mask his letching at their backsides.

'D'you think this Victor has stood you up, Mum?'

'No. I can see him. I'm going to watch *him* being stood up.'

Between checking his watch, he gazed over the traffic and caught her eye. She felt invisible.

*

When she gave John's latest letter a once-over, her hands quivered.

Dearest Elizabeth. Another sunny day!!! The sunrise was like Heaven was on fire. It was scary, almost, like all fires. But beyond beautiful! The robin was singing on my roof again. Woke me up at 4.45! So, I went straight to my writing pad. How are things with you?

She loved his handwriting, the flowery mixture of upper and lower case, rendered in fastidious lines, as if measured by a ruler. Lifting the paper to her face, she inhaled, imagining his palms brushing against the paper. Over the road, Ronnie was tugging on a cigarette. Her daughter was serving an elderly couple.

'Right, Nikki, petal, I'll be off. Wish me luck.'

'Oh! Has he arrived? Let me see, let me see!' Nikki dropped the plate so impatiently the man started. Coming closer, she rested her chin on her mum's shoulder.

Liz shrugged her away. 'Navy polo shirt, dark hair.'

'Oh, he's a honey! Listen, if you don't get on, send him over here!'

*

When the lights began dimming, Liz glanced at this man who'd swiped right. He was fidgeting with the third finger of his left hand, rubbing the skin. In that instant she knew he was hiding a ring in a pocket.

'Ronnie,' she whispered. 'Sorry. I have to go to the loo. It's come on me all of a sudden.'

'Of course, Liz.'

Placing a hand on her knee, he squeezed. She stifled a gasp of revulsion. Stumbling up the aisle, she found herself blinking in the foyer. Crowds shuffled towards Cameo 2, everyone gaping at her. Quickening her step, she headed for the exit.

*

She was thinking of the birthday card John had sent her. He'd sketched cygnets, very different to the Mute Swans she was used to in Holyrood Park. One was plunging its bill into the water, sending ripples towards the edge of the card. When the time came to take it down from the mantelpiece, she would have it framed.

When she tuned in to Gregor again, she shuddered. He motioned with his great hands, describing feminine curves. Was he enthusing about some ex? No. He was purring about his car. Although he was sitting right there, he didn't look at her. He was narrating to his pint. Minutes later, he was chuckling about some stunt on *Top Gear*. He didn't care he'd backed into a conversational cul-de-sac. Liz took a hefty gulp, grimaced.

'What do you drive, Liz?'

'I've got a bus pass.'

Liz polished off her drink, crunching the ice cubes. 'I'll get one for myself in the meantime, Gregor.'

Clutching her handbag, she strode towards the bar but went past it and out into the street.

*

Nikki placed another coffee before Liz.

'Thanks, petal.' Liz glared at the cinema's yawning entrance. It looked as if Tony had got cold feet. A past master herself, she still resented the affront.

'He can't have been meant for you, Mum,' Nikki sympathised. 'This'll cheer you up. Sasha texted me some more holiday snaps. Here, check them out.'

157

Nikki fiddled with her mobile phone, then placed it on the ledge.

'Thanks, sweetpea.'

Her daughter and seven mates had gone to Ibiza. Liz thumbed through a succession of gurning youngsters in bikinis. They brandished unwieldy cocktails at the lens the way Celtic warriors might have done heads. In other shots they were dancing, limbs frozen as if conjuring spirits from the dazzling lights. At one point, Nikki was emerging from the foam which had enveloped a dancefloor. In another photo, Nikki and Sasha were surrounded by shaven-headed lads, an improbable accumulation of bottles before them. The boys either sported Manchester United colours or were stripped down to chests that were sunburnt and hairless. All were mottled with tattoos that reminded her of mould. Nikki's left breast was being cupped by someone hiding from view. Liz noticed numbers missing from the sequence. Some had been censored.

But Nikki hadn't stopped gushing about the holiday since returning the previous week. The cheeky grins reminded Liz of her own photo albums: holidays, but also Nikki on her garden chute. Nikki in her pram. Her favourite was Nikki blowing out her first candle, her face the epitome of innocent joy.

'You going to show these to Johnny, Nikki?'

Nikki was wiping tables. 'You mean *Jamie*? He's seen them. Pissed himself. I've seen his of Magaluf. What happens on holiday *stays* on holiday.'

Liz smiled. Nikki had brought him round to the house for the first time the night before. Unlike previous boyfriends who cowered out of her way as if she had leprosy, Jamie had marched over, kissing either cheek. Smelling the smoke and cheap aftershave, she was reminded of her first serious boyfriend, a shy boy called Marcus. She recalled house parties, taking shelter from The Chemical Brothers and Underworld in bedrooms, she and Marcus plugged into each other's faces for hours, like lampreys.

Closing the photo album, she noted the time. This was payback for all the occasions she'd peered out of this window and opted to stay put.

'See you shortly, Mum.'

Nikki plucked the phone and stepped outside. Soon she was chattering excitedly between vape plumes. Liz opened her bag's zip compartment. There was a stack of letters here. She extracted the nearest.

I dreamed last night of where I grew up. I loved to swim. We swam by Farrars Island and searched for treasure. There were wrecks down below. Old gunboats, their canons rusty in the mud. I held my breath and explored. Sometimes I find bullets. My pappa once told about a diver, Robert Foster, from the Guinness Book, who held his breath for nearly 14 minutes! First, he had to breathe in pure oxygen. Imagine that, Elizabeth! Sometimes I imagine I'm a dolphin. Swimming through that river. I imagine I can hear our squeals as we came back for air, our fists round those orange balls, our treasure.

I love swimming. I love it when your ears go under. You can't here anything. As if you're alone in the world. There's no one else up there. I like it how you feel you can talk to me about anything. It was real funny, you talking 'bout the party where you "lost your cherry" as you wrote it. In some bed piled up with jackets, so drunk you hardly remember it at all. The Prodigy singing Firestarters. With me it was The Boss.

*

The rendezvous was in six minutes, but her view was obscured. A sudden downpour cascaded off the window. There was a confused huddle over at The Cameo. Simon could be one of many. If Simon was his real name. If he was there at all. Her phone trilled.

'Hello. This is Liz.'

'Oh, hi, there Liz! You're running late? How are you?'

'I'm fine. Eh. Nervous.'

'Never! Flirty forty?'

'*What?!*'

'Your profile description, babes?'

'Babes?'

'Five eight, medium, curvy, strawberry-blonde, GSOH, cinema, music, swimming.'

The description she'd mulled over for ages sounded ridiculous. And it gave her the impression of having been selected from a menu. Although that was exactly what had been happening all this time, her self-esteem plummeted. She realised how much she despised this situation - complete strangers adopting fake personas. Sometimes, flicking through all the random descriptions, or embellishing her own qualities, she felt her life was one big sitcom cliché. Now she could make him out, huddling into the cinema doorway, phone pressed to his ear. He looked old enough to be one of Nikki's exes.

'Listen, Simon. I have to ...'

'What?'

'I'm sorry, my daughter's sick.'

'Your *daughter?*'

'Bye, Simon.'

After deleting his number, she switched off her phone.

*

'Another one, Mum?'

'A blind date?'

'No. Another letter from your pen pal?'

'Yes, petal. Any bran scones left?'

'I'll get you one.'

Liz flicked the letter open at the second page.

I found a box. Inside was just mud. I took it to the local museum. They reckoned it would of been used to store stuff to write - a sailor writing to his sweetheart. The box was carved CSS FLORIDA, a reb ship, running the blockade they said. My momma looked up stuff at the library. Turns out the captain of that ship was Scottish, from Stone Haven. Makes me think of you, my dearest Elizabeth. I must have grown gills when I was a boy. I think of my own letters to you, now, so far away. What happened in between seems muddy, just like that river in Virginia. Where do you like swimming, Elizabeth? Do you have a favourite "loch"? Isn't that what you call them over there? Please describe it all to me.

'Right, Nikki, that's me.'

'What? I'm still buttering your scone.'

'I'm running late. This one sounds promising. Don't want him to slip through the net.'

Pushing herself away from her seat, she popped into the toilets. Scarcely 10 minutes had elapsed since her previous visit. She was nervous about this meeting. Danny had a wonderful

161

speaking voice, and this had formed a mental picture she was obsessing about. The tone was reminiscent of Sean Connery. Not the wrinkled guest of honour at Old Firm matches. The virile secret agent.

When she sat down, she noticed fragments of torn paper. The paper hadn't been there last time she used the loo. The cafe was quiet. She was the only customer and Nikki was holding fort while the owner, Graham, was at the bank. Feeling the need to tidy up after her daughter, she reached to the litter. She furrowed it open. It was a receipt from *Boots*. Squinting at the ruined print, she deciphered the letters a moment before it sank in. Pregnancy Test Kit £8.49.

Clambering out of the toilet, she rinsed her fingers then rushed into the cafe. Graham was leaning on the counter, glancing at a paperback.

'Graham, you're back?'

'Hi, Liz. Nikki's just popped out. Went to get a vape refill. Though she keeps insisting she's defo giving up. *After this yin.*'

'What? Why the fuck would she decide to stop vaping, *after this yin*, Graham?'

'Pardon, Liz?'

'Oh. Nothing. She's tried so many times. I see she's left her phone.'

'Oh, yeah.' Graham waved the mobile. 'She'll not be long, though.'

'Listen, I'm meeting a friend to go to the pictures. Can you pass on a message?'

'Of course.'

'Just tell her to phone me. The minute she gets back.'

'But you'll have to switch yours off for the film? Which film, by the way?'

'The film? Some comedy. Jack Black, I think. Just ask her to phone, Graham. I'll have it on silent. It's important.'

'Sure, Liz.'

She hurried to the pedestrian crossing. She remembered the big Victorian clock which used to stand by the traffic lights, with Roman numerals. There were angry Facebook comments when the Council removed it for 'health and safety concerns.' One guy stood out from the knot of figures by The Cameo. Clutching a Fringe programme to his chest. As she approached, he studied her hair. Danny smiled at her. She marched past.

Gulping air, she held this breath. At the traffic lights, she waited for the green man, chest welling. Her pulse began an insistent tattoo. Pain originated as a knot in her chest. Spread like a web. Her neck muscles tightened. Tears welled. Finally, she relinquished. She exhaled.

The traffic cranked up in intensity. Beeping horns, relentless techno beats, exhaust fumes, rattling taxis, blinking lights. Her heart was thumping. She pictured that Victorian clock, wherever it was now, its minute hand juddering to the top. There was never an exact time. How could there be, when it varied all over the world? There was no precise time, in Scotland, America, wherever. The moment she'd been dreading might have occurred when she'd been in the cubicle with Nikki's receipt, or it might happen before any of those cars reached their destination. It was all down to those vast swathes segregating the globe into time zones. And yet, paradoxically, *everything* hinged on the exactness of time. Every countdown.

She'd worked out John's time, 06:00, was noon in Scotland. Who had decided on his time, she wondered? Was there a committee with a little water jug and a minute taker? After the meeting, on the way back down the corridor, did they chat about the weather? The baseball scores?

Seizing another breath, she tugged out her wallet. John's sparkling eyes watched her. In January, she'd torn this from a magazine in the café, an advert for penpals. In the margin was another of her doodles. A square, a horizontal line, a stickman.

Her phone rang. 'Nikki,' she murmured. She felt its vibration, off and on, like a pulse. She didn't answer, just felt it massaging her skin.

John once said when the time came, he'd close his eyes and become that dolphin soaring over the sunken boats in the mouth of the James River. It would be easy for him to succumb to childhood memories. They'd never been that far away. Liz wasn't sure of the etiquette. Did he have learning difficulties? Was he slow? All his life, he would've been labelled a retard, a black retard. And much, *much* worse. Reports said his mental age was lower than his physical age of 41. But he was articulate enough in his letters. Maybe a kindly warder helped him out. Instantly, she pictured Tom Hanks in a uniform. He'd also went to great lengths to explain where he'd been the night of the murder he'd been charged with. During the lengthy timescale that had elapsed since the crime, someone else had claimed responsibility, although that person had since been murdered in prison, the truth dying with him. As if any of it mattered now.

Liz had absorbed so many facts from Google. She kept printouts in a dossier at home. Last night she'd read about Don

Harding. His last supper had been bacon and eggs, and toast with honey. Picturing his feast always made her hungry. It would have had the same effect on whoever gingerly carried it to him on a tray, with napkins. In April 1992 he lasted 10 minutes, 31 seconds.

When the cyanide reacted with the sulphuric acid in the gas chamber, you would hold your breath as long as you could. Of course, you would. Even while all that was going on, your lungs would fight for your life. You were only human.

They would numb John's skin before inserting the needle. They were only human.

COCK BLOCKED BY NICKY WIRE

Neil Renton

Ah used to have a theory about Nicky Wire fae The Manics.

When the show was at its peak, he would have made a great judge oan The X Factor. Him, Lily Allen, and Courtney Love. Maybe Louis Walsh tae maintain the level of casual inappropriate remarks now and again. Keep the Young Team in check.

Wire. Allen. Love. Walsh. The ratings would have been through the roof.

Wire was always a step ahead of everyone else. Wore dresses to wind the fuck up out of the Britpop scene, confusing the Lager Lager Lager boys of Lad Culture. Mascara warpaint, running aboot the stage with a sweat that never broke him, and a performance that he never phoned in. Always opinionated and not afraid to speak his mind. Fuckin' talented, too.

He's been a bit of a cunt, though.

He's oan one of the set of drawers in ma room, taking over from Iggy Pop on BBC Radio 6. His selection of songs has been decent as well—proper tunes that real indie lovers are into.

All of a sudden, without any warning, he drops The Jesus and Mary Chain and Hope Sandoval's song 'Sometimes Always.' It's a song of fuckin' beauty, and it stops me fuckin' the beauty that is Thingymebob.

When ye think o' The Chain, ye automatically revert tae images o' hair, primal screams, growls, and feedback. Ye forget they were capable of stuff like this. They always had those pop sensibilities and Motown intentions under the screeches.

Ah'm no longer in the bedroom at ma parents.' The one with an exercise bike that doubled as a wardrobe next to ma single bed and unwashed mirror.

Ah'm no wi Thingymebob. Ah'm wi Shona.

Thingymebob is all sympathetic. She heightens that American annunciation of words she's picked up from trawlin' through hours of watchin' far too many TikToks of her favourite Californian therapist. She's so obsessed she's let it sink into her psyche. It's left her wi a Yanky vocabulary, which explains why a minute ago she called it her "asshole." It's all a bit weird, as the closest she's got to the United States is when she's taken her nieces to one o' those American Candy Stores up the toon.

"You're in your own head," she says, suddenly becoming an expert on the brain. "You just need to get back out and you'll be fine."

Ah don't want tae get out ma heid. Ah like it in here. Wi Shona.

No one is better than me at makin' mix tapes. It's an art lost on the Spotify generation, where ye can blend wi another cunt really easily. Fuck all effort required.

Ah'd do it all. Plan them out on a notepad first, carefully record them to capture the complete song, and even write wi tiny letters in the wee lines ye got in the inlay cards, wi a bookie's pen chored fir the occasion.

Ah gave Shona it one night at Evol, the one wi The Chain on it. Shands, her man, ma mate, was standin' waitin' tae hand his coat in at the cloakroom. Head flicks, glance around to make sure no one was lookin' at us, then Ah passed it tae her all nonchalant-like. She put it intae her shoulder bag wi the expert ease of a pickpocket in reverse.

Her at the bar. Me cagouled up on the dance floor. Her sittin' wi Shands. Me drinkin' tae forget. Shona holdin' Shands's hand. Me gettin' her jealous.

Thingymebob now starts panickin,' sayin' that she's also in her ain heid and can't get out of it, as if we're having some joint thing.

In case of emergency, break glass. Ah open ma bedside drawer and rummage through the pack of ten pills encased in foil and plastic.

Under a pile of gig tickets and tags from when Ah could afford designer gear, Ah find the mix tape Shona made and gave tae me the week after Ah gave her mine.

Ah close the drawer, leavin' the Viagra untouched.

DEAD LAZY

Neil Renton

She sprinted in no particular direction other than as far away from the pack of chasing zombies as she could.

There was no grace in her ability. Her arms and legs propelled her up the street while hordes of flesh-eaters ran after her.

And every time she stumbled or tripped, they got closer.

All but Alex.

He was quite far up the group, kicking about outside Cameron Toll when they sensed and went after her. But as the pursuit went on, he struggled to keep up the pace and ended up falling further back. A run became a jog, which ended with Alex crouching as if he was about to take part in a hundred meters dash.

"Jamie," he wheezed. "Jamie."

His partner turned to see Alex struggling on the pavement. Reluctantly, she stopped the hunt and trotted back.

"What is it now?" she asked.

"I've got a stitch, and it's agony." Alex bent over and coughed up some claret-coloured phlegm.

"That's another one we've lost out on."

"You could have kept going. I wasn't stopping you."

"You quite literally squealed out my name," Jamie said. "You were screaming louder than the women who didn't want to be eaten alive."

"Sorry."

"It's always the same. Sorry. I've had enough."

Jamie marched past him with her arms folded.

"Jamie. Wait. It's sore."

Eventually, Alex pushed himself up and caught up with her trail.

"What do you want to watch on TV tonight?" he enquired, trying to defrost the atmosphere.

"Nothing. I want to watch you sign up for the gym."

"No, Jamie. I don't like them."

"I know you don't, but I don't like us yet again trying to live off the scraps of other people's leftovers."

"Okay," Alex said.

They passed a random zombie munching on the leg of a bin man at a bucket.

"I don't have any gym gear."

"You could easily pick stuff up."

"I'll be self-conscious. Everyone will be looking at me," Alex said, pulling the frayed hem of his T-shirt over his scar-ripped belly.

"Everyone's looking at you now, making a fool of yourself. What's the difference?"

They continued in silence, interrupted only by Alex's occasional pitiful moan.

"That hurt."

"You'll walk it off."

"No, what you said. Everyone looking at me."

Jamie turned and threw her one good arm and one half-devoured arm up in the air.

"Alex, it's true. You say you'll change, but you never do. And remember what the doctor said to us——"

"I wasn't to fill the sample container in the middle of the surgery?"

"No. He said that if we wanted to have a baby, we needed to change. We needed to get fit, to watch what we ate. We needed to get healthy."

Jamie watched Alex grapple with his lower intestines and pull them back into his stomach. He looked pitiful and helpless.

"I'm sorry," Jamie said.

"Me too," Alex said.

They ambled along the deserted streets back home, both of them hungry but too depressed to do anything about it.

"Jamie,"

"What is it, Alex?"

"Can it wait until tomorrow? The football's on tonight."

Jamie shook her head and ran off ahead.

"Jamie! Jamie! Wait! I've got cramp!"

WE'RE THE FLOWERS IN THE DUSTBIN

Mark Fleming

Never Mind the Bollocks, Here's the Sex Pistols, **The Sex Pistols (1977)**

July 1977. My 15th birthday fell during a week's Scout camp. Mum, dad, and wee sister, Anne came to visit on the Sunday. My main present was a new-fangled gadget, an electronic calculator, complete with function buttons for sines, cosines, and other long-forgotten trigonometric features, in preparation for the O-Grades I'd be studying after the summer. A bigger impression was made by that morning's *Sunday Times* magazine Anne brought to show me. Its front cover was emblazoned with the heading: "A happy group of punks enjoying a joke at a punk ball."

Inside, there was a feature about The Clash, whose debut album had been released three months before. That cover image was my first close-up glimpse of 'punk rockers.' I'd spotted the occasional garishly attired figure lurking outside Phoenix record shop on the High Street. Now I studied these denizens of some 'punk ball.' Shorn hair. Dog collars. Union jacks pinned to slogan-festooned garments which appeared to have been purloined from jumble sales. Although one punk was giving youthful attitude, a scowl, two-fingers to the lens, the others seemed consumed by excitement, grinning ear to ear.

Up until then, I'd dipped my toes into punk music. A religious listener of Jay Crawford's Edinburgh Rock show on

Radio Forth, over the past months I'd been compiling C90 after C90 of Deep Purple, Montrose, Thin Lizzy, Kiss, Ted Nugent, Rush, et al. Crawford occasionally gave airplay to up-and-coming bands purveying the more adrenaline-fueled end of the rock 'n' roll spectrum, like The Stranglers and The Sex Pistols. Throughout 1977, *Top of the Pops* had been featuring bands you could identify as 'punk' because they were often prefaced by 'The' (The Jam, The Adverts, The Saints, Eddie and The Hot Rods, The Damned, The Stranglers); equally by the underwhelmed reaction of the majority of the audience, hanging around to gyrate to Boney M or Abba. An avid fan of all rock music, whether the riffs were being churned out by Tony Iommi or Tony James, I balanced this devotion to the 'old wave' of earlier 70s groups and the so-called 'new wave,' until the summer of 1978.

My family was on holiday in St Abbs, the Berwickshire fishing village which had been our summer retreat, along with cousins, and friends from Middlesbrough and Manchester, for many years. We met here every August. That first night, a party was underway opposite our holiday home. The only album being played was *Never Mind the Bollocks, Here's the Sex Pistols*. 'Anarchy in the UK' had been amongst my Edinburgh Rock recordings, but this was the first time I'd heard the controversial band at length. As the night wore on, I became absorbed in this glorious rock 'n' roll: what *Sounds* magazine had described as 'a big, bad, beautiful noise.' From the marching jackboots segueing into Paul Cook's thundering intro to 'Holidays in the Sun,' through the profanity-laced vitriol of 'Bodies,' on to 'God Save the Queen,' the incendiary single the BBC refused to accept had topped the charts during Silver Jubilee week, to the finale, 'EMI,' and then back to the start, on repeat for the next 38 minutes 44 seconds rollercoaster ride. And the next. And the next.

Just turned 16, I had no real idea what I wanted to do when I left school the following year. What I did know was how vital this music sounded, how energizing. For hours, the swaggering riffs, harmonies, discordancy, and Rotten's acerbic urban poetry, crackled like sparks around a lightning rod. On returning to Edinburgh, one of my imminent tasks would be purchasing a copy. And I very much doubted I'd ever play *Rainbow Rising* ever again.

During that summer, I was also glued to *Revolver*, a TV series unabashedly celebrating the new wave. Peter Cook played a club MC introducing bands as if they were about to be inflicted on the audience. The Lurkers. The Vibrators. The Stranglers. Ian Dury and the Blockheads. The Jam. Buzzcocks. Siouxsie and the Banshees. The Rezillos. The Rich Kids. X-Ray Spex. XTC. Elvis Costello and the Attractions. Eddie and the Hot Rods. My mate from 'Boro, Jol, had brought cassettes with him. *Never Mind the Bollocks*. The Jam's *In the City*. The Stranglers' *No More Heroes*. The Clash debut. The Damned's *Damned Damned Damned*. We played them all to death.

We also marched around the village, the Pistols blaring from a portable cassette recorder, Steve Jones-style knotted hankies tied to our heads, because you didn't just listen to punk. You had to 'act punk,' too; although, by the summer of 1978, The Sex Pistols' meteoric rise had crashed and burned, culminating in a disastrous US tour and the band splitting. Many denizens of that

Sunday Times 'punk ball' had undoubtedly long removed the safety pins from their cheeks and now favoured the nascent New Romantic bands which sounded more appropriate for a 'ball'! Punk's limited three-chord thrashes had paved the way for the infinitely more interesting post-punk scene.

A smattering of lads in my year at Tynecastle secondary 'turned punk.' They hadn't gone the whole hog; there were no safety pins poked through cheeks. But their blazers were festooned in lapel badges. Back in Edinburgh, I got in touch with one of the schoolmates, Ross, who'd become a punk rocker. Over successive weekends, he loaned me pretty much his entire record collection. I taped over Rainbow and Rush with Ultravox!, Sham 69, The Killjoys, The Rezillos, Stiff Little Fingers, Alternative TV, Wire, Magazine, The Saints, and so many others. Within the year, Ross had formed his own band, The Accidents, who went on to be featured on John Peel's Radio 1 show. When that band eventually split, along with their drummer, Shug, he formed another, 4 Minute Warning. They invited me to play guitar. Three years after that *Sunday Times* story about the 'happy group of punks,' I was creating punk rock myself.

MENTAL HIBEES – SICK OF HIBS

Neil Renton

I'm at the cinema with only a bottle of water and a stomach bug to keep me company.

It's Saturday afternoon, and I'm floored with a 24-hour sickness bug that kicked in at approximately 11:38 on Thursday night.

It's absolutely laid waste to me. There's not an orifice on my body that hasn't been violated. I feel like I've brought the lining of my stomach up through my mouth, nose, and quite possibly ears.

I spent Friday trying to catch up on the sleep I'd lost, then Saturday searching for the energy that had gone missing the day before.

It's knocked my plans to pieces. I was set to look after my youngest daughter and take her to the cinema to see the Amy Winehouse biopic, but I don't want her to risk catching what I've got. So I decide to head into the public and isolate in a surprisingly busy cinema.

No snacks. It must be bad if I've not stocked up on popcorn, jelly babies, and Cadbury's buttons, all of which are unlikely to survive longer than the trailers.

Just water. I can't stomach anything fizzy or unsettling as I have no stomach left to stomach it.

On my way to the cinema, I stop off at a camera shop and pick up photos I'd taken on a disposable camera I'd handed in. The images are from a few years back, a few social events with my mates. It's safe to say that my photography skills aren't any better than they are on my mobile.

The swing table and recliner seat are wasted on me. Apart from my battered bottle of water, I've got nothing to put on the table, and I don't want to lean too far back in case I need to spring forward and run to the toilets.

To make matters worse, I'm sitting in the same row as a man with the most obtrusive smelling aftershave I've had the misfortune of encountering. On a day full of sunshine, this would be a faint irritation. In my current physical and mental state, it's attempted murder.

What is good about the cinema is it's cut off from society. There's no WiFi reception in Screen Two, located in the basement. Nothing works. Live Score is permanently stuck on the 97th minute of Arsenal beating Bournemouth 3-0.

It's an ideal haven for avoiding Hibs.

There should be no reason to fear anything. They're up in the Highlands playing Ross County, a side dangerously close to being relegated. They've given Hibs a couple of good games this season, but that was then. Now we're riding on the coattails of a win against the mighty St Johnstone.

Back to the film. Back to *Back to Black*. It's a weird one. It starts off like EastEnders: The Musical with some swearing, songs, and smiles. Then it becomes a bit Dickensian in its depiction of Camden. It takes a bit of time to get going, unsure of where the focus is. What impacted Amy? Her relationship with her dad, her gran, her boyfriend Blake, or drink and drugs?

It then skims over stuff, conscious that there's a running time to complete.

As it does so, it picks up a gear or two, and that's not just a cheap crack pun. I wish I were that clever. Marisa Abela, who plays Amy Winehouse, is no Amy Winehouse, but let's be honest, who is? She gives a good account of herself and deserves praise for her performance and singing. At some points, she reminds me of Britney Spears, which hopefully isn't a sign of things to come.

Aye, I enjoyed it. After making it to the toilet just as the closing credits come up for a game of 'SOLID, LIQUID, GAS,' I check my phone.

Hibs won 3-1 again. Happy days. I had a bet on that happening, along with a certain player to score at any point in the game, and even though I couldn't see his name, I can't complain. We can't be greedy.

Whatever bug I had must have made me delusional. Hibs hadn't won 3-1. They'd got beaten 2-1. And it's set off another meltdown.

Even the people who'd stopped caring seem to be past that point now. Everyone's getting blamed, from the manager Nick Montgomery to defender Rocky Bushiri, who gave away a goal after apparently kicking the ball off his own face. Another last-gasp lapse in concentration resulted in us getting beat.

I bump into a fellow Hibs fan outside the cinema. He's heading to see a later showing of *Back to Black* after watching the game. We exchange war stories and the scars left by Hibs in recent memory.

At home, I'm still not right. The fact that I'm feeling ill has made me needy. I long for attention, which is extremely shallow of me.

And I know how to get it: by turning into everyone's favourite character, 'Meme Man.'

Not all heroes wear capes. Some of them wear pained expressions, fighting the anguish of tummy contractions.

I'm all over this. Various snide remarks here, a trawl of my photo book there, anything that'll get me likes in a desperate attempt at self-validation.

And each time I do it, I swear on my life it'll be the last time I do it that day—before doing it again minutes later.

I don't know what's worse. A lifetime of having a sickness bug, relying on social media likes, or supporting Hibs.

Ross County 2, Hibs 1.

TEN THOUSAND CROWNS

Mark Fleming

'Fran the man. Wasn't even sure you'd show up the night. Karaoke's never been high on your agenda? Good to see you, though, buddy.'

Had Billy just spoken into the microphone? Everything in Francis's world was distorted. He'd been following the trails of bubbles in his drink. Convinced they were synchronized with the bald man murdering Ed Sheeran. He struggled to make sense of what Billy had just said. Mumbled, 'This soup's not right, Billy. Tastes rank as. Here. Try a mouthful.'

Snatching the glass, Billy gulped. '*Soup*, Fran? *Electric soup*, you calling it? Not that strong, is it? Tastes fine to me, buddy.'

'Soup? Did I say soup?' He tried to chuckle. He felt on the verge of something; hysteria or despair, it was impossible to tell. The former, he decided. Taking deep breaths helped to hold it back. Bunching his fists, he glared inside the tumbler. 'I meant lager. Fucksake, Billy. Mick Jagger. Tastes funny. My soup's bowfing as.'

'How much you been peeving in the house the night, Fran? Or you back on the wacky? Your pupils are so fucking dilated I can see number eights on them.'

Shaking his head, Francis clambered from the barstool. A weird chill had descended. Seeping into his bones. Weighing him down. His rib cage became ravaged with coughs. Each a detonation of agony.

'Okay, Fran? Not looking too clever, buddy?'

'That fucking soup.' Every motion was laboured. The flashing lights around the DJ's booth were burning his eyes. 'Going for a smoke.'

Shuffling outside, he joined the figures hunched in the doorway. Against the freezing wind, their grim features were like gargoyles, dragging smoke as if everything had reversed and these glowing sticks were precious as oxygen masks. Tugged out a deformed joint. Sparked it. How much of his unhinging mind was due to everything he'd been drinking? The tarry smoke he kept drawing into his lungs. How much just stress? The surrounding sniggers sounded like ruptured gas pipes.

*

Rocking in his chair, the motion adjusted from a hovering sensation to spinning around some monstrous whirlpool. He struggled to stand, laborious as an astronaut. The disco lights were flares, continually bursting. Flickering across the packed bodies shuffling to the loud beat. The relentless rhythm was pounding his spine. Billy was lurching amongst the bizarre silhouettes on the heaving dancefloor, catching his eye, indicating the teenager he was close to. Leering at her. The gesture was terrifying.

His mouth watered and he fixated on the vile brew swirling around his belly. He staggered towards the exit. Billy shouted after him, but the girl threw her arms around his shoulders, hauled him in, kissing him. Stumbling on past the smokers, Francis bowed his head to confront the gauntlet of pedestrians.

Headlights piercing his vision left brilliant tracers.

Careening towards the Roman bridge, his crotch was suddenly warm. Realising he was pishing himself, he teetered into the undergrowth, fumbling at his flies. Became enveloped by giant hogweed. Cars flashing by exposed their gnarled structures. He knew these weeds could grow three times his height. They came from Finland originally, introduced to Kew Gardens in 1817. In two centuries, they'd run wild, colonising woods, canals, railways. He wore gloves when removing them from gardens: in sunlight, they exuded a toxic sap that caused excruciating blisters.

The River Esk rippled by, sweeping away his frothing piss. As he gawked into its murky flow, someone cackled right behind him. Francis started. Instead of whipping his head around, he was mesmerised by the fireflies dancing out there. He smelt smoke, realised they were reflected fag ends.

'Fucking *dare* you, Sinky. Cunt's wasted. Go on.'

While he zipped himself, a hand sought his shoulder. Thrusting. The violent motion pitched him forward, the river transforming into a wall of icy water. Arms flailing, his feet struggled for purchase amongst slimy stones. Spitting out water against a background of hyena-like laughter, he snatched at weeds, hauling himself onto the bank. The silty liquid reacted with his stomach contents. He retched, too desperate to catch his breath to bother about the phones targeting him.

Feet scampered into the night. Francis fell forward, sinking into the brush, shivering uncontrollably. Heaved his guts out.

*

'The soup you said you had earlier, Fran. Wasn't exactly Heinz

Cream of Mushroom, was it, buddy? I could tell you were on something more than bevvy.'

Wrapped in a towel, hands hovering over a radiator, he shook his head. 'Picked a crop of magic mushrooms at work, Billy.'

'Fucking shrooms, Fran. At *your* age? We've not done that since we were teenagers. What were you thinking?'

'They're a class hit, Billy. You can make tea or soup. Some say heat kills the psilocybin, but it doesn't. It gets infused into the water. I've cooked up a pot of the stuff. Keep it in the fridge. Add lemon, ginger, mint.'

Billy grimaced. 'While the cat's away?'

'Did you say two sugars, Francis?' came from the kitchen.

'Aye, Kirsten.'

'Kristen.'

'Thought it was Kirsten myself, Fran,' Billy murmured. Winked at him.

Disgorging the mushrooms had taken the edge off the trip, the intensity fading into a stone. But his living room still seemed unnaturally bright. He faced the unfamiliar voice. Fleetingly, Kristen's face was there.

'Beauty and the Beast, Billy.'

'Fuck off, Fran. And less of the fucking *beast*.'

'Age is she, Billy?'

Billy whispered, 'Old enough to bleed.'

'Don't say *that*, Billy. That's horrible. What would Amanda say hearing you speaking like that?'

'Amanda? Fuck off, Fran. Fuck *her*.'

'Well, you'll not be doing that again in a hurry, mate.'

'Fuck off.' Billy's expression was fierce. 'Chase away a young team who chuck you into the fucking burn, get you home, into dry clothes, and you cast up that fucking bitch? Out of order, Fran. Should've been getting my rock 'n' roll off Kirsten by now. If we'd managed to flag a Joe outside the boozer, we'd never have even come across you, you cunt.'

'Kristen.' Francis shuddered. Tugged the towel closer.

Billy indicated the table. 'Still setting places for Lyndsey and Tara?'

'Force of habit, Billy.'

'Aye, well. She'll see sense. Might take a while. She'll get fed up with her Ma's cooking. Youse were so tight, Fran. I've heard through the grapevine, my Amanda's shacked up with some gadge from Dalkeith. About a week after she kicked me out. Taxi driver. He's fucking welcome to her.'

'You're talking like it was a normal breakup, Billy, and she's just moved on.'

'That's right, Fran. We've broken up. Both moved on.'

'It's only October, Billy. We were in Prague end of September.'

'Aye. St Wenceslas weekend. Their national flowers everywhere.'

Francis nodded. 'Picked up a bouquet of red roses the day we got back, as a reminder. Lyndsey loved the smell. Only just binned them.'

Kristen appeared with a tray with three mugs and handed them out. 'They hooligans,' she said, sipping from her coffee. 'I mean. They're fucking twisted, Francis, eh? Throwing you into the river like that. What for? For a laugh? A bet?'

'Aye, doll,' said Billy. 'When we got to the bridge, they were filming the whole thing, Fran.'

'Should go to the polis, Francis,' said Kristen. She leaned forward, hands cupping her mug.

Francis' eyes lingered on her low-cut top, her ample cleavage. Looked to the carpet. 'Doubt there's any CCTV nearby. That's an ancient bridge. Tara told me its history. They did a school project.'

'That your wee girl, Francis?' said Kristen, smiling at the framed school portrait perched on a display shelf. 'Lovely wee dimples. I love her picture pinned to the fridge. They bright orange flowers.'

'St John's Wort.'

'What?'

'Fran's a gardener, doll,' said Billy.

'I bring home a lot of flowers for the wee yin to draw. Her mum and me are … estranged.'

'Sorry to hear, Francis. You and your Amanda, too, you were saying, Billy? Must be something in the water. Sorry. Didn't mean that, Francis.'

Ignoring the comment, Francis continued. 'According to Tara, that bridge was the last obstacle before Edinburgh. Used by invading armies for centuries. Scots. English. Covenanters. Royalists.' He envisaged gangs of men trudging across it, heading towards savage encounters, champing at the bit, returning drenched red after hacking at strangers with hand-held weapons.

'Listen to Mastermind, Kristen,' said Billy.

'She also told me all about the Battle of Pinkie, fought in the fields on the other side of this estate, Kristen. 1547. An English army butchered thousands of ours. And their navy was offshore, firing cannons into our lads.'

'If they'd had mobiles in they days, wee radges would be filming it all,' said Kristen. 'They're not right in the head. You'll probably end up on TikTok, Francis.'

'Whatever, Kristen. Listen, guys. I'm shattered. Maybe hit the hay.'

'Can we at least finish our coffees, buddy?'

Kristen glowered at Billy. 'Don't blame you, Francis. We should leave you to it. Shall we, Billy?'

Kristen gathered the mugs, placing them back on the tray. 'I'll just rinse these, Francis. Least we can do for you.'

'You don't have to.'

'I insist.'

When she elbowed her way past the kitchen door, Billy plonked himself beside Francis, lowering his tone. 'You know the fucking saddest thing, Fran? We could *so* easily have got away with it.'

'How d'you mean, Billy?'

'Matthew's phoned while I was in the bog, while you were stripping off your wet clothes. Finally came clean about what went down.'

'Well?'

'Cunt left out his credit card statement. Simple as that, buddy. Emily's had a sketch. "What's CCBill?" she's said.'

'CCBill?'

'Aye. CCBill. He could've said anything. Fuck knows. Czechmates cocktails bill?'

'Czechmates? That they apple and lime concoctions that got

us all nuggets on the first night?'

'Aye, aye. Listen. Instead, he's said, "I don't know, Emily. Must be a mistake." The fucking rocket. "A mistake?" she's said. "Aye," he's said. "It's for ten thousand fucking Czech crowns, Matthew," she's said. "I'll get onto them in the morning," he's said. But she's not daft. She's only gone and fucking Googled it, Francis.'

'Ten thousand crowns?'

'It's just like any other business over there, buddy. The likes of us, out there on stag weekends, we just see skirt. But they've got it all worked out. When Matthew booked her, all he had to do was visit the escort agency's website, fill in his details. They use geolocation, he told me.'

'What?'

'Same as what's in our satnavs, Fran. That's how she found us in that beer hall. Would've had a virtual map, pinpointing her next clients.'

Fran pictured her elfin face, offset with a septum ring. The image was indelible. Wearing a PVC micro-skirt and matching fishnet stockings, both red as her dyed hair and the roses draped everywhere. They'd been rooted to her presence, the heady fragrance of her perfume, the tattoos weaving around her arms to her black fingernails. Matthew had introduced her as if she was a long-lost friend while she licked her lips and giggled at his "Scotch accent."

'And what is this CCBill?'

'It's one of they, what is it, *nom de plumes*, or something, is that what they call it, Fran?'

He shrugged.

'CCBill. It's a standard description gets printed onto a statement to cover up porn services. To save fucking embarrassment for whoever's due the bill, eh? So, Matthew and Emily have ended up having a huge fucking barney and he's blurted it all out. Confessed fucking *everything*. "It didn't mean anything, Emily. It was my stag do. One last fling for the groom to be, my best man, Billy. And Francis, and Josh. Meant fuck all. A laugh. But here's me coming clean, Emily. Only way our marriage is going to last is if we trust each other, from now on. I don't care what you did on your hen party in Newcastle."

Turns out all the lassies did was what most normal lassies do, got fucking melted, maybe snogged a few waiters. End of. Instead of his marriage lasting, she's at her sister's. And couldn't wait to spill the beans. To Amanda. To Lyndsey. To Kelly. She was gorgeous, mind. That lassie. The lady in red. What was her name?'

'Jannah. And hardly a lady.'

'Telling me, Fran. I was right in there, balls deep, boy. We all were.'

'Fucksake, Billy. I meant, age-wise.'

'Fran. She looked like a fucking model. Guys like us, in our thirties, ordinary gadges from Musselburgh? We'd never get a fucking stunner like that here. Not in a million fucking years.'

'What was that about *never getting fucking stunners*, Billy?' Kristen said, closing the kitchen door behind her.

'Just saying how lucky I am, doll,' said Billy.

*

Francis opened Tara's sketchpad. The first page was a bold design. Pink petals around an orange pistil. Sea pink. He'd told her what his father once explained to him. Centuries ago, people would slice their roots into milk, boil the mixture as a cure for obesity.

He turned over. Her next drawing was a purple explosion. Violets. As she'd been scoring the paper with her crayons, he was describing how folks in the olden days referred to these as the flowers of the dead. They thought picking them while they were covered in dewdrops would result in a loved one's death. Lyndsey had admonished him for going into those details. But he'd emphasised that was just the mythology. Flowers were all about life, not death.

Over the years, he'd held so many thousands of seeds in his palms. Planting them. Guarding them with protective netting. Anticipating their fragile shoots. He knew every species growing in his garden, in the neighbouring gardens. He knew which would be first to bloom. Which were already withering. He visualised the miraculous explosions of spring colour a matter of months away. He screwed his eyelids until tears came.

Now he was imagining Jannah's flaming locks writhing in that hotel room. Four times. Red as the roses garnishing the buildings in her sprawling city, the air thick with their scent. He wept as he waited for his next helping of soup to begin lifting him as far away as possible from this wilderness.

MENTAL HIBEES – IT WAS THE BEST OF TIMES…

Neil Renton

Why did I drop the knife?

Clumsiness, I'd say. I have a severe lack of awareness in tight spaces, often knocking glasses and banging my scarred elbow.

Maybe it was nerves about the day ahead.

The blade fell between my legs at the hotel breakfast table. The hollandaise sauce touched my jeans but didn't leave a stain or even a mark.

That was a sign. Don't overthink, over-worry, or overfill your plate.

The breakfast was superb. I could have done with an all-you-can-eat buffet, but it wouldn't have done anything for my already bulging physique, so I was relieved to be restricted to a menu.

Then we were off. Tracy and I talked about the gig we'd been to the night before and planned our next concerts.

I caught up with my two youngest. My son was about to go on holiday with his girlfriend, so I'd be spending time with his little sister.

We went to an old man's pub, the type that, despite having glass windows letting in the strange summer weather, was still pitch black inside. Juices with my pint-gulping mates. Catch-ups with friends I hadn't seen for months and family friends who didn't recognise me as I wasn't as tall as their hips.

My daughter and I had a good chat with my father-in-law. It had been too long since we'd spoken. We exchanged stories of concerts we'd been to and recommended albums.

Later, I met my mates. I had no idea how long they'd been drinking, but they had that scuffing-the-ground walk. They sat to stop themselves from wobbling.

I did the rounds during rounds, speaking to everyone. What had they been up to? How were their families? Showing genuine interest in them.

There were others too, people I'd only known through social media. I bumped into a couple in passing, spoke to one at the bar, and joined their table on my way back from the toilet. Hands washed, obviously.

I hugged one of them—it's that thing we do. Praised another for his weight loss, another reason why I'm glad I didn't overdo it with a fry-up.

Some people from my old work were here. I actually went outside to greet a couple of them—handshakes and well wishes, brief to avoid awkwardness. Then back inside for a proper chat with my former colleagues. I thanked them for what they'd done for me, we swapped gossip stories, and I promised to pop into their new office.

I was off to see one of my mates record a Fringe Festival show. I was at a loose end as I was by myself, phone on charge at a Starbucks. Then I was back in the sunlight watching couples sit next to each other while they invested in their phones.

For the first time that day, I went on The Artist Formerly Known As Twitter. A couple of notifications.

One of them was because I'd been mentioned. The person said it was great to bump into folk at the football and I was lucky enough to be included in the message.

Aside from the ninety minutes plus stoppage time, it felt like one of the best days I'd had in ages.

Hibs 0 Celtic 2

SONGS IN THE KEY OF STRIFE – POUR SOME TUNES BY SUGAR ON ME

Neil Renton

I'm greedy.

My mindset has changed, and I'm not as bad as I used to be, but it's taken years—far too long.

If there was anything free or discounted, I'd have it. I'd rather feel ill stuffing my face and adding to my waist than letting it go to waste.

Case in point: I was seventeen with a girlfriend, and since she was my first proper one, I knew nothing like it. Comparisons couldn't be made. Maybe I was in love with her, or in love with the feeling of wanting to love and be loved.

Anyway, she was going to stay at mine one Saturday night. I'd meet her after work, and we'd head back to my place. She'd have her overnight bag, and it was all very cute and sweet.

What was I going to do during the day? I was going to the cinema with my big cousin Stephen.

By "big," I mean a year older. Stuff like that means a lot when you're a kid. You always look up to them, even when you start to grow taller than them.

We were off to see the latest Jean-Claude Van Damme film, *Hard Target*, and I was excited as it was the English-language debut of esteemed action director John Woo. I was well into stuff like *The Killer* and his other films that featured slow-motion shootouts and doves flying about. It was stunning and appealing to a teenager.

Stephen and I skipped our usual pick 'n' mix and juice as snacks and instead went for a two-litre bottle of cider—a decision we made after chipping in together.

It was a lawless time when you could sit wherever you wanted in a cinema, none of this having to select a seat and find it in the pitch dark. We were in the back row of a nearly deserted screening. That's when it happened.

My cousin carefully opened the bottle, took a sip, then casually handed me the rest of the hardly touched giant bottle.

"I don't like cider. You can have it," he said.

And that's what I did. The entire two litres. I told you I was greedy.

At one stage, I was leaning back with my head hanging off the back of my seat. There was an usher checking on me. I was too busy trying to catch my eyes rolling to the back of my head to care about how I was.

The film was great. Van Damme won the day and saved the world, and thankfully didn't need any help from me, which was just as well as I had double vision.

After the movie, we went to the strippers. Because that's what you do when you're about to meet the girl you've been seeing and you've had two litres of cider and you're seventeen.

For those unaware, Edinburgh has quite a lively lap dancing scene. There's the Pubic Triangle with the holy trinity of The Western Bar, Hooters, and The Burke and Hare. Tipplers used to be just down the road a bit, separated by merely a few hundred yards.

These establishments weren't glamorous. This isn't a Hollywood cinematic version where silicone gyrates seductively in a Star-Spangled bikini. This is stretch marks and cellulite, and it was all the better for it.

The Burke and Hare definitely wasn't classy. There was no extravagant light display or Michelin-star bar menu. At this point, it had a pool table where Stephen and I played winner-stays-on. My cousin would remind me that strangers asked us if we fancied a "take on". I thought they meant pool, and my cousin thought they wanted a fight. Thankfully, it was pool, and to this day, I reckon I played the best games of my life.

Like dreams with no logic, I was soon at my girlfriend's work. She wasn't in a good mood; she'd had one of those days where you get blamed for everything, especially if it wasn't your fault. To make matters worse, I was steaming drunk.

We got the bus, had frosty chats to fill the silence, then disaster struck.

I got the two-minute warning that I was about to be sick, about one minute and fifty-two seconds later than planned.

So that's what happened. I made a valiant attempt to get off but made it no further than the door and covered the entire floor in vomit. My girlfriend managed to leap over it and ran off crying.

I went after her but couldn't reach her and fell onto my knees.

"Are you on drugs?" a concerned woman asked.

"No, I'm just on cider," I replied.

My girlfriend didn't stay that night.

When the spewing stopped and the hangover kicked in, I wanted to make amends. And that's what I did.

I wrote her a poem.

Technically speaking, it wasn't a poem. It was a song. But as I couldn't play any musical instruments, when we met days later, I handed her the folded piece of paper and she read the words I'd written for her.

And while we're at it, technically speaking, I hadn't written the song. It was Bob Mould when he was in Sugar. The song in question was "If I Can't Change Your Mind, Then No One Will."

I might have told a tiny white lie, saying it was me who came up with it, although I did go to the effort of jotting it down. My badly framed capital letters did well to mask the fact that there were some words I didn't know and just scrawled in hope.

She was delighted. No one had done that for her before. She smiled, and making a person happy is the greatest thing you can do.

It didn't make up for the incident on the number 10 bus. I was dumped about a week later.

EMPIRE BISCUIT STATE OF MIND

Neil Renton

You can gauge the roughness of an area when the taxi driver refuses to drop you off in it.

Hamish thought they'd gotten on well, but the mood shifted as they neared his destination. Instead of stopping at the exact location, Hamish sat in the back, carefully listening to Keith's instructions on how to get to the bakery from the safety of a shopping centre car park. A car park manned by a couple of kids in balaclavas.

As Keith sped away, Hamish convinced himself that the rush was just because the driver needed to charge the electric vehicle.

This wasn't a part of Edinburgh Hamish was familiar with. Since moving from Glasgow, he hadn't had any reason to visit. But today was different. An urge had taken over, and all he'd had that morning was the skin off his thumbs.

It was a fascinating area, populated by old ladies with sunken mouths and buckled tartan trollies, or pit bulls weighed down by bulging teats.

Eventually, Hamish reached the street he was looking for. He stood carefully in a doorway to avoid getting urine on his pink jelly shoes and observed the scene.

He wasn't the only one interested in what this dodgy part of Edinburgh had to offer. There was a queue across the street, everyone silent and wary, keeping an eye out for trouble.

The queue slowly dwindled inside a rundown corner outlet, only for the line to grow with new bodies at the back.

Hamish tugged nervously on the straps of his dungarees, handcrafted by partially sighted monks from Greenland, and waited for his mark.

She'll do.

She walked toward him, clad in a garish hoodie, leggings, and crocs. Hamish's stomach did a forward roll and six star jumps. He stepped out to block her path.

"Excuse me?"

"Why, what have you done?" she replied, built like one of those storage containers used for pop-up shops in Shoreditch.

Her cheek and confidence caught him off guard. He wasn't sure what he expected, but it wasn't the winner of "So You Think You're Funny."

"I need to ask a really big favour," he said, pulling out a crisp twenty-pound note from a wallet crocheted by New Zealand orphans.

"Steady, old man. I'm no a fuckin' hooker," she retorted.

Hamish looked confused. His twisty auburn moustache curled up at the corners before his face recoiled.

"No! No! I wasn't soliciting you—"

"Whatever that means."

"I need you to do something for me. See that bakery over there?" Hamish pointed across the road.

"The one with all the pretentious cunts like you outside it?"

"When you put it like that. Anyway, it's regarded as the finest bakery in Edinburgh, maybe Scotland. They sell Empire biscuits."

The teen shrugged, unimpressed.

"You know what they are?"

No reply.

Hamish took out a Polaroid and held it towards her.

"Ah, a German biscuit."

"Yes, that's what some people call them. If I give you twenty pounds, can you buy me two and get yourself something with the change?"

"Can't you get them?"

"No," Hamish whispered. "I'm the head of a movement. The Empire Biscuit State Of Mind. The biscuits hold a very special place in my heart. We've got a podcast, T-shirts, limited edition fanzines. I review these things but they've barred me from getting one because they're scared of what I'll say."

"So two German—"

"Empire—"

"Biscuits and I get something from the change?"

Hamish nodded.

"Deal."

"Oh, please ask for them to be boxed individually and don't swing the bag."

"Whatever."

She snatched the money and scuffed over, pushing herself halfway up the queue and threatening to punch a Cockapoo owner who dared to challenge her.

Hamish paced the pavement, trying to hold in a nervous pee. Maybe the elite bakers, who had learned their trade in Copenhagen and were extremely protective over their brand, had seen him. Word might have gotten around.

He'd take them home and set them up. One to be photographed, and the other to be consumed.

She was gone for ages, to the point that Hamish thought she'd conned him. She could have started an argument with staff, clambered through a small window, scaled a wall, and head-butted a cat.

He'd have to be more trusting with the next one. Less attitude.

Then she appeared, the branded brown bag in one hand like a pendulum while the other held a see-through plastic number. Stomping across the road with the grace of a destroyer of planets.

"There you go, yer two German biscuits."

Hamish took the bag and quickly studied the contents as if he was being handed his twins pulled from the wreckage of a car crash.

Slight icing damage. The oversized jelly tot on one of them was squint. Nothing he wouldn't be able to fix with his cake assembly kit held in his home-crafted bum bag.

"Thanks," he said, and he meant it. "Can I get my change?"

"What change?" she asked.

"I gave you twenty pounds."

"You told me to get something for myself."

"What did you get?"

"I went to the shop round the corner and bought a vape," she said, producing a device that resembled a weapon from *Star Wars*.

"How much was that?"

"Twelve pounds," she smiled. "You told me to get something with the change."

"I didn't mean for you to spend it all."

She didn't hear him. She didn't care. She went on her way, leaving a jet stream of purple and Hamish cradling the biscuits as if the fate of the universe relied on it. He wasn't in a rundown part of Edinburgh. He was at his grannie's.

THOUSANDS

Mark Fleming

FOR ONE NIGHT ONLY, YOUR FIRST DRINK @1984 PRICES!!!

His attention shifting from the posters to his Guinness, Alan relished digging out shrapnel instead of plastic. Cards were two-faced bastards, the way their casual swipes transformed into fuck off bank statements. Savouring mouthfuls, he took his usual seat near the widescreen TV.

Hearts' Conference League tie was being previewed. The dizzying heights of a trip to Fiorentina ignited past glories. That unforgettable night in September 1976 when the Jambos swaggered back from a two-goal Cup Winners' Cup deficit to trounce Locomotiv Leipzig 5-1 at a rammed Tynie. Drew Busby's flying header for the fourth. His old man losing his spectacles in the euphoric celebrations. The pitch invasion on the final whistle, guiding his dad over the hallowed turf, glimpsing the high school over the corrugated iron shed, distant enough to banish the thought of crashing back to Earth the next day with Double English and Mrs MacDonald, the torn faced teuchter.

Tonight, there'd probably be a goal deluge in the other direction. But that was football. He was reminded of one occasion he'd been barred from here, before a 1987 Euro tie, Dundee United soaring toward that season's UEFA final in

Gothenburg while England's teams were still banned after Heysel. An opposition player was captioned: 'Previously played with Young Boys.' The bar erupted. A barman, Sandy, gathering empties, kept going on about it.

'Fucking hilarious, eh, Al? Playing with Young Boys, the nonce. Ha ha ha ha.'

But Alan was picturing Reynolds, a Scoutmaster whose reptilian stare was avoided by all. In the era of Jimmy Savile and Gary Glitter hiding in plain sight on national TV, nobody batted an eyelid when he swaggered around the scout hall stripped to the waist. Anytime Alan caught a whiff of BO, he was dragged back to Abingdon Camp, the curls of Reynolds' chest hair like a matted ginger rug, the cloying stench when it was his turn for the horrible ordeal.

Alan had lamped Sandy. Burst his lip. Dismissing the memories, he peered over his shoulder. Like the football, or even just popping out for his morning paper, the daily ritual persisting into retirement, just about everyone was younger. His local had morphed into a sports bar long ago. Normally, the focus was on the slick Sky presentations. Against a non-stop stream of product placement, pundits analysed VAR decisions with the earnestness of doctors describing shadows on X-Rays. Tonight, though, to celebrate Hearts visit to Stadio Artemio Franchi, the landlord, Geoff, was commemorating Hearts' 1984 trip to Paris St Germain. The landlord at the time had organised a coach trip for his regulars to that UEFA Cup tie. Alan turned 22 during the foray, which was also doubling as his stag do.

The experience was far less memorable than the Leipzig match eight years before. After a plucky 2-2 draw in the first leg, the French stuck four past Henry Smith, while Alan ended up in a Parisian hospital having his stomach pumped. He'd sunk so much cheap wine over the four days, an Algerian doctor had warned of irreparable damage to his renal system. At that age, Alan had looked forward to bragging about the prognosis.

Earlier in the evening, *Now 1984* had been blaring from the sound system, taking those punters who could remember back to 'Frankie Says' T-shirts, perms and mullets, Lord Tom's, Bobby McGhees, and Gatsby's. Now, as the TV pundits dueled verbally, he glared into his pint. Aside from this having been poured with its creamy head infuriatingly short, pints were an exact science. His first was a lemonade shandy on Hogmanay the night before the 0-7 disaster. His first in a pub, The Blue Lagoon. The first *legal* one, when his old man took him to The Ettrick Hotel, both chuckling when the barman said, 'Your usual, Alan?' Where did his first Guinness of the night sit in the tally? Thursday to Sunday bingeing peaked in his 20s. He'd drink his way through 30 or more pints each weekend. Easily. The total would be tempered, slightly, during relationships. Easing off when he got married. Twice.

If his life's graph had always been a rollercoaster, he appreciated he'd been surfing upwards again ever since gaining access to his Standard Life pension. Head buzzing already, topping up from yesterday, he anticipated rushing to another crest, riding the wave onwards into the night. Especially if there was a miracle in Florence.

Demolishing his stout, he wondered why his mind worked this way. Aside from medical professionals, or the actuaries at work, who else would ever fixate on some 'grand total'?

Everyone else was just throwing it down their necks, not batting an eyelid while their tallies accumulated; some of the older faces he recognised succeeding his, many of the younger lads well on their way to emulating it.

*

Hours after the 5-1 hammering, he wondered why this figure was lodged in his spinning head? *Thousands*. Thousands of what? Disgruntled Jambos in Italy? Seagulls screeching over Wardie Bay on his stagger home? Now he couldn't find his key. Must've spilled out his pocket when he bought his last pint; coins, chewing gum, and bank cards scattering. Stumbling along the path leading to his back garden, his guts heaved. Pressing his face into the side of the building, he willed the sensation away. But acrid liquid fountained down the pebble-dashed wall, along the paving stones. He was furious. On 99.9% of occasions, he could rely on his bevvy merchant's cast-iron stomach. As he fought for breaths, he flashbacked to one time a DJ saved his life.

After his first divorce, he'd gone through a spell of dating much younger girls. Ended up with Shelley, a summer student at his office. This meant enduring raves. Dragged to some club in Grindlay Street, a long night splintered into delirious fragments. 'Thousand,' by Moby. Was that it? Shelley screaming into his ear, this track was in the *Guinness Book of Records* for the fastest rhythm *ever*, crescendoing at 1,000 BPM. Freaking out, trying to cope with the mental tempo on a crazy cocktail of alcohol and ectoes, he hurled over the dance floor, really losing it, swallowing too much of the poison back into his throat, curling into a ball of agony amongst the forest of feet stepping back, choking, tears streaming, Shelley shrieking, slapping his

205

face, the DJ rushing around from her booth, pumping his back, finally doing that Heimlich thing, clearing his windpipe.

Then it came back. As the night had worn on, those bothered about the result drowning their sorrows, Alan just drowning, he could see himself scribbling on a beermat. A stab at his life's tally. Estimating the pints per year, 1978 onwards. 30 x 52 x 44. About-turning, facing the torn-faces in maroon shirts, Guinness stains down his own, his latest pint aloft like a trophy. 'Fifty fucking thousand … ya fucking beauty!'

Muscle spasms continuing to wrack his body, he swayed over the trampoline; bought for the grandkids who seldom visited, and when they did, remained morosely rooted to their phones. Feeling purged, he clambered aboard, leapt into the cold night air. Again. Higher still. Giggling with the abandonment.

Shelley had escorted the ambulance to A&E at the old Infirmary where his stomach was to get pumped. Exiting, bleary-eyed in the stretcher, he noticed her pointing heavenwards. 'Wow! Check the stars. I've never fucking seen so many! D'you know, Al? Some are so far away, their light's taken so long to reach us, they aren't fucking there anymore. How mental is that?!'

He'd really liked her, but she cooled it after that performance, the most extreme of several, with many still to come. Laughing, he emulated Drew Busby, head lashing. Raising his arms, he craned into the infinite majesty of the skies, seeing double the amount of the stars fleeting past his vision. Those that were still there. Those that were just a void.

THE WARS

Mark Fleming

Sunday, early morning

I clock my bruised face in the all-night garage's CCTV monitor. Smirking. A kid entering a sweetshop. Not the Willie Wonka factory we've all dreamt of. More one of Fagan's urchins, poised to cram pockets before bolting. Waiting for the guy to appear, I toy with the debit card, aware this might've already been blocked. More likely, the owner is currently conked out. I scan the shelves. Filled sandwiches. Crisp multipacks. Chocolate bars. Energy drinks. Coffees. Croissants. All you can swipe buffet.

Saturday, early evening

A gang of women troop in wearing the same T-shirts. I try to avoid gawking at the face/slogan emblazoned across their chests. *Cheryl the Peril. D Club No More.* Away from that fuzzy blown-up selfie, the star of the show is much prettier. Her mates' tops are pink, but Cheryl the Peril's is white. She's also wearing a veil she keeps tugging out the way so she can join in the communal fun, firing down pints, shorts, and shots. Snorts, too, given the gear changes whenever they come back from the bogs.

Waiting for Doug to pour my own JD and cokes, I'm

listening in. Turns out the 'D Club' are mostly divorcees. Cheryl's on marriage number three. But the interesting snippet is what's happening *after* last orders. The party's continuing at Auntie's Chevonne's. Cheryl's fiancé, Rab's entourage are joining them after *their* night out. Hens and stags combining to rave into the wee small hours. I like that. Old-fashioned. Apart from Cheryl's Mum, Aunties, and Nana, Cheryl and her mates are 80s or 90s kids. Some even 2000s. Maybe I've danced with a couple of the Aunties at Busters. Zenatec. Danced and the rest. Not that this factoid would be crossing anyone's mind; my skinhead renders me invisible. Slightly pee'd off the lassies getting served aren't flirting with me. Just a wee rub of my bald head.

The joint celebration reminds me of my grannie, once upon a time. I was brought up by my grannie. She told me, before she and my grandad got hitched, their respective nights out converged at the Palais at Fountainbridge, where Grannie sometimes danced with Tam Connery before joining her pals in the chillout zone, the 'sit-ooterie.' Where she met my grandad, ayeways a big show off. 'Yin of the finest of the Palais jivers, in my day. I could have out jived any of they fucking GIs.' Heard that many a time, at family parties. When I was wee, I'd watch, amazed, when he got up, spun on his heels. Over the years, he'd get too pissed to master that, usually crumple in a heap. Then he'd not even bother getting out his armchair, just click his fingers for Grannie to refill him. Life as a party piece.

My ears prick up when Chevonne's on the blower describing the refreshments awaiting. Crates of this and that; cider, lager, Buds, Becks, Coors. Blue Bols. Strawberry dakharis. Passion fruit liqueurs, at which point Cheryl roars 'lick yours' and buries her face in a young lad's crotch, seated too close but lapping up the attention.

'Top flat,' says Chevonne. 'Name on the buzzer: C Colquhoun. Cock swoon.'

When she says this, I catch her staring right at me in the mirror behind the bar. She winks.

When they clutter out of the pub, I'm dwelling on times gone by. I was a serial party crasher. One time, Oasis or Blur blaring from every jukey, I headed to Broughton Place to a flat cloaked in darkness. Must've misheard the address, the Brum accent actually meaning *Brighton* Place in Porty? I used to traipse to parties all over. Before Joe Baksis had central locks, it was easy enough to get from A to B for free. After that, you'd to rely on cashies with lanes next to them. *Stop here, buddy, need to get your sheckles.* Then offski like trap 6 from Powderhall.

The party crashing began in my teens. Hung around The Tap. Earwigging the drunken chat from the floppy-fringed art students or goths in massive, sculpted hairdos. All getting loaded before The Hooch or Wee Red. Back then, with my crimped barnet, dyed raven-black, and chiseled but acne-riddled cheekbones, I looked like a bargain basement Nick Cave. Nick Grotto, my mates cried me.

You'd get the addresses of two or three post-club parties every week. Mostly student gaffs. You didn't even need a carryout. Just rock up. Perfected long before Liam Gallagher, I would swagger into the kitchen, grab a cluster of cans by their ring pull. Straight onto the dance floor, throw my arms around the closest of the pished lassies.

Because my folks' house backed onto Prestonfield golf course, every September I started harvesting shrooms. By the thousands. Painstakingly plucked. Dried. Stashed in money bags. They *were* money bags. I was turning over a tidy wee sum from my fungi. Didn't even have to gatecrash parties anymore. I was guestlisted. *Here's Fun Guy! How much for a wee poke of your fungi, mate?* Stalled that for a while after a customer took far too many and ended up in the Royal Ed. Angie McGuirk. Emulating Syd Barrett on her first trip.

In any case, that income was sporadic. Seasonal. I moved onto solids, The Hooch still my patch. Actually, there were two clubs under one roof. Yin and Yang. Downstairs, Outer Limits. The dark, I thought of it. Like the Mos Eisley spaceport bar. Wretched hive of scum and villainy. But paradoxically, Europe's first laser disco. Chart fodder. 'Radio Ga Ga.' Pointer Sisters. Wham. The cavernous dance floor strafed by vast curtains of silver light, broken by flickering strobes. Long before ectoes hit the clubs, a lot of them were my customers. Lapping up Fun Guy's wacky and wizz. The seething throng of hundreds of sex-starved Edinburgh youths and laser-eyed soccer lads transformed into a single, amorphous entity, tentacles stroking the beams. Or swinging punches.

After the bouncers locked the main doors for the night, I spent my time ghosting up and down the stairs. You could sneak through a fire exit and upstairs to The Hooch. The light. The mushies never guzzled for a trip, just sampled for a buzz. Bringing the punters up for shuffling to cooler vibes. Alternative rock. Post punk. Psychobilly. House when nobody else had ever heard it or even heard *of* it. Funk and soul classics. James Brown.

Prince Charles. Hamilton Bohannan. Frankie Goes to Hollywood doing a live performance between *The Tube* and Trevor Horn making them superstars.

Sleight of hand exchanges in dingy corners of dingier pubs, like a dodgy magician; gear or powder for crumpled notes. Hash cubes. Skunk. Inevitably falling in with the wrong guys. Johnno McGuire. Ants Allison and his ugly twin, Gerry. Heavy cunts who offered bigger and bigger slabs to sell on, on tick. Stashing the quarter-weights under my garden shed; smoking too much myself, getting well para. Then, my life caved in. There were always tremors but this was Richter Scale 10. One Sunday morning, St Mark's hymns in the background, I discovered spade marks and a gaping hole where five grand had evaporated. The Allisons and McGuire going banzai for me being so careless, although I suspected they were the prime suspects. They trashed my car anyway. Fleeing to London for a few months to lie low. The terrible trio crossing an even heavier crew from Glasgow but getting grassed up, ending up doing stretches.

By then, my nerves shot, I'd lost the plot totally. My stretch was three months in a locked ward in the Royal Ed. In the TV lounge, chainsmoking with the other zombies, I'd think of that lassie, Angie all those years before, maybe sat right here. Another of life's complete circles.

Sunday, later

Finding the name on the intercom is one thing, but the first hurdle was always getting past this point. As it's stags and hens' night, the main door's been left on the latch. Trudging up the stairs, unlike many a party brazenly signposted by thumping music, the silence is ominous.

There's Colquhoun on the front door. Uncannily quiet. Maybe they've peaked. Emptying the bottles, a few last tokes, the older guests already snoring in their chairs. Sit-ooterie, right enough.

Many moons ago, I gatecrashed a party in the next street. After I barged in, a guy tearfully embraced me. Told me I was the spit of his wee brother, Norrie, a junkie who'd conked after cooking up and set his flat on fire. A neighbour saved him. Handed me a Cally Special and a spliff. With an ironic snort, I said, 'Drugs, eh?!'

Another stroke of luck. Chevonne's left her front door on the snib, too. Nudging it open, heart pattering, I pad into the hall. Judging by the bottles and cans, the D Club party was in full swing at some point. Muted music beyond the living room door. Cackling.

'Wake up, Rab. You're as bad as Cheryl. Some fucking pair youse are for the alpha male and female of the party animals. I'm taking photies. Maybe even put thegether a fucking slideshow for my speech next week.'

The music alters. Somebody's decided to up it a gear. Young Fathers. I can hear bodies roused onto the carpet. Feet stomping. When I was on the slippery slope to rock bottom, this would've been my cue to slink into the bedroom. Jackets hanging on the door or strewn over the bed. Aladdin's Cave. Nick's Grotto. Rifling through pockets like a rat delving its greedy snout into litter.

Saturday, late evening

For as long as I can mind, my life's been filled with clouds; sometimes black, billowing in with twisters and lightning forks, like the horizon that would terrify residents of US Prairie States. This makes the occasional silver linings more uplifting.

I've exited the bog, didn't even notice anyone standing there until a fist connected. An occupational hazard of so much past behaviour, crossing people to varying degrees. A skelp from a stranger quickly melting into the crowd, making my head ring, is small fry. Compared to the chib scar below my ribs.

Swaying towards my seat, sinking to my knees, I spy the tiny plastic rectangle on the carpet. Someone's making a fuss over me, but I fend them off.

'I'm ok, I'm fucking ok, right? Leave it, eh? A flesh wound.'

My fist tightens over that card and it's in my back pocket long before the bar towel is pressed into my bloodied eye socket.

Sunday, later

I go back outside the front door. Gaze down the stairwell. Then I rattle the letterbox. Keep at it until the music gets turned down. The door swings open. Chevonne peers at me.

'The fuck do *you* want?! Here. I know you. Spied you earlier. You alright there? Been in the wars the night, pal?'

'Chevonne?'

'Aye!'

'Found this in the pub.' I hand her the card. 'I'd overheard you saying the address for your party. Stags and hens. Stuck in my mind, cause that's what my folks did, a long, long time ago.

But I minded the address. Anyway. I was passing. Thought it'd be quicker handing it straight over than trusting the barstaff, eh. Chevonne Colquhoun.'

'Wow. Hadn't even noticed I'd lost my card. Been on the fucking peeve big style, cause my wee niece is getting hitched. Aren't you a proper Prince Charming, by the way? You been eating Wotsits? Your goatee's orange.'

'Eh? I'm really sorry, eh. Bought the yin packet at the garage. Had the munchies. And a Four Four Two.' Patted the magazine jammed in my back pocket. 'Hope you don't mind. Finder's fee.'

'I'll let you off, pal. Least I can do for going to so much trouble!'

My earlier days summed up. Spending all my time going after trouble. Chasing trouble. Being stalked by trouble.

'Excuse my manners, pal. What's your name?'

'Drew.'

'Drew. You are a fucking star. You want to come in? Bar's still open. Anything you want.'

SONGS IN THE KEY OF STRIFE – THERE'S NO BUSINESS LIKE AFTERSHOW BUSINESS

Neil Renton

I knew Princes Street Gardens like the back of my trembling hand.

There was the other part, nearest Waverley Train Station, where there used to be a putting green at the bottom of the hill. It's gone now, replaced by more space for sun worshippers to take advantage of the rare appearance of the yellow globe we see in Edinburgh skies in April. There's Scott's Monument, which I've never climbed, and the bus shelter I've frequented countless times.

Then there's the part I'm in now, with the bandstand in the shadow of the castle. Along from it is the play park, often overlooked by parents and much quieter than it should be. Imagine the rent on a soft play arena right in the centre of Scotland's capital. A decent place to take your screaming kids after they've dragged you away from the shops they didn't want to be in.

I also knew my way around concerts. I'd survived the front row at the infamous Oasis show at Irvine Beach, where hundreds of gig-goers pushed me this way and that. I'd made it out alive of the chaotic beer queue on Friday night at the Stone

Roses' Heaton Park comeback and managed to get out of Dodge before those over-friendly locals turned against us.

Yet here I was, sitting alone in one of Edinburgh's most picturesque settings on the eve of a Courteeners concert that was to be held in this very location. And I didn't know anything anymore.

I was wishing the park bench would swallow me up and chew me through its mahogany slats so I wouldn't have to see one of my favourite bands. Failing that, I was hoping for an email saying the whole event was being postponed to a date when I had an unavoidable conflict.

The gig came at a bad time for me. My mental health was in a mess, but it wasn't Liam Fray and Co's fault that their show coincided with my breakdown. They didn't know. To be honest, as a result of keeping it mostly to myself, no one really did.

I was besieged by panic attacks that made me jump at the slightest movement and the faintest sound. How was I going to make it through an outdoor concert with drunk folk accidentally bumping into me as they belted out songs?

So I took it upon myself to go down before the gig and sit on a bench. I visualised what would be happening, where I'd be standing, and how close I'd be to any exits in the event of the mother of all panic attacks. All while the roadies ploughed through a soundcheck.

That's when I heard "Aftershow."

It's a blistering start to their first album. A gentle lament to a relationship before all hell breaks loose in the frenzied guitars heralding the breakup about to happen. It was unintentionally fitting as my mind was fracturing all over the place.

It might have been a rough and ready version of the opening track of The Courteeners' debut album *St Jude*, but instantly it took me away from my staggered breathing and transported me to where I wanted to be: amidst a crowd of likeminded music lovers having the time of their lives.

I'd never heard the song performed live. "They'll play it at the gig," I told myself. "Go for that alone and head home right after."

That's what I did. I returned to the gardens with more than enough support to ensure I was okay if things didn't go well. At first, I felt as though I had time-travelled to a different era; everyone seemed far younger and livelier than me.

I might have felt out of place among the barely dressed girls and the lads setting off flares.

I might have stuck to a carefully judged couple of plastic pints of lager. I might have asked to stay anchored to a spot away from the madness, even though it was on a slope that wasn't kind to my ankles. However, I felt good. I felt like I was back to some semblance of normality.

The only disappointment was that The Courteeners never got round to playing "Aftershow." I suppose there's always next time.

I WALKED INTO THE DOOR AGAIN

Mark Fleming

***Solitude Standing*, Suzanne Vega (1987)**

I had a major psychotic episode when I was 25, culminating in an ambulance trip to a psych ward where I was formally sectioned. After weeks of being heavily medicated inside the intensive psychiatric care unit of the Royal Edinburgh Hospital, a nurse informed me I was being transferred to an open ward. With a staff escort, I'd be allowed to pop out to Morningside shops, cafes, or the nearby library. I'd eventually be considered for weekend passes to visit my family.

When I was introduced to the young lad sharing my dorm, Andy, it turned out he was a big music fan, constantly plugged into his Walkman. When I phoned my mum to break the news about having transferred wards, the first thing I asked her to bring along to the next visiting hour was my own Walkman. Mum duly handed over my portable cassette player, and the following day, Andy loaned me one of his extensive cassette collection: Suzanne Vega's second album, *Solitude Standing*. For the first time in many months of being trapped inside a depressive smog, I finally experienced an unfamiliar sense of optimism; the proverbial chink of light at the end of a long tunnel. The New York songwriter's emotive folk rock became the soundtrack to my recovery, and I played it until the batteries ran out.

The introductory song, the album's prologue, is a two-minute acapella, 'Tom's Diner' (based on an actual Broadway diner; a few years later, I discovered this was also the café portrayed in 'Seinfeld'). 'Luka,' released as a single, was about an abused child, which I found out was an autobiographical reference to her own stepfather. 'Ironbound/Fancy Poultry' was an ambitious track, over six minutes; actually two companion pieces. 'Ironbound' was melancholy but beautiful, flowing into the more upbeat 'Fancy Poultry,' based on an advert for the cheapest cuts of chicken — the wings are 'nearly free' — and culminating in a gorgeous melody. Elsewhere, the tracks were multi-layered, featuring an array of talented musicians. My personal favourites were 'Calypso,' memorable for its uplifting guitar solo, and 'Gypsy,' a heartfelt love song containing a line about being held like a baby that won't fall asleep.

Coincidentally, 'Tom's Diner' also mentions the bells of the nearby cathedral ringing. A few days later, the staff organised a Christmas shopping trip for some of the inpatients. As we trooped onto a bus and headed to Waverley Market, I couldn't help but dwell on the getaway arranged by Randle McMurphy for his fellow patients in a stolen school bus in *One Flew Over the Cuckoo's Nest*. At one point we entered the branch of James Thin in the Market. I treated myself to a Raymond Carver anthology containing his three seminal short story collections, up to his final publication, *Cathedral*. Unlike novels where you'd read the story in order, with short stories, I liked to dip in randomly. I'd skim the contents pages, then start with the shortest. This was 'Popular Mechanics,' in *What We Talk About When We Talk About Love*, using less than 500 words to describe a terrifying domestic dispute. This reminded me of a similar short short story by a Scottish writer I was really into, James Kelman, called 'Acid.' I'd first heard of Kelman in 1983 when the NME reviewed his groundbreaking debut collection, *Not Not While The Giro*, praising it, despite, according to the reviewer, one story, 'Nice to be Nice,' being "written in Glaswegian." So, in tandem with rediscovering my love of music through Suzanne Vega, I got into reading again. I'd had a few short stories published before falling ill, and rediscovering fiction led onto me writing again. When one of the doctors was doing his rounds, he came across me plugged into Suzanne Vega, jotting some story ideas into a lined pad. Shortly afterwards, I was granted my first weekend pass.

CHORED

Neil Renton

"Let's make sure we don't go to jail."

Kat dipped the garlic bread into the macaroni and pointed the residue at the TV news.

"What?" Paul asked.

"The council is going to fine residents if they don't use the correct bins."

"You'd have thought they'd have more important things to concern themselves with."

"You'd think people would be able to put the rubbish in the appropriate bin. It's not rocket science."

Kat and Paul smiled at each other—a couple who had thumbed their noses at those who said childhood sweethearts never make it. Both understood the importance of not just having a relationship but building on it, stamping on molehills before they became mountains.

Paul took the dishes through and placed them in the sink while Kat got her bag and diary and moved them to the cleared dining table. Jacob sat watching an iPad that his mum and dad swore he'd never need and that they were better than that.

"The eBay stuff. That's all been sent?"

"Did it yesterday after work, went to the post office at Asda," Paul said, appearing with a dish towel on his shoulder.

"Good stuff. Thanks."

Kat checked a lottery ticket in her purse. She crumpled it up and added it to a pile of useless receipts.

"That means going to work again tomorrow?"

"I'm afraid so," Kat replied.

Paul bathed Jacob while Kat caught up with her emails. She used her diary to cross-reference dates and respond accordingly. She felt a massive sense of achievement in doing so.

She passed Paul, who was on his way to sort out his Fantasy Football team in time for the midweek fixtures. Meanwhile, she read Jacob a bedtime story about Jason and His Red Sneakers and kissed her son's freshly shampooed head as she did so.

"I'll take the bin out tonight," Kat said as she sat on the sofa next to the iPad she shut off for the night.

"But it's Tuesday."

"So?"

"We've got our routines." Paul looked over from his struggles with his new formation.

"Take advantage of the generous offer. It's the last time I'll be doing it."

"Only if you're sure."

"I know what I'm doing."

Kat took the rubbish bags out the back and around the side. The night was silent, the garden still. She separated the plastics and paper into the relevant bins. She grinned when she saw where Paul had been putting the cardboard.

She stopped at the crumpled-up lottery ticket and took out her mobile. A quick glance to see if any of the neighbours, by chance, could see her—only if they were staring at her from the darkness.

Kat fired up the lottery website and placed the ticket under the numbers on her phone, matching a number at a time. Her finger moved from the one at the bottom to the one above it. She felt weak and steadied herself on a stinking bucket.

This changed everything. She could go. Vanish. Start again. She would. Tomorrow. Paul was in at the office and doing the nursery drop-off. Tomorrow too soon? Maybe the day after. Soon, though.

You know what this meant, she told herself. No more worrying about You Know What.

She rubbed her unborn child with the ticket before folding it neatly and putting it back in her pocket.

SONGS IN THE KEY OF STRIFE – THIS MORNING A DJ SAVED MY LIFE

Neil Renton

I was about to kill myself when a miracle happened.

Chris Moyles played a song on the radio.

Wait, I hear you ask. Isn't that his job? He was once the self-proclaimed saviour of Radio 1, a profession where you play music to the public and get paid for the privilege.

Surely he wouldn't be getting a substantial wage just to talk? Relentlessly?

That's what you'd think.

Moyles and I have history. Years ago, I was in hospital recovering after an operation. Because of patients wandering about, kind nurses checking on us, and sick people generally sounding unwell, I couldn't sleep. Which would have been a nightmare if I were able to dream. Just as I was beginning to drift off, one of the staff put on Radio 1.

Good, I thought. A diversion. A song will come on, and I'll doze off.

Unfortunately, Moyles was on, and he was on a roll.

I realised that for the first thirty minutes of his show, it's all about him. He might be in the studio with his team, who occasionally get a word in. A bit like wiping your diarrhoea-strewn arse with tracing paper, they don't do much as they're aware they can't stop the flow.

He just keeps going and going to the point that I wondered if it would have been as painful having the operation without anaesthetic as listening to him rabbit on.

I put my reservations about him aside when he joined my favourite radio station, the indie-themed Radio X.

He's probably not that bad a person. You know what they say about first impressions. He's made a lot of money and become famous for doing what he does. And there are times I find myself agreeing with his rants. His Platinum Hour, which used to be on a Friday when he'd play any type of music, is good. I like it when he plays music.

Anyway, it's time for me to be a narcissist. January. Just after seven. That First Day Back At Work After The Festive Period when, to be honest with you, the last thing on my mind is an egomaniac broadcaster.

For one, it's not a Monday, so I'm off-kilter. Daft as it may sound, I like to start things on a clean break. New year, new month, new week, new work shift, Monday. Nothing good ever started on a Tuesday.

I was on my way to a job that I hated, and the job hated me. To this day, I still think another CV was submitted when I went for the position, and they were mixed up like in a Hollywood comedy where two opposite characters end up swapping bodies. There was nothing funny in this.

For some reason unknown, most of the people I worked with didn't like me. Or if they did, they had a funny way of showing it. I was very rarely part of conversations at work, and my opinion on topics I knew about was rarely asked for or listened to. Being in the middle of a busy office with a group of workers who didn't acknowledge my existence was one of the loneliest experiences I've ever had.

My safe space was the stationery hub, where I made idle chit-chat with others who passed through it. I liked the photocopier, but I couldn't get it working. Even an inanimate object hated me.

The easy way out would have been to apply for another job. I don't like doing things the easy way. Instead, I worked myself up into such a panic-laden frenzy that the only option I felt I had was to take my own life.

There was also the spectre of an unknown medical condition hanging over me. It could have been multiple sclerosis which, if I'd taken a moment, I would have discovered wasn't the be-all and end-all that my overworked health anxiety had led me to believe it was.

Bizarrely, this made me worry that my life was going to end, which in turn made me want to end my life. I know. But that's how I thought, and unfortunately, I'm not the only one.

I didn't know what exactly I was going to do, just the end result. Like being told that BIG SECRET SPOILER for that film you want to see. I knew the ending, just not how it got there.

I waited at a set of traffic lights that had changed without me knowing. Workers headed to offices wearing formal clothes and New Year's resolution-inspired gym trainers. Students on their way to the nearest Starbucks to make the most of the free WiFi and tap water on offer.

Meanwhile, I didn't want to be here.

And then the miracle happened.

Chris Moyles played 'Don't Stop Me Now' by Queen.

I don't mind Queen.

There's the heavy Rangers connection that I understand, despite it not being for me. There's also the epic Freddie Mercury, the complete talent of one of the greatest frontmen, and the famous Live Aid performance that struck me for its sheer excellence from an early age.

As I stood at the traffic lights, hoping a runaway juggernaut would plough through me when I stepped onto the road, the song started to raise me from my slumber. I believe it's about masturbation, but don't let that ruin my tale. And when you think of the title, it could have been me saying I'll do the unthinkable no matter what. Don't stop me.

It didn't. It's one of those tunes you can't help but fall under its positive mindset. It's gloriously overblown. You can see lead singer Freddie Mercury charging about in his lycra and Adidas like a Pied Piper, leading us all away from the black cloud we're under and off to sunnier climates. Even during the grey of the first month of the year when the good times are just a distant memory.

You know what, I said to myself. I'm going to go into work and try my best not just in my role but with others. If I fail, I learn. If no one listens to me, I'll talk until they do.

Don't stop me now.

It was still a horrible day, but thanks to the double act of Chris Moyles and Freddie Mercury pulling me through, it wasn't as bad as I thought it was going to be. I might not have had a good time, a ball, or a wank, but I survived.

On reflection, what would have happened if Moyles had played another song? One that wasn't as optimistic? He was on a radio station famed for playing indie guitar music, a percentage of it being gloomy in its outlook.

Who knows? I dread to think. I might not have been here to write this. I wouldn't have been able to fight through my medical ailments. I wouldn't have got another job. One where I made friends. One where I was supported with my mental health issues. And more importantly, one where I got on with the photocopier.

RED HANDS AND STONE ROSES

Mark Fleming

The Stone Roses, The Stone Roses (1990)

On a bipolar scale of 0 to 10, 0 represents severe depression, and 10, mania. People who are not bipolar typically sit somewhere between 4 and 6. During 1987, my outlook on life slid way beyond 4, sinking ever further into a red zone where I began harbouring horrendous delusions, suffered from severe insomnia, and at my lowest ebb, succumbed to suicidal ideation. Three years later, my moodswings skyrocketed past 7, into hypomania, then mania.

In 1990, everything was happening at once. I'd moved away from my parental home and into a flat (aged 27, I was a late fledgling!) I was excited about getting my first fulltime job after my breakdown. My personality undergoing a transformation, fueled by visits to The Penny Black or The Guildford over the road from the Scottish Record Office where I worked, I would flirt shamelessly with female colleagues. Bumping into a longstanding hero from the post-punk scene, Mark E Smith of The Fall, in the latter pub, enjoying a starstruck chat over beers, seemed ample justification for my unconventional 'tea breaks'. I was also smoking a lot, constantly tapping workmates to fund the next 20-packet. Or pint.

A litmus test of my mental state was always my erratic relationship with football. Despite living in Shandon, just over the railway from Gorgie, I grew up supporting Hibs. But in the vacuum following that pedophile assault in 1976, I'd often fixate on Dad's side of the family's Northern Irish roots. A schoolmate insisted this connection gave me all the credentials to follow his team, the Glasgow Rangers. Their fans were the apex predators of mid-70s hooligan subculture, even 'taking' Manchester United's Stretford End during a 'friendly.' I was fascinated by his scarf, too, festooned with red hand badges. At some subconscious level, maybe I assumed wearing that scarf would've made me less of a nonce target. (Here I imagine a Mark E Smith lyric about nonce/nonsense!)

This Hibs/Rangers dichotomy got more pronounced. Not the sectarian bile - I had mates of every cultural background, not to mention girlfriends, and couldn't have given a flying fuck about which particular church any of them never went to. For a few seasons, on/off, I did go to Rangers games, listening out for the Hibs result on the bus back. Go figure.

During my one and only visit to Ibrox for Hibs away, I endured a squirming 90 minutes of my 'first team' being showered with abuse: the verbal equivalent of medieval prisoners in stocks getting pelted with rotting vegetables: an appropriate analogy since most of these insults seemed to date to the Reformation.

It was dispiriting enough to hear the away fans being roundly booed whenever they broke into 'Flower of Scotland.' I also overheard a brief ditty to the tune of 'What Shall We Do with the Drunken Sailor?' fancifully suggesting what one charming Glaswegian might do with the Virgin Mary. Clue: afterwards, she'd simply be Mary. Still the mother of God, though, which was how Prods were also supposed to regard her. (The crushing irony of a million whistling flutes, shrill as nails down a blackboard, metaphorically silenced by historical fact over conspiratorial fiction: at Derry, Aughrim, Enniskillen, the Boyne, and every other battle of the Nine Years War of 1688 to 1697, William of Orange and Pope Alexander VIII were on the same side.) One raucous wit achieved the blend of vitriol and satire some football fans occasionally master so effortlessly. Reflecting Edinburgh's then status as Europe's HIV capital and Hibernian's history as the club where Celtic originated, he bawled: 'Youse are Celtic with AIDS.'

But when Hearts' Chairman, Wallace Mercer attempted to consign Hibernian FC to history by becoming their majority shareholder, I proudly attended the 'Hands Off Hibs' rally at Easter Road stadium, passing around flyers I'd photocopied at work.

A Hibee succumbing to bluenose tendencies? Weird as that sounds, things got even weirder. I pinned a Northern Ireland banner to my bedroom wall next to my 1972 League Cup souvenir poster, and when I felt my mania soaring, I'd touch that flag's red hand emblem, my delusional brain informing me this was how I could control my spiraling moods to bring me back down to the 4-6 meridian zone. A nine counties' Ulster flag would've worked just as well! The first time I 'touched the hand,' imagining it had calmed my racing pulse and overactive thoughts, I was so chuffed I ran through to where my parents were still sleeping, waking them, jabbering excitedly about how my mental health would never be an issue again. Rather than placating them, I must've totally freaked them out.

This delusion originated during that psychotic episode in 1987. I had been taken to psychiatric hospital by ambulance with a police escort after violently self-harming. Dosed with heavy duty tranquillizers, strapped to a straitjacket, I spotted a red light in the back of the ambulance. My crazed mind insisted I only had to say 'red' aloud, like a spell, and everything would fantastically revert to how it had been before I was banging my head off my bedroom wall. But I couldn't get the word out. So, in 1990, on a bipolar high, that delusion resurrected. I became convinced the colour red was an antidote to my mental health issues (as opposed to the reality: it was a vivid symptom!)

More recently, I applied to the NHS for a copy of the case file covering my periods in the Royal Edinburgh Hospital from 1987 to 1990. Among the psychiatric reports and nurses' observations, here are two telling entries from the latter spell: "Mark talked of how touching something red can ward off bad feelings. He showed me a red object he was holding in his pocket. Mark remains on CLOSE OBSERVATION due to risk of unpredictable behaviour." Also. "Still needing limits set. Twice he put his hand in the fish tank to try and catch a red one."

Round about the time of the Hands Off Hibs rally, I got talking to a Northern Irish Rangers fan in the pub. He was studying at Edinburgh Uni and was an organiser for the Federation of Conservative Students. Mistaking my manic ramblings for genuine adherence to his narrow-minded attitudes, he insisted I should be an FCS spokesman! By then, I was struggling to separate my manic delusions from reality.

My elated moods were also coinciding with binge drinking. Most nights, I used my credit card to stock up on booze from

Victoria Wine. I'd start writing short stories, worked on the novel I knew was going to be a bestseller. I tore up as many draft sheets as I wrote. I was spinning so many plates, I was struggling to cope at work. I was existing on a few hours' sleep.

That summer also saw an explosion in indie music with the so-called Madchester scene. The posters on my bedroom wall: Inspiral Carpets 'Cool as Fuck.' The Stone Roses splattered in paint. Happy Mondays 'Rave On.' When I heard The Stone Roses eponymous debut album, I was blown away. The meld of sugary Byrdsesque 60s harmonies with shuffling, baggy rhythms, and John Squire's mesmerising fretwork had me hooked.

Like many patients experiencing a hypomanic episode, I also thought I'd discovered Jesus. For the first time since adolescence, I began attending church; sometimes the morning after boozy sessions or following a toke. On one occasion, bleary-eyed in a Scottish Episcopalian cathedral, when the priest began waxing lyrical about *the resurrection and the life*, I assumed he was referencing the blistering climactic track on The Stone Roses album.

Because my family recognised I was crashing into the red again, albeit in the opposite direction to the far more disturbing psychosis of 1987, I was admitted to the Royal Edinburgh Hospital once more, to Ward 1A. Over the weeks, I got pally with a fellow patient, a South Asian maths student who'd burned out; and a patient from Ward 1, a Hearts Boy from Clerrie who owned The Stone Roses album on cassette. The three of us listened to this all the time. The psychedelic treats of 'Elephant Stone,' 'I Wanna be Adored,' and 'She Bangs the Drums' became the soundtrack to my spell in Ward 1A. In fact, the album became integral to my well-being.

When my mania was getting so bad the staff had to try calming me by issuing PRN medication ('as required,' over and above the daily dosage), my mates would escort me to my dorm, ensure I was relaxing on my bed, then play the Roses. On many occasions, I'd lie back, waiting for the onset of a 100 mg dosage of Largactil, my mind drifting to the soothing sounds of 'Fools Gold' and 'Waterfall.' Bliss.

The 'red object' in my pocket, a Lego brick, was forgotten about.

WHAT'S THE EXCUSE THIS TIME?

Neil Renton

One ring. Click the fuck into voicemail now.

Another ring. Fuck. Someone is going to answer. I just want to leave a message. I don't want a big conversation. This isn't the time or place.

"Hi, Reilly and Andrews absence line, Ronnie speaking."

Fuck, Ronnie. Fucking Ronnie.

"Eh, Ronnie, it's me, Declan."

"Declan," Ronnie says. "I can't really hear you."

"Yeah, it's a bit noisy here," I say.

"Can't you go somewhere with better reception?"

"Eh, that's the problem. I can't. There's a chance I'll be late for work this morning."

"Declan, you know what that means. You're one late away from being sacked."

You're not even my manager. You're just a do-gooder who's on the same level and pay as me. You've been here for years and never progressed. They just get you to do the jobs they don't want to do themselves. More grief. Same wage.

"I am trying to make it in."

"Last week, a stray dog got on the bus and had sex with another dog, and when the driver tried to shoo it off, the stray dog sat on his seat and the driver refused to drive the bus. What's the excuse this time?"

"Godzilla is blocking the road."

"What was that? I can't hear you for the sound of planes flying low past the office."

"They're probably on their way here. To be fair, I'm not sure if it's the actual Godzilla, but it's some big massive fire-breathing lizard thing at Haymarket, and it's fucking everything up."

The bus had stopped in a traffic jam. At first, I knew something was wrong but wanted to play it cool. I didn't think it was anything too bad because all you heard was the driver tutting, so I just kept reading the letters page in the Metro.

Then it appeared. The worst case of Monday Morning Dread I've ever seen. Tall as fuck, towering over the flats in the West End and sending everyone scattering.

The creature takes a swipe through the train station with its tail, which emerges with a Marks and Spencer's chilled cabinet on it.

I'm heading towards the door of the bus, but it's too late.

"Declan, watch your language as the calls are recorded. I really can't hear what you're saying. If the bus has broken down, get off and get a tram—"

"I'd love to, but it's picked us up and it's about to launch it as if it's earned a call-up to the Silver Wing darts team."

"Wait! Did you hear that? It was like an explosion," Ronnie said.

"Hear it? I fucking felt it. The fucker's raging. He's got lasers coming out his eyes. Platform Number Four is now Platform Two and a Half."

The double-decker airport bus is hoisted above Haymarket as its claws penetrate the windows. Tourists are screaming and praying to gods in their own languages. Tynecastle has popped up in the near distance. Please don't let that be the last thing I see.

"Well, expect to see you as soon as you can get here."

"Wait. Another one has turned up with wings and fangs and everything. I've no idea if it's pals with Godzilla or enemies. Or if they've just bumped into each other."

The winged creature lands near that Indian restaurant on the corner. It's shrieking like fuck. Godzilla does the same back and I'm regretting not charging my iPods last night.

"Just get to work, Declan. I need to go as there are other calls coming into the manager's line. You'd think the world was about to end."

ELIXIR OF LIFE

Mark Fleming

Larry appears, creaks the doors aside just as the first chime turns everyone to statues. In her stationary mobility scooter, one of his regulars, Mary, mouths a prayer. The mournful clangs are drowned by seconds of music blaring from the boutique opposite; Larry seethes until there's a raised voice and a sheepish assistant extinguishes the noise. Water over fire. Shug makes to barge in. Larry stays put.

'Wait, Shug. This is for you.'

Shug sighs, finds a spot on the pavement amongst the dowts where his eyes can rest. Studying scuffs on his shoes, tears come, and the present falls away.

*

Beyond this farm's pockmarked buildings, the ruins of Heidelberg Castle loom, destroyed in some war centuries before. Which troops stormed its ramparts, and whose soldiers rained rocks and boiling oil down? Shug doubts many of the locals even know.

He thinks of the charred corpse floating down the River Neckar yesterday. You couldn't identify the uniform. War swiftly makes its victims anonymous. Watching that body tugging with the currents, Sergeant Lewis said, 'You know where we are, boys? Wurttemberg? They're all papes here. Hope thon's a fucking pape.'

Ahead, Lewis is squirming through the undergrowth, but Shug can track the lummox's progress like a Churchill tank. Lewis beckons him. Shug stoops beside him in the caked mud.

'Can you hear that McNulty?'

Shug can make out a skylark's trill. A donkey baying. Then something else, so incongruous he must hold his breath to listen closer. A child is singing Marlene Dietrich's 'Falling in Love Again,' in German.

They crawl by cattle carcasses, flies investigating their dappled hides. Wriggling up to a breach punched into a wall by 17 Pounders, they scan the farmhouse. Lewis cowers across the cobbled courtyard, halting at the front door. Heart hammering, Shug trails him. The voice is louder still, seems to be coming from below. Lewis's eyes widen.

'*Look,* McNulty,' he hisses. 'Steps to a cellar.'

Shug follows him down to a rickety wooden door. They peer through the slats. Inside are two figures, candlelight flickering over the singer, her back to them. A scratchy record plays on a gramophone, the female accompanying. Her companion swings one hand in time to the music while slugging from a bottle.

'Sweet mother of Jesus, McNulty. A little blonde *fraulein*. A blue-eyed Aryan to suck our cocks.'

Lewis kicks so forcefully the door spins off its hinges. He yells, waving his Lee Enfield. Shug shadows him into the gloom, while the shocked occupants leap to their feet, hands stretching to the ceiling.

'*Nicht schießen! Don't shoot! We surrender!*'

The singer is a boy, mid-teens, blond fringe drooping over

his features in lank strands. Shug stifles a relieved sigh. While Marlene Dietrich persists, Lewis pokes his rifle barrel into the lad's neck. Shug trains his weapon on the other one, white hair poked into a grey cap. Both are in shabby, ill-fitting uniforms, with red and black *Volkssturm* armbands. The older German wears lance corporal insignia on his right arm. A quick assessment of the cramped cellar reveals there's no one else. As Shug's eyes grow accustomed to the musty confines, he registers rusting tools: hoes, shovels, a scythe; a crate with the turntable perched, a wine bottle decanting its contents onto the straw flooring.

Lewis gestures towards the gramophone. 'Stop the music, Fritzy.'

The youth's spindly arms thrust to the needle, raising it, his jerking movement scratching the disc.

'Pick that up,' says Lewis, indicating the bottle. The man hesitates. '*Fucking pick it up*, Grandad. You're fucking *wasting* it.'

The fellow snatches up the bottle, passes it to the sergeant, hand shaking. His attention rooted to the boy, Lewis gulps the remainder down. 'Nice bit of kraut plonk, McNulty. See if there's anymore.'

Shug peers around the older German's muddy jackboots. 'Quite a few bottles, sarge. Maybe a dozen?'

Lewis winks. 'Youse were having quite a party down here, eh, lads? Careless singing like that. That's the demon drink, mind. Don't blame you. Makes the war go away for a while, eh?'

The white-haired soldier looks to his comrade, back to Lewis. 'Your accent? I am sorry.' His eyes drift to the tartan regimental patches on Lewis's sleeve and he reads the insignia.

'Fifty second division. KOSB. *Scottish?*'

Lewis ignores him.

'That's right, pal. We're the Kosbies,' Shug says. 'The Blue Bonnets.' It means something to him. To Lewis, it's just another excuse for his bullying.

'You speak our lingo, Fritzy?' says Lewis.

'My daughter was English teacher. Before.'

'What's *your* name, boy?'

'Klaus.'

'Fetch me another, Klaus.'

The youth delves, seizes a bottle. Makes a show of biting the cork, tugging it out with his teeth, holding the neck out. Giggling with nerves. Lewis hacks a throatful of mucus, spits, snatches the bottle.

'To your fucking Fuhrer. He better pray we get to him before the fucking Ivans. Especially the slitty eyed ones from over the Urals. They'd've been Genghis Khan's hordes. They'll gang rape your beloved Fuhrer *and* all his Nazi high heidyins. After fucking their way through every town and village from Danzig to Dresden. They'll even be digging up the bodies from the RAF firestorms, Klaus. Fucking *them*, and all.'

Lewis gulps the wine, rivulets running down his stubble. After satiating himself he belches, the ugly rasp amplified within this dank cell. His breathing has altered, each intake urgent. Already he stumbles to one side, rights himself, spits again. When he passes the bottle, Shug makes a point of rubbing the neck with his sleeve. He takes a welcome mouthful of a full-bodied red, tasting of cherries. Lewis clicks his fingers. Shug relinquishes it.

'Fucking tasty drop, this,' says Lewis.

'Elixir of life,' says the elderly soldier, grinning.

'Fucking right, mate. Elixir of life, this stuff? Eh, Klaus? Did you try any?'

The youth nods. 'Elixir of life, yes, sir.'

As the sergeant swallows, his rifle tip works its way down the boy's buttonless tunic to his emaciated belly. The youngster's head droops with shame.

'McNulty. March the old bastard outside. Take your rifle across his fucking napper if you have to. I just want to hear Klaus singing some more. Good enough for the Alhambra, so he is. A couple more drinks, McNulty, then we'll join you. An order.'

Shug peers at the kid, hands thrusting into the air as if he is still the schoolboy he would've been months ago. He waves his rifle towards the old man. 'Right. You. This way.'

When he scuffs by, Lewis sticks a boot out. The German tumbles, hits the ground, spectacles flying to one side. 'Clumsy old bastard. What a fucking shower their beloved Fuhrer is sending out to die for the Fatherland while he hides in his bunker. Eh, McNulty?'

Ignoring him, Shug clutches his prisoner's fingers, heaves him to his feet. Then he plucks his spectacles, their wire frame buckled, the left lens cracked. He places them into his grazed palm.

'Never mind the Home Guard, McNulty. I'm sure the old bastard's a Waterloo veteran. When he would've been on *our* side.'

The boy nods at Lewis, colluding. 'Yes, yes, Tommy. *Waterloo*. Against the French. Wellington. Von Blücher. Together.'

Quivering with nerves, the words spilling, his English is good. 'Rolf, my stepfather, was in the last war. He fights for Kaiser Wilhelm. Your Tommies, fighting for King George. Cousins, yes? Queen Victoria married our Albert Saxe-Coburg. Your royal family and ours. Together, yes?'

'Shut your fucking geg, kraut.' He takes another mouthful of wine, smacks his lips.

When the elderly chap is upright again, Shug jabs his gun into the small of his back, steers him out the shattered doorway, back up the steps. 'Face the wall.'

Shug delves into his pockets. A crumpled cigarette packet with two remaining. His heart soars. A torn letter. He's struck by the elegant handwriting. A photograph of a family catches in the wind. Flutters away like a butterfly. Shug lights a cigarette, passes it to him.

'Dankeschön, Tommy.'

Shug stares into the back of the German's head. If only this old man and child had removed their tunics, they'd have assumed them civilians, eking an existence in the ruins of their farm. But the greater fear would be their own soldiers discovering them out of uniform. They see the evidence everywhere, in village squares, in copses where rooks lurk: hanging from nooses, placards pinned to their chests. *Deserteur.*

He is mumbling. The Lord's Prayer, in his own language, to the God they share. Now the boy is singing again, voice quavering.

Lewis snaps: 'In English this time, boy. Can you sing along, Fritzy, in English?'

As the German falters, Lewis starts clapping, shouting

encouragement. '*Men come to me like moths to a flame, and if their wings burn, I know I'm not to blame.*'

'Yes … I try … Men come to me … Like …'

'Right, Fritzy. That'll do.'

'No. Please. I sing for you. Englisch, if you teach me.'

There's a slap. The boy squeals. 'Bitte.' He cries more urgently but is stifled. Shug senses Lewis's great, calloused palm closing over his lips.

'What happens, Tommy?' says the corporal.

'What happens? We'll take you to field HQ. Two mile down the road. Your war's over, at least. You should be thankful.'

He will also be thankful he is not the boy whose muted whimpers are now rising to an anguished bleating while Lewis grunts rhythmically, horridly. Shug's stomach churns. He spies the photograph snagged against weeds. He'd retrieve it for Rolf, but he's so repulsed he's rigid. Lewis emits a lengthy sigh, as if he's squatting over a latrine. The boy's sobbing is curtailed by a muffled blow. Another. Presently Lewis stomps back up the steps, buckling his belt.

'Where's the other prisoner, sarge?'

'Bastard had a knife tucked into his jackboot. Went for me.'

When he tells this lie, Shug's eyes waver to the blood around the butt of the sergeant's rifle. Lewis grasps the old guy's tunic, pokes his weapon into the material, wipes it clean. 'Klaus may have sung like an angel, but he was a sneaky devil.'

He awaits Shug's approval, even a forced laugh. There's an unearthly screech in the distance.

'*Das kaninchen,*' the corporal says, cigarette bobbing. 'Rabbit. Hawk catch him.'

A crackle of gunfire comes from woodland below the castle, the vista shimmering in the afternoon haze.

'They don't all surrender as easily as these two did, McNulty. No time to hang about. We need to find the rest of the lads.' Taking the cigarette from the German tenderly, he feeds it between Shug's lips. 'Here. That the old kraut's family?' Lewis steps over to the photograph, snatches it up. 'Handsome boys. Your grandsons?'

'Meine enkel … Yes, sir. My grandsons.'

'I'll keep this. Spoils of war.'

Studying the image, Lewis nods, tongue darting around his lips. Like a snake, thinks Shug. Intent on the family posing in their Sunday best, they fail to notice the German skulking away until he's almost made it into undergrowth. Lewis chuckles, raising his Lee Enfield.

'Hawk catch him.' Squeezes the trigger. The retort makes Shug wince, bite into the cigarette filter. He tastes cherries.

*

Two weeks later, Lewis was killed when their position was strafed by US Warhawks. No one mourned him. During these silences it's Rolf and Klaus who are always with Shug. He forces the rest of it from his mind, leaving Klaus singing, Rolf savouring the wine.

'Right. That's it for another year, Shug. Apart from the fucking rockets with the satellite dish sized poppies on their bonnets. Your usual coming up. I can already hear your comment after your first taste. Every time, Shug. Elixir of life.'

THE MAESTRO, GEORGE

Neil Renton

She puts on the telly to keep her company. Presenters interview talking heads about politics and stuff. Everyone has an opinion on everyone else's opinion.

Covering the early shift and the late until Saturday. Last week of doing this, promise, until the next new starter decides during their induction week that it's not for them. There's a pile of Monday morning washing, remains of the weekend, that she'll sort out tomorrow. Depleted six-packs of shop-brand lager that she kept in the fridge for Friday night emergencies. She'll get up in a minute and get stuff done once the second coffee has worked its magic.

They're now going over to LA.

Eyes adjust. It can't be. It is.

He did it. He fucking did it.

He's in a line of guests being ushered into a party. He gets a tap on his back shoulder and he's facing a camera.

She goes to get her phone. Why? Maybe message him, message others about him. She changes her mind, leaves her mobile where it is, and turns up the volume.

"Congratulations on your Oscar win!" says a host with an accent that's mid-Atlantic, thrown about in turbulence and not sure if it's going to land in New York or Newhaven.

"Thanks, mate," he says, holding the gold statue in one hand and a folded pair of sunglasses in the other.

"What was going through your mind when they said your name?"

"I dunno. There was a part of me that was delighted, obviously. But I've got that very Scottish thing of being embarrassed about public adulation."

"You shouldn't be! This is amazing!"

"Thanks. I think this proves some people wrong. I've had a lot of good support over the years that's helped me get here. Not everyone believed in me."

"Those doubters must be kicking themselves."

"They could be. I'm no bitter. Honest. It's the fuel that fires me up."

He looks so at ease, taking the questions and paparazzi in his stride. He belongs there.

"Right, let's talk us through the outfit."

"Yeah, sure. Kilt from my mate Howie. He made it especially for this, invented the tartan and everything."

"Gorgeous. The shoes are a bit different?"

"Yeah, Rockports. I don't think they were ever big in the States, but back in the day these were all the rage. My mate Hez still had them in his cupboard, thirty years old. He gave me them as long as I mentioned him in any speech if I won. Cracking deal."

"And the glasses?"

"These are my lucky shades. George."

"Giorgio Armani?"

"Nah, George from Asda."

"Seriously?"

"Aye. When I had nothing, they were all I could afford. Two pounds fifty. Grudged paying more in case I broke or lost them. When you're going to a soup kitchen, you still need to look the part, eh? They're not to everyone's taste, but so what?"

He's asked what's next, and he's all excited about projects when the interviewer meant what party he was heading to.

She switches off the telly, deciding she doesn't want to hear people just now. Time to get a shake on.

She brushes her teeth with intent and a clenched fist as white as the toothpaste. She spits into the sink and cleans up all the mess.

Her brush goes back in the cup, where there's the one that's been unused for ages. The heads are facing in the opposite direction as if they've fallen out.

PROTECT YA NECK

Neil Renton

Benny rolled into the bank stinking of Buckfast and unfiltered optimism.

He pulled down the collar of his beaten leather jacket so as not to give the impression he was a bank robber. He wasn't a fighter, man. He was a lover.

A lover of life.

There were a few wooden desks surrounded by high chairs. At one of them sat a young woman whose eyes widened as soon as she looked up. She'd probably seen him at TRNSMT or at The Eldorado homecoming show at The Liquid Rooms. She seemed to be the type. Benny made a beeline for her.

"Alright, pal!" he said.

"Eh, hi," she flustered. "How can I help you today?"

"I want to insure something."

"Okay," she said, leaving behind her celebrity blushes and slipping effortlessly into business mode. "We offer a wide range of insurance products. What are you looking to insure?"

"This," Benny said.

He then tilted his head slightly to the right.

"Sorry, what was it you were looking to insure?"

"This," Benny smiled before he shifted his neck.

"You want to insure you tilting your head?"

"Aye, pal. It's my thing. The head tilt. Everyone knows me for it."

"I see," the cashier said with no actual idea of what to do next. She typed some random words into her keyboard while Benny looked about the bank with amazement before he returned with a collection of leaflets.

"If I lose my ability to move my neck like that, I lose me. I can't have that. And neither can everyone else."

"I'm sorry, but I don't think we can actually insure a physical movement. I'll contact head office for clarification if you want."

"Please," Benny grinned at her unintentional joke as he read up on pension transfers. "Just tell them Mariah Carey insured her voice for $10 million. And I'm a better singer."

The cashier got through to a colleague and managed expectations that the customer was in the branch at the time, which explained her hushed and slightly embarrassed tones.

"Hi there, yeah," she said as she hung up the phone. "They'll look into it. Can I take your number so I can keep you updated?"

Benny scrawled it on a slip for paying in cheques and dashed his signature next to it.

"There you go, pal," he said before heading for the exit and wishing her a good and pleasant day.

He held the door open for an elderly woman wearing a jacket too big for the summer.

"Thanks, son," she said.

"No problem, love," Benny said right before he tilted his head.

"It's you! The singer boy! All my grandkids love you. They went to see you up Victoria Street recently and keep going on about it."

"They did? That's amazing."

"Could I get a selfie?"

"Yeah, sure. I'll get my pal to take it."

Benny stood next to the old woman, who was cheesing out of her nut. The cashier snapped away as best as she could on a phone almost as old as the woman.

"Wait, one more." And with that, Benny tilted his head, and the old woman almost fainted.

GUERRILLAZ

Mark Fleming

'Back on speaking terms? Where to Gallaghers?'

'City Cafe next, mate,' says Liam. 'I'm on Maps, so don't think of ripping us off with detours up and down these cobbled closes.'

Glancing at the rear-view mirror, I tap the details into the meter. Gone 11, pitch-black, but these clowns are still in shades, Liam's aping John Lennon's circular lenses. Noel's lugging an acoustic guitar painted with a Union Jack. Maybe he senses my irritation, cause he shoves a flyer through the gap. Nodding, I skim it.

*"Couldn't get an Oasis ticket? Here's the next best thing! The Wonderwallies are an Oasis 'guerrilla group' who hijack stages to perform a sidesplitting cocktail of Manc mirth: raucous revamps of all your favourite Oasis classics AND standup comedy." Keith Waterman. The List ***** reviews.*

I sense Liam awaiting my approval. Noel just slouches in a replica 90s City away shirt. As I mull over an insincere but tactful reply, Noel suddenly coughs a mouthful of barf over the 'Brother' sponsorship logo.

'Warned you about those cocktails, Trevor!' snarls Liam-alike.

That they react by belly laughing instantly boils my piss. I slam on the anchors.

'Steady,' says Noel. 'It's just on my shirt. Not on the floor. Here. I've got a bag. Somewhere.'

'There's the hat we use for collecting the dough.'

'I'm not being sick into a Stoney bucket hat.'

I glare into my mirror. 'If you *are* sick on the floor I'm charging you fifty notes on top of your fare. Cleaning costs. Not to mention my other customers having to endure the fucking smell. Only so much a pine air freshener can cope with.'

Liam digs into the pockets of his jeans. Out comes a wallet. He extracts a red note. Waves it, as if to waft away the acrid tang. 'Fifty on top of the fare. Agreed. Now. Drive the fuck on.'

'What did you say?'

'I said fifty pounds, driver. You'll get two if you get us there in five.'

Gritting my teeth, I place their flyer onto the dash, check my wing mirrors. If I had a fifty for every time I've had to grin and bear it, I'd have retired yonks ago. Every August, Edinburgh's population doubles and the EH1 publicans rub their hands. This year customers have told me they've been lapping up Bangkok Ladyboys. Hip-hop Shakespeare. Nearly nude ballet. Whatever this idiotic duo performs. I glare into the rear-view again. Liam-alike has fished a T-shirt from his rucksack, handed it to his partner. Noel-alike starts dabbing, creating a stinking Jackson Pollock.

Flashing readies. One step away from clicking fingers. In perfect character for when the real Gallaghers have been on the marching powder, I suppose. Not that I begrudge the genuine working class Manc lads having made good. If I'd stuck in at Hutchie Vale and signed for Hearts like my Uncle Deek, I might well have got some capital from the bragging rights. Deek never shuts up about his almost football career — and that's when he corners you in The Diggers, rather than ching's narcotic megaphone.

I'm just thankful for the opportunity to work my arse off for three full weeks on hiked fares and the generous tips Festival punters can afford. I hate myself for it, but now I'm thinking of him brandishing his wallet. The possibility of a healthy tip from these arseholes. So, at the next red, I decide to pass the time.

'All I want to do is rock, eh Liam? If this was last year's festival, I would've asked if punters were still bothered about Oasis. Oasis tributes. But that was before the comeback tour was announced and their fame went through the fucking stratosphere. I seen the queues outside the pop-up shop in George Street earlier. Every second punter in a bucket hat.'

'There'll always be love for Oasis. Oasis will always get a crowd rocking. Anyway. We're not a tribute. Any monkey can grab a guitar and learn Noel's three chords. We're a proper show. Satire. We prefer to think of what we do as guerrilla gigs.'

'The Wonderwallies do guerrilla gigs?'

'Of course, driver. That was how it all started for Liam and Noel. Hitched a lift to King Tut's with another Manc band, Sister Lovers, who were supporting Boyfriend and 18 Wheeler, both Creation bands. Gatecrashed the bill, played four songs, including I Am the Walrus. Alan McGhee happened to be there. Loved their audacity. Signed them on the spot.'

'My brother-in-law, Rab, saw them at La Belle Angelle, buddy. April 94. Just passed that. Says to me, "Went to see Whiteout last night, Colin. Greenock band. They're touring with a band from Manchester. Taking turns about headlining. The English lads defo had something. Watch this space. Oasis." A fucking Wednesday night, in front of about 50 bods.'

'That's mega, mate. Trevor and I started this routine years ago. Knocked it on the head after Standing on the Shoulders of Giants flopped. But throughout the 90s, we'd show up in random venues. I'd do five minutes stand up. Play a couple of our versions of Oasis songs. Pretend to do a line on stage. Powdered lactose. Stage a mock fight. Head to the next venue. Not before I'd passed around my Stone Island cap. Tonight, we're back on it. The Oasis just rammed Murrayfield, so we're going to relaunch our guerrilla gigs at your city's fabulous Fringe, mate.'

'Wonderwallies, eh?'

'That's it. Three five-star reviews so far.'

'Is there a Blur guerrilla act? You could have face offs. Double bills with fucking aggro. They'd be the Guerrillaz.'

'That rivalry was just marketing genius, wasn't it, driver?'

I'm thinking, comparing music is one thing. And since musical taste is so subjective, impossible to quantify. But the personality clash is more nuanced. The Gallaghers spout hyperbole, which they get away with because it's mostly been tongue in powdered cheek. And the real Liam's a natural comic. Albarn's just a ring. Refusing to have his photo taken after being on Joolz Holland if James Blunt was also in it? So, James gets locked in his dressing room until Albarn and his fucking narcissism have left the building. Decent cunt. Cunt.

'Don't you get chucked off the stage? Infiltrating somebody's gig? I mean. That'd be like pitch invaders at Tynecastle getting fucking handshakes from the players!'

'We're usually well funnier than the main act, lad.'

An idiot in a tux steps in front, waving his arms. Slamming my fist into the horn, I swerve. What's also going through my mind is the guy's use of the word *satire*, because that so often gets plucked out the blue, especially during the Festival. It can be a grandiose description applied to third-rate dreck classified as comedy because that's the heading they've requested to go under in the official programme. As for guerrillas. Pussy Riot were guerrillas for crashing some Moscow cathedral in protest at Orthodox leaders supporting Putin's regime. A few minutes trashy punk rock got each of them two years in Russian prison. Cabaret to fleece pissed-up punters out of drinking vouchers is just busking.

My attention is arrested by the treacherous human slalom I must negotiate all the way through the West Port. Until. Just when the Oasis banter's warming me to my passengers, a snap-snapping Zippo jolts me like a car backfiring. Liam's trying to spark a fat doob.

'No way. Stub that out, buddy. Right now.'

Almost dismissively, he flaunts his wallet again. 'You'll get a decent tip, driver. I promised you, didn't I?' In his cod accent. 'A Burnage boy's word is his fooking bond, lad.' Posh boy again. 'I'll leave you a few draws, too. Bonus.'

Balling notes, he flicks them through the gap. Crinkled blues, browns, and a couple of reds tumble onto the floor amongst the chewing gum wrappers. 'There you go, you Jock cunt. That's you sorted.' He thumbs up towards my mirror, then puffs out a noxious cloud that catches my throat like tear gas.

Hacking, I clock my greying beard in the rear-view. My dad stares back at me with a clarity that takes my breath away. I see him the last time I spoke to him. Three weeks ago. Telling him how much I loved him moments before I listened to him exhaling for the last time in St Columba's. A lifelong non-smoker, biopsied at the Infirmary for a persistent tickly cough, diagnosed with advanced lung cancer that had spread to his brain before slipping into a morphine-induced coma, all within a week. An acrid veil drifts over dad's photo pinned to my dash, masking him beaming at my camera with a bowls trophy. Just months ago. When this year's Fringe brochure would've been getting proof-read.

I feel something shifting inside. Becoming molten. Lifting my foot from the clutch, the taxi kangaroo jumps. Stalls.

'What gives, driver?'

'Fucking flat battery, buddy. The motor's been bugging my fucking happiness for a couple of days, like. Can I ask you lads a favour? Just needing a wee jump start, is all. It'll take seconds. If youse'd give me a push, I'll pop it into second, hit the throttle.'

Liam rouses Noel and they exit, taking position at the rear. Gunning the engine, my cab lurches forward, sending them stumbling. Stomping on the accelerator, I watch them shrinking in my rear-view. Killing the engine again just as suddenly, I climb out.

I hold Noel's guitar aloft. With its patriotic colours, I'm reminded of that iconic photo of US marines raising their flag over Iwo Jima. But the image I'm fixating on is Jimi Hendrix at the Monterey Festival, lifting his guitar, swinging it into the deck, setting it on fire. Light years beyond audacity.

I smash the guitar into the Old Town cobbles, its discordant chimes echoing against the ancient tenements. Again. And again. And again.

Cruising away, sweeping up their petty cash, I unfurl one of the tenspots. Powdered lactose my fucking arse.

BETTER LIVING THROUGH CHEMISTRY

Neil Renton

"I never had Debbie down as someone who loved chemistry."

"It's always the ones you least expect," Megan replied, half-heartedly. She wasn't fully engaged in the conversation with her mum, her attention focused on preventing an impending disaster.

Megan's mum banged on the kitchen window and enthusiastically waved at Debbie on the street below.

"Oops. Didn't mean to give her a fright. Looks like she's spilled all her homework on the pavement."

Megan leaned over the kitchen sink, watching her friend frantically gather up pills, chasing after a rogue one that had rolled away. She tapped the glass herself, giving Debbie a shrug. Debbie, now standing, returned the gesture.

"I'll need to phone Rachel's mum and thank her. It's so nice of her to let you all stay over for a revision session the night before your exams."

"She's never really in. Well, she is, but she's always busy, always on the go." Megan was careful not to trip herself up with her words.

"I should get her some flowers as a thank you. That would be nice."

"Have you seen my savings? I'm sure they were in a tin in this cupboard."

"There you go, behind the soup tins. Thieves would never think to look there," Megan's mum said, reaching into the back and pulling out an old shortbread container.

"I'm sure they wouldn't," Megan said, a touch of sarcasm in her voice.

"What do you need money for?"

"I'm actually going to head into Leith tomorrow and open a bank account. Just to be on the safe side in case any burglars fancy tomato soup or mushy peas when they break in."

"What's her favourite colour?"

"Who?"

"Rachel's mum."

"She'd be insulted, Mum. She's a professional gardener, so you wouldn't want to just grab a random bunch of flowers. It'd offend her, and it would have the opposite effect of what you're intending."

"It must be so hard for her."

"What is?" Megan did her best to stay calm, but inside she was screaming.

"Being a professional gardener when she lives in a top-floor flat."

"And that's why she's always busy—working with the restrictions."

Megan darted into her bedroom. Her school stuff was meticulously laid out. She closed her eyes, prayed to a God she didn't believe in, and packed it at the top of her bag.

"Good luck," Megan's mum called as her daughter headed to the front door.

"For what?"

"The exam tomorrow. All you can do is your best."

"Thanks, Mum," Megan replied, feeling a wave of guilt. "Come here."

She hugged her mum, who seemed to be shrinking as she got older. At first, her mum stood stiffly, unsure how to respond. Then she embraced Megan, first loosely, before grabbing hold of her as tight as she could.

Megan felt herself starting to get emotional. She remembered the time she'd convinced her mum to watch *Pulp Fiction*, telling her it was a PG. By the time her mum realised it wasn't a Disney family comedy, it was too late.

There's that bit where Bruce Willis and John Travolta circle each other when they first meet. You just know something's going to happen between them, but you're not sure what.

That's what it was like in Megan's house since her dad had gone—her and her mum tiptoeing around, waiting for the right moment to say the right thing, a sign that never seemed to come. They were both on edge, waiting for the other to make a move.

"Right, I'm off. I'll see you tomorrow after the exam," Megan said, pulling herself free.

"And after you've set up the bank account."

"Nothing gets past you."

Megan shot outside and looked disapprovingly at Debbie.

"For fuck's sake," Megan muttered.

"What do you think will happen to a cat if it swallows an E?" Debbie asked.

"Fuck knows, Debbie. But I tell you what, it's coming out of your stash."

The pair of them hurried up Hawthornvale—a route they'd taken millions of times on their way to school, Vicky Park, or up the town. But today, the trip was different.

Today, they were going to London.

WORKING 9 TO MAMBO NO. 5

Neil Renton

Charlie knew it was going to be one of those calls when the customer muttered those immortal words.

"I'm not having a good at you."

Then the caller proceeded to have a go at Charlie—her pronunciation of certain words, the fact that she hadn't been quick enough when she had him on hold, and that she was female.

Charlie didn't mind. For once, she was oblivious to it all, worded bullets bouncing off her.

She was going on a date after work with Scott. A few drinks on George Street, then back to his place as his parents were away on a city break.

Scott wasn't like the rest. Wasn't like the others. He was respectful towards her, and it was a breath of fresh air.

"You still on the phone?" Francis mouthed. Charlie nodded and rolled her eyes while the caller called her a stupid little fucking girl.

Whatever.

After issuing her fourth final warning, Charlie ended the call and went over to see Francis.

"I'm not sure how else to say this, but you've been summoned downstairs to the restaurant. Dolly Parton wants to see you."

Charlie frowned, trying to take this in.

"Is that the new head of customer service?"

"No, it's not! And you should know who that is and who Dolly Parton is!" Francis said.

After a moment, when she felt the coast was clear, Charlie shrugged.

"Dolly Parton! The country and western superstar! Cultural phenomenon! Feminist icon!"

Still nothing.

"Sang 9 to 5."

"Oh," Charlie said. "Eh?"

"Do you know why Dolly Parton wants to meet you?"

"No idea."

"Right, run down and see what she wants. You can't keep her waiting."

Charlie headed off for the lift, wondering what was going on.

"Remember to put yourself into a code. We're working on one for meetings with celebrities. In the meantime, use code 12."

She wasn't too sure how to greet her. When she was younger, her school had a visit from royalty. She couldn't remember which one it was—one of the Queens or Kings. She was told if they ever approached her, she had to curtsy. That'll do.

There she was. Nursing a flat white, sitting at a table with that guy who was in charge of the social media stuff.

"Charlie! Bring it in, honey," Dolly said, getting up and hugging her. "It's so nice to meet you."

Charlie recognised Dolly Parton without actually knowing who she was. Straight away, she was at ease.

"Excuse me, young man. I'd love to stay and talk about digital footprints, but me and my gal need to have a chat. Can we go somewhere quieter, Charlie?"

And with that, Charlie took Dolly Parton round the side of the building, linking arms as they went.

"You're maybe wondering what I'm doing here," Dolly said as they sat on a bench, answering David's set-up splattered with seagull shit.

"Yeah. You could say that."

"You know a guy called Scott Turnbull?"

"Yeah! We're dating. I'm meeting him tonight."

"That's what I was worried you'd say, darlin."

Dolly took out her phone and carefully unlocked the screen with the greatest set of nails Charlie had ever seen. It was clear she hadn't been to that place that did them in The Gyle.

"I'm really sorry to show you this."

"What?" Charlie asked inquisitively. "Spotify?"

"Not just any Spotify. My own account."

"Okay…"

"See, Charlie, why this is important is because of this. Artists can see when we get on people's playlists. It's kind of cute in one way."

"I'm listening."

"And Scott Turnbull has been making a playlist which he's added one of my songs to. Have a look at what he's called it."

Charlie leaned down to stare at the screen as best as she could without her reading glasses.

"On Friday Night I'm Going To Take Charlie Up The—"

Charlie stopped, open-mouthed.

"And that's Scott? The Scott I'm seeing?"

"Farid so, honey."

Charlie scrolled through the songs Scott had lovingly picked to soundtrack her seduction. She'd never listen to 'Mambo No. 5' the same way again.

"Anyway, whatever you do in the privacy of your bedroom is up to you. But I thought I'd better give you the heads up."

Charlie thanked Dolly Parton and headed back up to her desk. She told Francis and the rest of the team that she'd fill them in later. She'd head to the night out after work, after all.

All she needed to do was make a quick change of plans.

DEAR TAN

Mark Fleming

During lockdown, I wrote to my great grandpa. Like everyone used to texting, it was a pain getting back into using a pen. But he was all alone in Liberton, eyesight and hearing poor. He didn't do gadgets, but he could read my long letters with his magnifying glass. I was devastated when the virus got him. Rab Cavendish. Escaped Afrika Korps bullets only to die at the hands of a fucking germ.

I've written a letter to Tanya. To tell her the news, I'm breaking up with her. Tomorrow, we'll resume sitting with our mates opposite sides of the canteen. Wrote two paragraphs, giving my reasons. Now it's tucked into my jeans. A ticking timebomb. No way could I tell it to her face. It's much easier to be a coward than to be courageous. Fuck courageous. Life isn't like the movies, with earnest speeches, smiles all around as relationships glide effortlessly into platonic, 'Hallelujah' on the soundtrack. I visualise the other punters in this bar. Smirking at the guy, red faced after the slap to his chops. The tirade of profanities drawing mobies like magnets. Her Bacardi Breezer all over my Tommy Hilfiger shirt, the moment captured, replaying on TikTok ad infinitum.

Tan deserves better. Haven't worked out the logistics yet, as timing is everything. Somehow, I need to slip the envelope into her jacket. A pickpocket in reverse. Causing just as much grief.

As Tan fishes out her card to swipe the machine, I study my phone. When first world problems like this arise, I check my screensaver. A black and white family photo. Great Grandpa on a camel, a pyramid in the background. Grinning at the camera in his Eighth Army uniform, a target for the souvenir photographer. Before going back to being a target for snipers.

Our romance began as another Christmas party encounter inspired by mistletoe and shots. Unlike all the other couplings that dissolved into cringing denial, we started going steady. Until yesterday. There was a new start. Nadine. The moment I was assigned to show her around the department, she toyed with me, like a cat with a mouse. Giggling at my attempts at humour, squeezing my arm each time she guffawed. Intoxicating perfume. Top buttons undone. She might as well have stuck a hook through my lip and reeled me in.

Tan was oblivious. No seething jealousy. No confrontational tantrums. That, more than anything, sealed her fate. She was already blinded by what she referred to as love. Although I've said it back, usually after a skinful, I know it's really lust. We're both 21. Tanya can already see into our future, and she's often described it. A cul-de-sac in one of the Gilberston newbuilds, close to Musselburgh train station, and the new school currently at the planning stage for the kids she already has names for.

Watching her, I continue weighing pros and cons. Tan's been giving me driving lessons. Whenever I stall and lose my rag, she resolves the crisis by ordering me to place the gearstick into neutral while kneading my groin. She's an enthusiastic lover. Well up for experimentation. Oils. Dressing-up. Tying up. Toys. Outdoors. Nadine looks like a *Love Island* contestant, but unlike most of the ones on TV, amount of cosmetic surgery in inverse ratio to their IQs, she loves a laugh. Knows her music, her football, her films. And if she moves on to someone else, I'll be a free agent. My mates in the 5-a-sides liken single women to Russian conscripts. No matter how many are taken out, there are always fresh ones to take their place.

'One Stella Tortoise for sir,' Tan coos, placing the pint before me. I notice the tiny mole on her right cheek. I've never paid it much attention. Now I find my eyes drawn there. The light also exposes downy fluff at her chin. I imagine the lads in the office crowing. *Darren's dating the bearded lady.* Was dating.

She winks. Those eyelashes still get my pulse racing. And as she turns towards me, she presses her ample chest close, a jolt immediately shooting to my groin. The music alters to 'Take Me Out.' I love this track. Tan's old man's got the album. We listen to it during sex, Fridays, when she's got an empty while her parents go to their local rugby club. Tan wraps an arm around my shoulder. We snog. Nadine fades like the bubbles bursting in my Belgian lager. I curse my uncertainty. What's wrong with being in love so young? Been a staple of pop lyrics for fucking decades.

The bouncer's shouting on everyone to drink up. Clamping my mouth, I suppress hiccups. Tan is swiping through her phone's gallery, showing me photos WhatsApped by her cousin, Tegan, who got married in Santo Domingo. Gorgeous swimming pools. Pico Duarte, the highest point in the Caribbean. Like 12 Arthur's Seats, according to Tegan. Arm around her shoulder, my free hand removes the letter. Slides it into her jacket.

Drizzle washes the pub windows. There's a taxi rank around the corner. It's Friday tomorrow. We'll go our separate ways. I'll give her half an hour to get home to Northfield. Text her. Tell her to check her pockets in case she hangs the jacket in the wardrobe and doesn't even notice. Then I'll switch my phone off. Surely, she'll absorb the information lucidly. But what if she assumes it's a love letter? Opening the envelope would become such a cruel anti-climax. Is Nadine really a better option? Bird in the hand, and all that. It's not too late to salvage it. I'll embrace her. That's when I can delve inside. But my mind changes again. I'm all over the place. The bouncer's bullish voice impels me to arse the lager. I realise how much my head's swimming.

I picture her about to open the letter, hair falling over her face, her breasts heaving in her silk cami top, the scarlet one. What have I been thinking? She cannot read that fucking letter, even if I have to plunge a fist into her pocket and screw it into a ball.

My thoughts ebb and flow. Her fuzzy chin. The alcohol swilling in my gut. Screwing my eyes shut, I picture Nadine. When I demonstrated the photocopier, she insisted she'd clamber aboard at the next drinks do in the office. Imprinting a vision of lacy knickers at her ankles, flashes striking her thighs, her voice husky with laughter and lust.

I tune in to what Tan's saying. Wedding marches on steel drums. Nadine's a total fucking tease. Even the senior managers ogle her, the ones who only ever get hard-ons when they score

Birdies. Her lips aren't just bee stung. She's been gorging on honey around a hive entrance. Naturally so, rather than the horrific blow-up doll look craved by wannabe celebs. Tan's letter can stay put. I've a Health and Safety course at the bank's training centre tomorrow afternoon, so I might not even see her until next week.

'Just going for a leak, Tan.'

I pretend to trip. She gives her own infectious titter. She'll immediately be delving into her handbag for her makeup mirror. A glance over my shoulder confirms this. Mirrors hold a magnetic allure for her. We've been rendezvousing in the office car park at 08:50 each morning. I spy her from a distance, bending to wing mirrors, teasing her fringe, pouting. I love watching as she'll crouch towards a car, puckering her mouth to dab her cherry-red lipstick regardless of whether there are still occupants. When we meet at lunchtime to dine by the miniature loch in the park opposite our office block, salads in matching Tupperware boxes, I know she'll have left her desk 10 minutes beforehand to prepare. This aftie, she clocked off early, went to *Cheynes*. The way she treats our dates compared to my apathy, rocking up in the same shirt and tie from work, I'm amazed it doesn't seem to bother her. If it does, she pretends it doesn't.

Today's also pay-day. The reward for another month staring at spreadsheets. The lager's giving me a glow, makes me giggle as I head for the bogs. Two guys are standing in the way. Arguing. Disagreeing rather than either of them getting het up. But with slurred voices. I tap the shorter, heftier guy's shoulder.

'Scuse us, mate. Get past you there?'

The man's maybe in his 30s. Doesn't even look at me. He peers inside his drink. A half pint tumbler. As I ease between them, my sole catches the carpet. I nudge against his elbow. 'Sorry, bud,' I mutter.

Clattering inside, I take my leak, rinse, run my fingers through my hair. Out the corner of my eye, I spy the door opening. Somehow it looks odd. Only opens half-way. Poking the dryer, I'm aware of being scrutinized through the gap in the doorway. Then the two blokes barge in. The stocky one mouths something. I frown, shrugging my shoulders, indicating the dryer. The three of us stare at the appliance until it cuts out.

'You've ruined my new shirt, cunt,' he rasps.

I gawk at him, shrug again. Bravado gets the better of me. 'What's a shirt cunt? A shirt that goes over a cunt?'

I crouch to a mirror behind the sink, bring my face up close. 'That was an accident, mate. Just give it a quick rinse. Fuck sake.'

'An accident, mate?'

His fist flies, the glass he's still clutching reflecting the overhead light, sparkling. A wave of nauseous darkness.

*

Alone in the corridor, I'm gazing at posters. Weirdly named clubs. I hate dance music. Even at my age, I feel a generation gap with the hotheads fuelled with uppers dancing to moronic rhythms concocted in soulless studios. I prefer the rock albums my dad abandoned: Led Zeppelin, Springsteen, Neil Young, Rush. There's an honesty about them. Music as genuine communication, not manufactured noise. Although I also get how you can lose yourself to Chemical Brothers as much as the Allman Brothers. First got together with Tan on the dancefloor to Shakin' fucking Stevens, fuck sake. It's all relative.

I notice the carpet. The scuffed design is peppered with lurid crimson blotches. Mesmerised, I stare. The pattern is evolving before my eyes. I feel a draught against my right cheek. I touch the skin. I realise how crazily my fingers are shaking. My fingertips can feel but my face can't. A tremor courses through me, raining droplets to the ground. Drawing my hand away, it looks like Ulster's flag.

Tan is hysterical. Has she found the letter? I'm being helped to a seat, a barman pressing a towel into my face. It stinks of stale beer. The barman is forcing the cloth in tighter, stemming the flow. Blood trickles down my neck. It tickles. The barman is asking me things. I register his accent, not his words. Glaswegian. I can smell his last cigarette. Everything's happening in slow motion. When they fight to save lives in *Casualty* all is panic, but controlled panic. Doctors bellow orders. Staff scramble to deliver shocks from defibrillators. The barman just squats beside me, rocking on his heels. There's blood on his shoes. Tan is trying to drag me to my feet, but the barman orders her to step back, give me space.

I close my eyes. Wait for things to pass. When they struggle open again, I see blue lights flickering against the pub windows. I'm led through the staring crowds. They part for me, as if hanging on my every movement. Like I'm a pop idol.

*

Someone is discussing significant tissue damage to my cheek that will eventually recede to a scar. Crescent-shaped. It's too early to discover if the surgeons have saved the sight in my left eye. I'll look like a gangster, not the guy who did it.

*

Tanya is rubbing my shoulder. I try mumbling but she applies a finger to my lips. The crimson of her varnish makes me feel queasy.

'The police have caught the culprit, Darren. Detectives are waiting to interview you. There are photographs to identify.'

There's another dimension to that night. Shock has erased most of it. Propelled me through a time warp from ordering another Stella to waking up in St John's. But something else lurks in my memory. Occasionally drawing closer. As Tan stretches over me, it shoots back. The letter. Through the painkillers, a pang of alarm.

'Where's your jacket?'

'What's that, lover?'

'Jacket?'

'My jacket?'

'The jacket … You wore it in the pub …'

'What? My favourite Katherine Hamnett jacket? It was covered in your blood. Went straight into the washing machine the next day. Handed it into Bernardo's.'

I smile but wince with pain. She kisses my forehead. I inhale her scent. The humid quicksand is drawing me in again. As her footfall fades, I sink into the pillow.

*

An image of red footprints on the carpet. Like a dance pattern. I picture Tan's jacket bundled in a rack. And I imagine some silver-haired woman selecting it, admiring herself in the mirror.

Twisting and turning, transported to a dancehall. A vast dancehall where the band are wearing tuxedos and playing old time music with instruments so polished they dazzle. And before them are so many courting youngsters, gliding effortlessly. There's Rab. My age. Grinning at his sweetheart, catching his mates' eyes, a wink here and there. All of them in khaki. Abandoning themselves to the notion of being in love and to the music lifting their souls, to laughter and joy and forgetting the darkness waiting for all of them outside.

BURNS NIGHT

Neil Renton

Frankie had creepy admirer, but Frankie didn't mind too much, as her creepy admirer had really good taste.

She'd been sent an Agent Provocateur lingerie set and a pair of Christian Louboutin heels from a mysterious source identified only as 'RB.' She didn't even need the gift receipt that had been thoughtfully included. Even more impressive was that she hadn't requested any of the items on her online wish list. It all fitted her perfectly, as the constant vibration of complementary alerts on her social media images told her.

The doorbell interrupted her bedroom posing. She waited for one of her parents to get it, assuming it would probably be for them, then remembered they were both away at a Burns Night do at her dad's Masonic club. So inconsiderate. She threw on the matching negligee that came with the barely-there bra and knickers and tottered downstairs to see who it was.

Frankie opened a hint of the door, which was more than enough to let in a putrid odour that made her dry-wretch. Standing outside, she could just about make out a man wearing an old-fashioned combination of a fluffed shirt bursting out of a tailored jacket and breeks. It wasn't his clothes that caused her to panic—although, to be fair, they left a lot to be desired. It was his wide-eyed, dead-eyed expression. The rotting skin around his lips. The greasy, swept-to-one-side lanky hair with wild sideburns that made him look like he was off to the indie club Evol with her big brother back in the day.

Then it hit her. RB.

Her admirer was Rabid Burns, the sex-obsessed Scottish poet zombie.

"Alright, hen! You look sexy! And I'm glad I paid for same-day delivery!"

Frankie screamed a really high-pitched squeal, the kind you only get in horror movies, and bolted back up the stairs to her room. Again, with the kind of logic only reserved for scary films, she managed to leave the front door open in her wake.

As he was a decrepit brain-dead creature with only one thing on his non-existent mind, Rabid struggled through the doorway and stomped his way towards her slowly.

"I'm a wee bit smelly 'cause I've no washed in a while. But if ye gimme a chance, I'll make ye smile!"

Frankie went to yank open her bedroom window but had second thoughts. She didn't want to jump out of the first floor, as she'd no doubt hurt herself when she landed on the turfed garden outside. She turned to the bed to hide under it but bemoaned the fact she'd gone for one of those Swedish flat-pack ones with a series of drawers filling any space. Why did she not consider the practicality of hiding from a crazed killer when picking furniture?

She could hear him climbing the steps. He was taking his time, mind you. Old bastard. He couldn't have been that up for it.

THUD went his foot on the step.

"Ye may 'ave heard a rumour I've goat an STD!"

THUMP went his other foot.

"But that's all shite as I'm drug and disease free!"

You're also a fucking shite poet, thought Frankie. She flung open the doors of her wardrobe to find a place to conceal herself, and her heart sank.

Why did she have so much clothes?

Not only was the rail buckling under the weight of the hangers, but there wasn't a floor in the cupboard. It was lined with shoes and piled on top of them were bin and designer bags. Frankie squeezed herself in and peered through the slatted door, which was a fantastic design feature you only seemed to find in slasher pics. Or Corstorphine.

Eventually, Rabid Burns made it into her room. He was well and truly puggled, so he was. She felt a bit sorry for him. Mere mortals don't appreciate how tiring it was, spending all day on the internet buying naughty underwear, especially when you've been dead for hundreds of years. She felt his pain.

He leaned on the bed and caught his breath, with a clenched fist patting his chest, trying to work out where she was. He surveyed the closed window and kicked the drawers under her bed with a heavy boot.

The only other place she could be is in the wardrobe.

Inside the closet, Frankie closed her eyes. She hadn't held in her breath this much since she'd been sprawled in her bed for an Instagram reel about ten minutes ago.

Rabid flung open the closet doors. Frankie shrieked, grabbed the contents of the first bag that she could reach, and charged at her assailant.

And as she did so, she speared him in an eye with a stiletto.

"What d'ya dae that for? It's no very fair," Rabid whinged. "Ye stabbed me in ma peeper and ma heid is very sare!"

Then he was dead. Well, until the inevitable sequels, spin-offs, and origin stories came along.

Frankie froze in terror. Not at the dead monster on her bedroom floor, but at something far, far worse.

"I can't believe my mum had put my Jimmy Choos in the charity bag!" she shrieked.

QUICKSAND AND CAFFEINE

Mark Fleming

My mind was whirring, but for a moment, I was smiling again. Trainers sinking into the wet sand, then extricating, the sloppy sounds took me back to Craiglockhart primary, my mate Sparks shoving his hand under his oxter, delighting as the rasping drew giggles, basking in Miss McKenzie's disgust. Next to him, my cheeks would flare like the time Johnny Hamilton caught us pocketing marker pens after our paper rounds. When the ex-Hearts twat sacked us on the spot, Sparks guffawed in his face. But I thought of Tina. Pushing Gemma's buggy along Porty Prom, must've been 20 years ago, I pointed out the floodlights at Starks Park had just come on. Riveted to a dog walker skirting the shore, she announced her greatest fear. *Quicksand.* Now another night of insomnia seemed the least of my worries.

My heartbeat increased as I slalomed in the gloom, around puddles, seaweed clumps, and jellyfish. Last time I checked my phone it was 03:51. Another four hours or so before a sliver of red would show above Berwick Law. What the fuck would I do if I struck a sludgy patch, found myself unable to lift my feet out again? Who'd hear me screaming? Glancing around, my only company were wraith-like gulls drifting in from their roosts in the Forth.

Heading back towards the Prom, the crashing waves faded.

I'd enough fresh air in my lungs. I'd make an Ovaltine, sip it while sinking into the couch, bury my nose in Val McDermid's crime scenes, Brian Eno soothing my eardrums. The combo worked sometimes. Climbing back under the duvet, I'd try not to wake Tina. She was sometimes aware of me getting up to go to the loo. You overhydrate, she'd mumble. She'd no idea I'd started going out for these walks. Explaining would mean broaching the shite going on in my head. It's *my* shite. Don't want to add it to *her* shite, with the NHS contract expiring next month. But when sleep abandons me after a few hours, my brain just switches on. Thoughts immediately churn, like the swell buckling the groynes. Imagination on overload, each daylight anxiety magnifying a hundred-fold.

Clambering up to the walkway, I stopped to spark a cigarette. Another vice I've resumed, but only outdoors so the salty air removes the smell. The time Tina commented when gathering laundry, I blamed it on the Persy after the last match. Focusing on the clean smack of my soles against terra firma, loosening the sand, I was aware of my footsteps echoing. Altering. Someone was right behind. How'd I only become aware of them? Dark clothes? Mugger attire? Teenage memories of being jumped on the long trek along Fountainbridge after Outer Limits. My senses screamed: Go! The stomping feet were gaining. I readied to break into a run. But I also wanted to see my mystery stalker. Confront him. Inner turmoil can transform me into the Tasmanian Devil. Bunching my fists, I burled around.

He was only a boy. I recognised him. Pictured him in the lunchtime queue outside Greggs, in a Porty High prefect's blazer. Was he on something? I studied his eyes. No, the closer I examined him beneath a lamppost's stark glare, I could see tears glistening. He seemed to be waiting on my reaction.

'You alright, mate? Thought it was only me struggling to sleep the night.'

He motioned as if he was about to answer. Didn't. Instead, he looked over to the surf. Piping oystercatchers drew our attention. I waited for him to speak. Brushing at his eyes, words struggled out. 'Not really, mister.'

I noticed his jeans, soaking up to his thighs.

'Been paddling?'

'Nup,' he mumbled.

'Well?'

A great sob funneling up from his chest, he burst into tears. 'Was going to do something really stupid.'

I felt something sparking inside me, shining a light on my own internal nonsense. 'How stupid?' But his expression panicked. 'No. Ignore that. Stupid question. What's your name, mate?'

'Josh.'

'As in Doig? Campbell.'

Almost a grin. 'Nah. As in Ginnelly.'

I nodded. 'I'm Tony.' We shook hands; his limp, ice-cold. 'I'm just at the end of Esplanade Terrace, Josh. Where d'you stay, mate?'

'Mount Lodge.'

'Least I can do is drop you off. Your jeans are soaking, eh. But you fancy grabbing a quick coffee first? Help you thaw out. My wife bought a coffee maker few weeks ago. We use it all the time. I was blaming it for keeping me up at night. But that's not the reason.'

'Oh.'

'I can talk for Scotland when I get going, Josh. But I'm a good listener.' Flicked the dowt into the ground.

After he followed me up the path, I halted by the door, touching my finger to my mouth, winking. 'Tina, my wife, can be a light sleeper. Our daughter would sleep through an asteroid strike on Inchkeith.'

Relaxing, Josh nodded. We skulked inside. Flicking on the hall light, we headed into the kitchen, blinking.

'This is, eh … Really kind of you, by the way, Tony.'

'Think nothing of it. You want a latte? Cappuccino? This gadget does the lot.'

'Eh. Can it do an Americano, Tony?'

'It'll do anything you want, mate.' Switching on the machine, I flipped open a cupboard, grasped the sack of coffee beans. 'Grab a pew, Josh. I see Gemma's headphones on the chair. She was hunting high and low for them. Just pop them on the table.'

Lifting these, he sighed but seemed to lighten up. Taking a seat, he rubbed his hands together. Focusing on the wires, he spent moments untangling them, then watched me adding coffee to the percolator. 'Ayeways have instant at home.'

'Gotta love modern gadgets, Josh.'

'What'll they think of next?'

'Who knows. One that's Bluetoothed to Alexa? *Double expresso and Sunshine on Leith*. You could ask for Hearts Hearts, Glorious Hearts with your next coffee.'

'Was thinking more of one you could shove your knob into

and have it suck your balls dry.'

There was that split second when I processed what he'd just come out with. Then we were both chuckling beneath our palms, hissing hysterically, reminding me of Sparks antagonising the teacher all those years ago. As we both stifled laughter, I nodded to the machine, made a show of caressing it.

When the laughter stopped, we started talking.

SEAL'S BROKEN – DEATH OF THE TWINS

Neil Renton

"Seal's broken."

"You've just been. You've got a bladder like a burst baw." I love Carpet, but it's no a day for folk being up tae ninety. No the day.

"Aye, when I was in the bog, Seal phones me. He's left you a message, big man's gutted that he can't be here for you."

I shouldn't have snapped. It's no a day for snapping at folk. No the day.

"Aye, he's a good cunt, that Seal. I knew he'd be upset. He loved the twins."

"We all did, Keith."

Ah wipe my nose on the sleeve of the suit I got from Slaters. Ah cannae look anywhere as everyone is in tears, and it's makin' me upset.

My old man is sitting in the corner, tryin' like fuck no tae complain about the prices o' the Hibs Club wi' his pals. No today, please. No today.

Christine, ma rock, ma fuckin' diamond. She's pursin' her lips, tryin' to hold it in. As hard as this is for me, it's just as hard for her.

Ma pals, all reunited. Even Dempsey, who's flown over from Australia just for this. Last time Ah think we were all together was that time we went to the Hibs and Celtic final years ago. A good day oot at the fitba ruined by the fitba.

"Bud?"

"Aye, please. Thanks." Ah'm no sure how many Ah've had. Ah can't remember how many I've tasted.

"Tell you what, Keith, the service was beautiful."

"Aye, it was one of those humanist ones. Done by a boy called Mark. Decent boy, big Hibee. I think he's kickin' aboot. Does mental health drop-ins at Easter Road. I can see me going along."

I'm in the walkway, standing in the way of folk wanting tae go for a pish or a vape. Ah remember bringing the twins here for the first time. It feels like it was yesterday. I wish it was tomorrow.

Christine showed me how tae make a folder on ma phone for photos. Ah scroll through them, smiling at the memories.

Ryan and Lindsay approach me. They've been great. What a way to spend their birthday, eh.

"You alright, Dad?" Ryan asks. His suit is too big; it's like he's goin' tae court and he's hoping the fashion police don't get him on the way.

"Aye, I'm good, son. Thanks. How's you?"

"Bearing up."

"You're being so brave," Lindsay says wi' a tap o' my arm. "We're so proud."

The three of us stand for a moment and cry. "It's better out than in," the grief therapist I'm at told me.

"Right. Let's get a drink. That sly bastard Carpet went to get me a Bud. Ah bet he'll expect me to buy it now."

"We'll get you one," Lindsay says.

"Cheers, kids. Tell you what, when all is said and done, they're in a better place just now. Warriston Cemetery, buried next to my Sambas and Stan Smiths."

www.ingramcontent.com/pod-product-compliance
Lightning Source LLC
Chambersburg PA
CBHW072005210726
48294CB00013B/1572